WHITE F

DAVID STEVENS was born in Winnipeg left school at the age of sixteen and worked on the Canadian Pacific Railroad on the west coast, later joining a Canadian paratroop battalion in the Arctic Mobile Striking Force in northern Canada. Since then he has been a professional actor and has worked over the years in Jamaica, England, Canada and New Zealand as an advertising writer, a TV and radio producer and a playwright.

He eventually settled in New Zealand in 1965 where he is now devoting himself to writing full time.

DAVID STEVENS

White for Danger

FONTANA / Collins

First published in 1979 by William Collins Sons & Co Ltd
First issued in Fontana Books 1980

Made and printed in Great Britain by
William Collins Sons & Co Ltd, Glasgow

Prologue

The dogs pulled tiredly but resolutely, the drift from behind ruffling their thick coats. The sledge bumped over waves of sastrugi, fluted ridges carved from the snow by the sharp knife of the constant wind, and the man found it increasingly difficult to keep his feet as he stumbled along in its wake. Often he went down to his knees, but, drawing on the last resources of his exhausted body, he would hang on to the sledge and drag himself upright. Occasionally a patch of clear came in the swirling drift snow and he would catch a glimpse of a peak on the horizon. Mount Huggins?

Even if it was Huggins, what good would it do? He put the thought from his mind. The mountain, he knew, was still many miles from base over some of the most difficult terrain in the Antarctic and he would postpone thinking about it until he was sure.

He let the swish of the runners on the hard crust take his mind back and away from the unknowable future stretched whitely ahead. Two weeks? Or was it three? The sun constantly in the sky made it difficult to calculate.

No matter. If the time past was hard for his tired brain to recall, the event that left him alone in the Antarctic barrens was not. He had been with two companions from the university, Bill Claydon and Steven Rourk, two of the most experienced south polar explorers on the continent. Where had they gone?

He had been several miles ahead, pushing on to set up camp while Claydon and Rourk had made a detour to a high, oddly shaped nunatak to take bearings for their survey map. The whiteout came without warning, the sun's light bouncing between brilliant snow and a low, thin cloud cover until nothing could be seen in the radiance. Even his feet blended into the overall whiteness. He had stopped immediately. So close to the South Magnetic Pole, his compass was next to useless and without landmarks to navigate by it was more than foolhardy to go on.

He had set up camp and waited. And waited. After ten hours he began to worry. He knew that even in the whiteout his companions should have been able to follow his trail. He gave them another two hours and then packed up his sledge and started back.

The whiteout had dissipated by the time he had returned to the spot where Claydon had turned the sledge off towards the nunatak. The crust was hard and even and he made good time along their track. The nunatak, piercing up through the ice cap, rose ahead, looking almost exactly like an ancient Egyptian pyramid, very regular and about three hundred feet high.

He found their dog team picketed at the base of the steep rock. Or what was left of it. Some of the dogs out of hunger had eaten through their traces and wandered off. The sledge was near by, its contents strewn in the snow. At first he thought the dogs had ripped it open until he noticed the metal boxes that had contained Claydon's survey maps and Rourk's many sightings open and empty. No dog could have done that!

He looked up. The wind soughed a thin spume of snow around the edge of the nunatak, but nothing else was evident on its heights. Suddenly, he had felt very alone. Not the aloneness of a single man in an empty wilderness, but the aloneness of the unknown. Fear crept coldly into his belly. Claydon and Rourk were far too experienced just to wander off and leave their dogs without food. And the sledge? Rifled?

The wind picked up and the dogs howled hungrily, but it wasn't the cold that sent an involuntary shiver through him. Everything looked so . . . abandoned.

With an effort he got himself back into action. He dragged some frozen seal meat from the upturned sledge and the big huskies snarled over it and then quietened as they chewed into the icy bits of carcass. Once the dogs were settled, he began to cast about for footprints, some sign that might tell him to where his friends had disappeared.

There were plenty but the wind had long robbed them of any distinguishing features and none that he could find led away from the area. Again he looked up at the rock above. Could they have climbed up there and fallen? The nunatak looked largely featureless from where he stood, but he knew that he would have to go up there and look.

The wind was stronger now, plucking at him as he scrabbled awkwardly up the rock. It wasn't a hard climb, but his bulky clothing slowed him considerably. By the time he had reached a place where he could get around the peak to see what was on the other side, the wind had risen to a demented scream that whipped up clouds of brittle ice crystals that stung his eyes and face. And that was on the lee side of the nunatak. When he pulled himself around to the windward side, it felt as if he was pushing into something nearly solid.

He didn't find Claydon or Rourk, but before the weather closed in he saw something else. Or was it an illusion, one of the famous Antarctic mirages? Now, struggling back to Scott Base, the reality of it was fretting at the edges. Did he really see it?

Once again he stumbled behind the sledge and once again hauled himself up. He realized his feet no longer hurt. Frost-bite? The thought cleared his mind. He no longer doubted what he'd seen. The question was, would he ever make it back to tell anyone else?

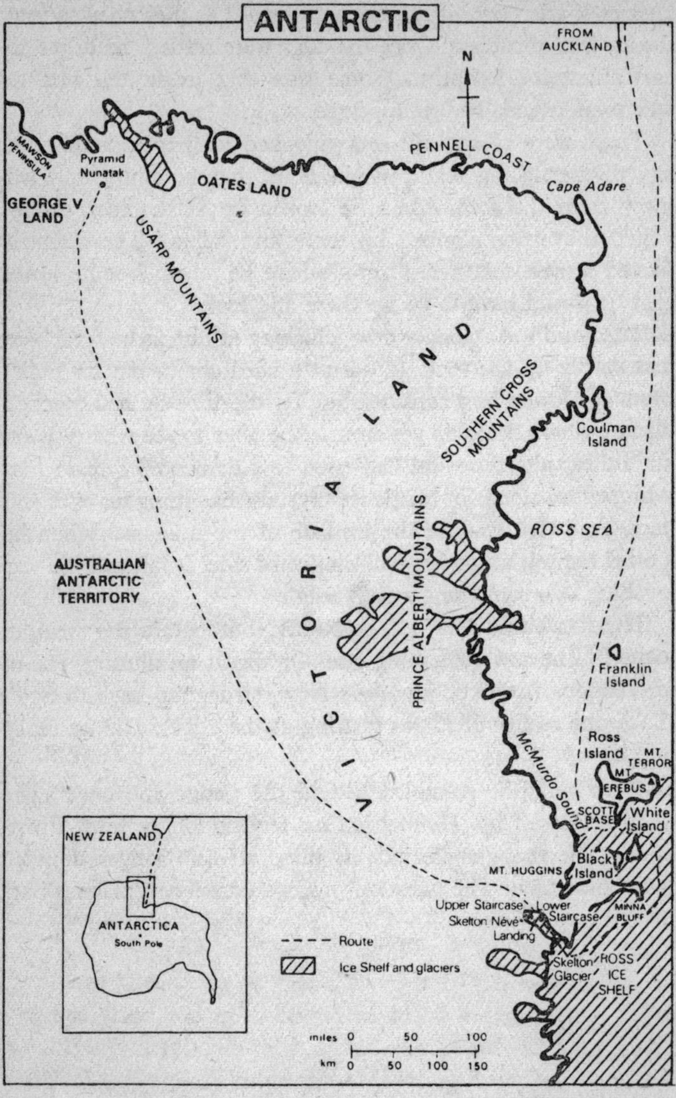
ANTARCTIC
FROM AUCKLAND
N
MAWSON PENINSULA
Pyramid Nunatak
GEORGE V LAND
OATES LAND
PENNELL COAST
Cape Adare
USARP MOUNTAINS
VICTORIA LAND
SOUTHERN CROSS MOUNTAINS
Coulman Island
ROSS SEA
AUSTRALIAN ANTARCTIC TERRITORY
PRINCE ALBERT MOUNTAINS
Franklin Island
McMurdo Sound
Ross Island
MT. TERROR
MT. EREBUS
SCOTT BASE
White Island
Black Island
MT. HUGGINS
Upper Staircase
Lower Staircase
Skelton Névé Landing
MINNA BLUFF
Skelton Glacier
ROSS ICE SHELF
Route
Ice Shelf and glaciers
NEW ZEALAND
ANTARCTICA
South Pole
miles 0 50 100
km 0 50 100 150

Chapter I

'I want you to go with Howard.'

My younger sister sat across the small table in the airport lounge looking steadily at me over her Drambuie. I hadn't seen her for nearly six years, but I remembered that look. When she wanted something badly, she gazed right into your eyes as if daring you to say no.

'To Antarctica?' She might as well have asked me to join her husband on a trip to the moon. 'Is the university sponsoring Howard again?' I asked.

'No, he's quitting the university to go.'

'But how?' I said. 'It's expensive as hell.'

'It's a privately sponsored expedition,' she explained. 'A man named Warden Grampion is setting it up.'

'And he wants to take Howard along?'

'Howard is the reason he's going.'

I finished my Glenfiddich and took her glass. 'I think you'd better start at the beginning, Jenny. Let me get fresh drinks.'

I waited for the barman to finish serving another customer at the far end, needing the moment to recover from Jenny's little bombshell. I glanced at her. She had inherited the Norse part of our Scottish ancestry, blonde, square-jawed, wide-set blue eyes. I leaned more to the dark, Celtic side.

As wholesomely good-looking as ever, she looked tired, too, with dark smudges under her eyes. Even her smile couldn't hide the skin drawn too tightly over her high cheekbones. I hadn't seen much of my kid sister since I'd left New Zealand at nineteen just to prove to myself there really was a rest of the world. When I wrote her that I was doing a promotion tour of

Australia for my latest novel, I wasn't surprised when she wrote back insisting that I fly across the Tasman to New Zealand to see her. What did surprise me was the odd urgency about the letter.

Armed with the drinks, I went back to the table.

'Jen,' I said, patting her hand, 'you'll have to start at the start.'

'Yes.' She looked at me levelly. 'What's your opinion of Howard?'

'I hardly know him. Quiet. Unassuming. Good at his job.'

'Do you think he's a man who would stand up in a . . . a crisis?'

'How would I know, Jenny? I've only met him twice.'

And that, I thought, was a long time ago. The first time was when he and Jenny had visited me in Canada on their honeymoon. I had been a captain in a Canadian airborne battalion, full of brag and swagger. Howard Turbott was a quiet man by contrast, all diffidence and apologies, and I rather overplayed the rough, tough paratrooper in counterpart. What a pig I must have been. The second time was six years ago when I'd returned to Auckland for my father's funeral, smoothed out by civilian life.

'What are you getting at, Jen? Biology lecturers aren't usually judged by their ability to function in crisis situations.'

'You know about Howard's trip to Antarctica last year?' she said.

'You filled twelve pages telling me the details,' I replied patiently. 'I even know what kind of underwear he had to take.'

'I guess I was pretty excited about it. It was something very new for Howard.'

'Yes, I wouldn't normally connect Howard with the South Pole.'

'I suppose, compared to you, he does sound a bit of a stick. Lab, library and home to the family. Outdoors means a stroll in the park of a Sunday. I was as surprised as anyone when he said he was going to apply for a spot on the expedition.'

'And keen too, I'll bet. You used to love it yourself when I'd take you for tramps into the hills when we were kids.'

She laughed. 'I imagine that's what gave me such a vicarious pleasure. David never stopped telling his chums about his dad being an explorer.' Her face lit with inner warmth. 'Which made it a change from hearing him continually go on about the adventures of his fantastic Uncle Logan.'

'I haven't seen David since he was about six. What stories could he possibly tell about me?'

She laughed again. 'I suppose I sing your praises, and there are your books, of course.'

'They're fiction!'

'Not to David. However, Howard's Antarctic expedition upstaged even you.' She stopped and the sparkle went out of her eyes. 'You remember I wrote you that he and two other men from the university were lost on a field trip?'

I nodded. 'Only Howard made it back.'

'It was amazing he survived alone. It was just luck that he came upon another field party on the Skelton névé. He was so exhausted that he almost passed their camp without seeing it, only the dogs wouldn't go on.' Her lip quivered. 'Oh, Logan, he came so close to dying!'

'And now he's going back?'

'Yes.'

'Where do I come in?' I asked, perplexed.

Her voice shook. 'When he was found, he had Claydon's and Rourk's equipment, the ones who didn't make it back. Howard said they just disappeared and – ' she drank some of her Drambuie – 'and that he was sure they'd been taken to a city he'd seen.'

'A city?'

She nodded, her head down.

'He'd been through a lot, Jen. He was having delusions.'

'He still says it. I think his colleagues feel that an accident happened, and Howard just left them.'

'Is that what they say?'

'No, but I'm sure that's what they think.'

'How do you know that?'

'Bill Claydon and Steven Rourk were experienced polar travellers. They wouldn't just wander off. You only have to see the faces of the faculty and the students when they see Howard to know what they think.'

'Do you agree with them?' I asked gently.

'Even the kids at school say it to David – that his father's a coward and ran away and left two men to die. It's all I can do to make him go in the mornings.'

'But do you agree with them?' Sharper this time.

'I don't know what to think!' she said defiantly. 'It's such a crazy story. Would you believe it?'

I shrugged. 'Well, why is Howard going back?'

'To rescue Claydon and Rourk,' she said in a small voice.

I poked at the dottle in my pipe with a dead match. If Howard Turbott believed two men could live for nearly a year in the middle of Antarctica, something was very seriously wrong with him. I was beginning to understand my sister's worry.

'Where does this chap Grampion come in?' I asked.

She gazed a long time into her glass, gathering herself up, and then she started, speaking slowly and precisely.

'Even after they'd flown Howard out to a hospital in Christchurch,' she began, 'he stuck to his story and fully expected a rescue mission to go back. They thought he was delirious and paid no attention. When it finally got through to him that they didn't believe a word he said, he smashed up the hospital room. He was very weak and he'd lost three toes from frostbite, but he still caused a lot of damage.' She sounded almost proud of him. 'After that he stopped yelling and started letter-writing. Winter was closing in by that time and it was too late to organize anything then, so he concentrated on trying to get a party set up for this coming summer.

'The university soon made it plain what they thought about it and nobody else was interested either. They didn't believe him. There was no proof. The refusals were short and barely polite.'

'Except Grampion's.'

'Yes, he heard Howard's story in England and flew all the way out here to speak to him personally. When Howard told him the details, he agreed to finance an expedition this summer.'

'What's Grampion like?'

'Very rich, very pushy, the kind of man who always talks in commands.'

'What's his interest in all this, then? Surely not just to clear Howard's good name?'

'The city Howard's supposed to have seen. He's some sort of archæologist and he's got a crazy theory that Antarctica once had a warm climate and supported a flourishing civilization. He thinks Howard saw the remains of one of its cities!' She sounded as if she thought Warden Grampion would benefit by a visit to a sympathetic psychiatrist.

'Not interested in finding Claydon and Rourk?'

Jenny laughed humourlessly. 'The only thing he's interested in is proving his silly theory and making himself a big deal to his archæological friends.'

I put another match to my pipe to regenerate what was left of the tobacco. 'And you don't want him to go?' I said through the cloud of smoke.

Tears showed in the corners of her eyes. 'I can't stop him. But I'm so afraid for him. Since he got back, there's been so much pressure on him, so much doubt, even from David and me. If things went wrong, he might . . .'

'Crack up,' I supplied.

She wiped the tears away and nodded. 'Grampion's only interested in his city. He doesn't give a damn about Howard or his reputation.'

I sighed. 'Jen, what can I do? Can I help?'

'You can look after Howard for me.' Her eyes pleaded.

Finally I said, 'You know Howard won't agree to my going

along to Antarctica to nursemaid him.'

'I've already arranged it.'

'Oh, for God's sake, Jenny!' I expostulated. 'How?'

Her mouth set in a determined line. 'I've told him that I'll leave him and take David with me if he doesn't take you along. And I mean it!'

I was flabbergasted. 'You don't even know if I want to go!'

Her face softened and her eyes glistened again. 'Oh, Logan, I know you're supposed to be in Australia promoting your book, but there's no one else I can ask. When you wrote to say you were coming out this way and you'd be able to stop for a while in New Zealand, it seemed as if my prayers had been answered.' She tried to smile.

There's not much you can say to that. 'Okay, Jen.' I tried to put together a reassuring smile. 'I'll go if Howard agrees.'

'He will,' she said with more confidence than I felt.

Chapter 2

Jenny explained that she had wanted me to stay with her and Howard and their son, David, but she didn't have a guest-room and I told her I didn't at all mind staying in a hotel. When we left the airport bar she drove me to the White Heron Motel which, she said, was at least close to their home in Parnell, a pleasant suburb near Auckland's city centre.

It was a long, hot, enjoyable drive from the airport at Mangare to the city centre. Auckland is squeezed between two beautiful harbours on a narrow isthmus of land made up largely of extinct volcanoes. The Waitemata borders it on the Pacific side and the Manukau on the Tasman side, but it manages to spill out of the ends until it is as large in area as

Los Angeles although only about a half a million people live in it. New Zealanders like a little space around their homes. Lots of green, small parks, well-kept gardens, it was much as I'd remembered it.

I checked in at the Heron and arranged with Jenny to go over that evening and discuss my going south with Howard's expedition. It wasn't something I was looking forward to. I arranged with the woman at the desk to get me a rental car, then went to my room, unpacked, had a shower and flopped on the bed with my emergency bottle of malt whisky and a pipe.

Antarctica! It hadn't really sunk in yet. The last largely unexplored continent in the world. A place that few would ever get to see, unless they were scientists or working for some government. The more I thought about it, the more exciting the prospect became.

Jenny's house was on one of those sections of land peculiar to New Zealand that has no road frontage. When the older, larger estates were broken up, there was often no convenient way to turn them into lines of neat little rectangles and many of them only have access by means of a long driveway cutting between other properties. Jenny's even had a meander in it that hid the house until you were almost up to it. It was an old stucco affair surrounded by trees and bush and the warm glow from its leaded windows made it seem very peaceful.

As I parked, the front door burst open and a boy, all arms and legs and excitement, leaped along the path towards me. He stopped about ten feet away, suddenly realizing that though I might be the uncle he'd heard so much about, I was still a stranger. He looked at me uncertainly.

'Hi, David. You're about twice as big as the last time I saw you.'

'Uncle Logan?'

'Your only one.' I put my arm over his shoulder and turned up the path.

His initial diffidence fell to pieces under the pressure of questions bubbling up inside him. By the time we reached the doorway where Jenny was waiting, I was hard pressed to stem the onslaught.

'Give your uncle a chance, Davy, you'll get plenty of time to pester him.' She turned to me and her smile was strained. 'Come into the lounge. Howard's in there,' she said, trying to sound bright and normal.

She led the way into a small lounge made even smaller by the many well-filled bookshelves. There was a fire in a good-sized hearth and the comfortable chairs placed around it and bright cushions on the window-seats made it inviting and cosy.

Howard rose as we entered, limping slightly as he moved. I remembered the toes sacrificed to the frost.

'Hallo, Logan,' he said without warmth.

His hair was a little thinner than I remembered, his forehead a little higher and, although he was nearly as tall as I am, his slighter frame and habit of looking down made him seem shorter. I'd previously thought his open, even features rather bland, but now a determined set to his mouth and a dark, far-away look in his eyes gave his face a certain resoluteness.

'How are you, Howard?'

He thought about this for a moment as if looking for some hidden meaning. 'Fine,' he said finally. 'Would you like a drink?'

'Whatever you're having.'

'Are you going to write a book here in New Zealand?' David asked. 'I told the kids at school all your books were true and that you were a real adventurer.'

Jenny smiled at her son, but this time it was warm and genuine. 'I'm afraid I might have oversold you in the hero market,' she said to me, 'but boys like to have someone to look up to.'

As soon as she said it she snapped her jaws shut and I could see Howard's hand tremble as he poured the drink.

'Will you show me some karate tricks, Uncle Logan?' David chattered on, unconscious of the drop in the emotional climate. 'Like how to take a gun off a guy like you did in that book about diamonds in Africa.'

'Later on,' I said.

Howard brought the drink over, his lips tight. 'Perhaps we've all heard enough about your uncle's exploits already,' he said sharply.

David's open, enthusiastic face clouded as he looked at his father. There was pain there and incomprehension too. Howard made a tentative conciliatory gesture towards him, but the boy looked away, embarrassed now.

'I think it's about time for your bed, David,' said Jenny.

The boy made a half-hearted protest, but the tension in the room was so palpable that I don't think he was too unhappy to leave the adults to their problems.

'Will I see you again, Uncle Logan?' Solemnly.

'Sure. Maybe we could have a look at the museum together on Saturday when you're off school.'

His face cracked into a grin. It's hard to keep a small boy down. 'That'd be great!' He gave me a quick hug, his mother a kiss, and turned to go.

'Davy,' Howard called after him. He stopped, his grin gone, and returned to give his father an embarrassed peck on the cheek, then disappeared out of the room. Howard's expression was stony, but I caught a small shine in the corner of his eye. He took a long swallow of his drink.

'Sorry about your toes,' I said to break the descending silence.

He looked down at his feet absently. 'It was only three of the little ones. Doesn't bother me much.'

I didn't think I'd be so sanguine about having my toes amputated, but Jenny and I sat down while Howard remained standing, prodding at the fire with a poker. The silence stretched out embarrassingly. Finally Howard turned to me.

'So it's big brother to the rescue, is it?' There was no mistaking the tone of his voice.

'Jenny asked me to help,' I said.

'I don't need any help now,' he said bitterly. 'And I particularly don't need you as a bodyguard cum wet nurse.'

I was beginning to see how silly this all was. 'Look, Howard . . .' I began.

Jenny broke in. 'Howard – ' she sounded tired – 'let's not go through it again. You know why I asked Logan.'

'Because you think I'm two steps from a nervous breakdown!'

Jenny's eyes blazed. 'Yes! Maybe that's right. And maybe I'm not far behind. You nearly died last year. And now you're going back. Why shouldn't I be worried?'

Howard began to reply but Jenny held up her hand. 'Howard, I'm not stopping you going back,' she said more quietly. 'I just want someone to go with you who isn't . . . who . . .' She put her hand over her eyes and her voice tightened in her throat. 'I just don't want anything to happen to you.'

The flare went out of Howard and he reached over and stroked her hair tenderly. 'Okay, Jen. I said I agreed and I have.' He gave me a baleful glance. 'But I don't have to like it, and I can't guarantee that Warden will go along with it.'

'When will you speak to him?' I asked.

He took his drink and sank morosely into a chair. 'I'll see him in the morning.'

'What will you tell him? I mean, are you going to explain the real reason I'm along?'

'I'd prefer not to,' he said, looking away.

'I know how you feel, Howard,' I said placatingly. 'And I don't want to put you in an awkward position if I can help it.'

His eyes came swivelling back coldly. 'You know the best way to avoid that, don't you?'

I ignored the thrust. 'I've thought a bit about it since Jenny asked me to go with you this afternoon. I've had a good deal of Arctic training in the Canadian army and you could say that you've been trying to interest me in going on the expedition for some time, and that only recently have I been able to organize my commitments to fit in. I am your brother-in-law so it doesn't sound too offbeat.'

His face was impassive, far away. 'Yes, that sounds reasonable,' he said. I got the impression that Howard wasn't going to be over-zealous in pushing my case.

He resumed poking the fire, but there were many things I wanted to know. 'These men, Bill Claydon and Steven Rourk,' I started, 'you think they're still alive?'

'Didn't Jenny fill you in on the details?'

'Some of them. But her version's second-hand and probably not without a little bias. I'd prefer to hear it from the man who was there.'

He took his time, weighing up what I'd said, then remarked, 'At least you don't seem to like jumping to somebody else's conclusions.'

'I didn't say I'd believe you.'

For the first time that evening he smiled, but it was an inward, cynical smile. 'You're not without company,' he said.

But evidently he decided to chance his story one more time, like a gambler who always thinks the next one will be a winner. He told me how his two companions, who had been doing the surveying work in the party, had turned off towards a uniquely shaped nunatak to take some sightings while he pushed on; how a whiteout had pinned him down for a considerable time; and how, when he'd back-tracked, he had found their sledge and dogs abandoned and all their geographical work for the area apparently stolen.

'Couldn't they have wandered off and got lost in the whiteout?' I asked.

Howard shook his head. 'They were too experienced to do anything so foolish as that, and why would they take all their papers with them?' His eyes took on that far-horizon gaze that sailors often have. 'Anyway, I saw where they went.'

'Yes?' I prodded.

'I climbed the nunatak to look for them. The wind was getting up by the time I got into a position to see over the other side of the peak, but I had a clear view, nevertheless. There was a valley on the other side, a narrow valley but deep, cutting away from the nunatak and widening slightly. The ice cap piled up from its edges, even overhanging at the far end, but the valley itself was dry.'

'Dry!'

'There are a number of valleys in Victoria Land that are dry,' Jenny supplied. 'It's uncommon but not unknown in Antarctica.'

'At the end of the valley,' Howard continued quietly, almost to himself, 'there was a . . .' He paused.

'A city?' I said.

He almost visibly detached himself from that distant southern continent and brought himself back to his own living-room.

'For want of a better name, I call it a city. It seemed to have towers and some type of buildings.'

'Grampion thinks it's a ruin from some long-lost civilization,' Jenny filled in.

'It was no ruin!' Howard said vehemently. 'I could see smoke coming from it.'

'Just how long did you see it for?' I asked.

A doubtful shadow flickered across his narrow face. 'Only two or three minutes,' he said defensively. 'A blizzard was coming up and I had to get off the nunatak.'

'How far away was it?'

His lips compressed. 'A few miles. It was hard to judge distance with nothing to scale it by.'

When he'd been telling his story, I'd almost been there with him, so graphic his description and so sincere his tone; but looked at coldly it was pretty hard to take – a quick look down a valley with a blizzard starting to blow; you're liable to see anything.

'You think Claydon and Rourk went there?' I tried not to sound too incredulous.

'I think they were taken there.'

This time I couldn't hide the disbelief.

'There were a lot of footprints around the sledge, too many

. . .' he began to explain heatedly, then clamped his mouth shut at the look on my face.

'Why didn't you go down into the valley?' I asked quietly. To me this seemed the crunch question. If he was so sure his buddies were in the valley, why didn't he go after them?

He looked at me pityingly. 'You think you know all there is to know about tough country, ex-paratrooper, dilettante adventurer! Don't you think that was the first thing I did – strike camp and circle around trying to find a way into the valley? But I told you, a blizzard was coming up and a blizzard in that country is the end of the world. I was lucky to survive at all and by the time it blew itself out I hardly knew where *I* was, let alone the nunatak or the valley! It was more dumb luck than expertise that I picked up some landmarks to find my way back towards Scott Base.'

I tried to sound reasonable. 'Couldn't Claydon and Rourk have got lost in the same way?'

'Don't you see,' he said agitatedly, 'they were trained surveyors, I'm a biologist. The Antarctic is a continent of ice, tens of thousands of square miles of ice, an ocean of ice. They navigated us over that ocean, I was just a member of the crew. I wouldn't know which side is up on a sextant, and a compass that close to the magnetic pole is about as reliable as finding moss on the north side of a tree. I had trouble finding my way back; they wouldn't have.'

It began to sink in what an incredible journey Howard had made on his own. But it only served to underline the probability that the ordeal had twisted or blotted out much of what had really happened. 'I hope that we can find what you're looking for, Howard,' was all I could say.

'I'll find them,' he said, but he wasn't talking to me.

Chapter 3

I slept late the next morning and was awakened by bright sun filtering through the drapes on the sliding glass doors that opened on to the motel's terraced patio and pool. The telephone was ringing. It was on a table by the bed, a convenience that I'd meant to install in my apartment in Toronto every time some friend decided to ring me in the middle of the night.

'Logan Adams here,' I said.

The voice on the other end of the line was very cool, very urbane, with an English public-school accent. 'So glad I caught you, Mr Adams. My name is Silas Bannister. I'm Mr Warden Grampion's secretary. I take it you know that your brother-in-law, Howard Turbott, has put your name forward as a possible member of our Antarctic expedition?'

'Yes.'

'Good. I wonder, if you're not too busy, whether it might be possible for you to pop around some time this morning and have a word with Mr Grampion . . .' I heard a gruff voice in the background say, 'Not some time this morning, right now,' but Silas Bannister never missed a beat. 'Perhaps in half an hour would be convenient?' he continued.

I smiled. It sounded as if Grampion needed a smooth front man like Bannister. 'Suits me,' I said. 'Where do I go?'

He gave me an address in a suburb called St Helliers and then began to outline directions. 'That's all right,' I said, 'I know the area.'

'Good. We'll see you shortly then, Mr Adams.'

He hung up and I dressed and went out to the car and headed for the Tamaki Drive, a wide road that winds for about six miles along the Waitemata foreshore out towards St Helliers. I cruised along enjoying the sight of the long beaches, pleasant homes and apartment buildings and the incredibly crowded marinas. It seemed everyone in Auckland owned a boat. The green cone of Rangitoto lorded it over the many small islands in the immense harbour, and yachts tacked their way among the freighters anchored in the stream waiting to berth.

Tamaki Drive petered out at St Helliers into a maze of winding streets; but I soon found my destination, a very large, rambling home at the end of a cul-de-sac. Its rear side looked back towards a steep broken cliff at the water's edge, and the spacious grounds had the casual but well-tended appearance that bespeaks constant attention. I pulled into the short driveway and stopped behind a powerful-looking Jensen. For a man who presumably was only visiting the country, it didn't seem that Grampion was going to let himself go without his creature comforts.

The red scoria drive crunched under my feet as I went up to the heavily panelled door and searched for a bell. Before I could find it, a tall man, immaculately dressed in a conservative grey suit, whiter than white shirt and a public-school or regimental tie, opened the door.

'I'm afraid the bell is disguised as a grape in that carved bunch.' He pointed. 'Damned silly. Mr Adams?'

'Right.'

He held out a well-manicured hand. 'Silas Bannister. Do come in.'

We shook hands and I followed him into a large hall that would have done the average family as a lounge.

He saw me looking around and waved his hand deprecatingly. 'Not my taste, I'm afraid, but a friend of Mr Grampion's has let us use the house as a base for the six months or so we're here.' He turned to one of the doors leading off the hall. 'Mr Grampion's in the study. It's a bit of a shambles, but you no doubt understand the large amount of detail and organization that is required on a project of this sort.'

He didn't wait for a reply and I trailed him into the study. It *was* a shambles, but an orderly shambles. A great pile of boxes was stacked neatly, almost completely obscuring the laden bookshelves behind. Ice-axes, bamboo marker sticks, crampons, coils of Terylene rope, glare goggles, Primus stoves and a myriad other articles were neatly arranged on the thick Axminster carpet. Skis with ski skins and poles leaned against a wall next to a mound of thick down sleeping-bags. The large desk at one end of the crowded room was covered with lists and bills of lading. From behind it rose a shortish, solid man with thin, iron-grey hair, a round, meaty face, sharp grey eyes ledged with heavy eyebrows, and a large meerschaum clamped in his mouth.

'Logan Adams – Mr Grampion,' Bannister introduced us.

I picked my way through the welter of equipment and offered my hand. He wrapped a big, square paw around it. 'Howard says you're a writer,' he said, not taking the pipe from his mouth.

'I've done a few books.'

He pointed to a chair now occupied by a box of heavy wool socks. 'Dump that on the floor and sit down,' he ordered and thumped back into the swivel chair behind the desk.

I cleared the chair and settled myself in. Grampion's eyes darted over to where Silas Bannister leaned against a stool lighting a cigarette and obviously intending to include himself in the interview.

'Better give Stan and Ari a hand in the garage packing those sledge rations,' he said. 'I'll find out what all this is about Mr Adams joining us.'

Bannister, it seemed to me, would prefer to have stayed, but he said, 'Of course, Mr Grampion,' and left unhurriedly.

'Good man,' Grampion informed me when Bannister had shut the study door. 'Got an absolutely extraordinary ability to find the things we need and get them here on time. Could charm a starving man out of a meal.'

I took out my pipe and scraped the bowl clean with a small penknife I carry. Grampion looked me over coolly while I busied myself tamping in the tobacco.

'Bit out of the blue, isn't it?' he said in a clipped British accent.

I raised my eyebrows.

'Howard wanting you to come with us. Never mentioned you before.'

'We've always been close,' I lied glibly. 'He didn't know I could get away until just recently, so I imagine he saw no reason to bring it up.'

Grampion just grunted. It was plain he didn't believe that. 'You've got some cold-weather experience, he says?'

'In the army. I was in a paratroop battalion that was part of the Arctic Mobile Striking Force. We were supposed to stop the Russians if they decided to attack that way.'

He snorted with disgust. 'What did they expect the bloody Russians to do, walk across the North Pole?'

'The military mind,' I said.

His eyes narrowed. 'Is that why you got out?'

'One of the reasons.'

'And the others?'

'I like to be able to choose what I do and when I do it.'

'Why do you want to come on this expedition? You don't even know why we're going.'

'I know why Howard's going.'

He gave me a bleak look. 'The chances of finding out what happened to those men are nil. My thought is they're at the bottom of some crevasse or long drifted over with snow. I'm sure you are not so naïve as to think that I'm going to all this trouble, putting up all this money, to look for Howard's friends . . . or whatever.'

That was blunt enough.

'Howard also mentioned a city,' I said.

His basalt-grey eyes flashed. 'And what's your interest in this city?'

'None whatsoever.' I glanced at the gear strewn around the room. 'Except to wonder why anyone would go to so much trouble and expense looking for such a chimera.' I could be blunt too.

Surprisingly, he laughed. 'My archæological ideas are considered by many of my more traditional colleagues to be well out of the mainstream.' He scraped a bit of dottle out of his pipe with a match and relit it. 'However, they said the same of Schliemann when he set off to discover what was thought to be the purely mythical city of Troy.'

'Heinrich Schliemann at least had Homer as a basis,' I pointed out. 'I've never heard of cities or people having been thought to have existed in Antarctica, even in mythical poems.'

'You'd be surprised at the evidence.' He rummaged around in the desk litter and brought forth a black rock. 'What do you think of that?'

He passed it to me and I turned it over in my fingers. 'It's just a chunk of coal,' I said, perplexed.

'Precisely. From Antarctica.'

'Yes?' He seemed to think I should see some significance in that.

'Use your head, man!' He thrust the coal under my nose. 'It takes whole forests of trees to make a coal bed. And trees have to have a reasonable climate. At the moment, outside of a few species of lichen, there isn't a plant on the entire continent.' He took the coal. 'But once there were trees and that means a climate that people could live in.'

'But surely coal beds were laid down millions of years ago, long before there were even any monkeys in the trees to get the idea of coming down on to the ground?'

He tossed the black rock back on to the desk. 'That is the theory of the moment. But it, too, is riddled with anomalies.'

He's not only on the lunatic fringes of the archæological fraternity, I thought, but well out to the borders of geology, too.

Grampion saw the look on my face and must have guessed

what I was thinking. The animation that had filtered into his expression when he began to talk about his theories was quickly replaced by a businesslike mask.

'You don't know much about why I want to go to Antarctica and care even less. You also, I surmise, feel the futility of Howard's quest.' He paused for a moment, his eyes boring into me. 'Perhaps you'd be good enough to tell me what your reasons *are* for wanting to come on what could be a very arduous expedition?'

There wasn't much point in telling him that I just wanted to go along for the ride. He might have some science-fiction ideas about his pet hobby-horses, but he didn't strike me at all as a stupid man. I told him the truth.

When I'd finished he sat back in his chair and looked at the pastel-blue ceiling. 'Hmmph, I thought there was something that didn't quite sit right,' he mused. 'Howard came over here this morning looking like someone had kicked him in the groin and insisting that his good friend and brother-in-law be included in the trip. The funny thing was he could hardly bring himself to say anything good about you.' Grampion lowered his gaze to me. 'He isn't your friend, you know.'

'Jenny feels that Howard is in a very bad mental state, that he might – ah – break down,' I murmured in explanation. 'Particularly if he can't find Claydon and Rourk.'

He gave a little grunt. 'He won't find those men, you know. Certainly not alive. That's ridiculous.'

I couldn't quite understand this man's reasoning. 'If you think Howard is foolish to try to locate his lost companions, why are you so sure his story about the city is correct?'

Warden Grampion puffed his big-bowled pipe for a moment, then shrugged. 'Who can be sure? Of course the whole story from beginning to end might be nonsense. I realize that.' He smiled a touch and for the first time I saw that there might be a little humour in the man. 'But you must admit, there aren't many men returning from Antarctica these days with stories about lost cities. If it's true, it would dramatically prove many of my contentions about that continent. Schliemann's Troy would seem picayune by comparison! I could hardly pass up such a chance, no matter how remote the possibility.'

'And if there is no city?'

'It won't prove me wrong, it just won't prove me right.' I looked dubious and he went on, 'It doesn't matter at the moment. We'll have plenty of time in the next few months for me to indoctrinate you with my theories.'

I was surprised. I thought he would fight against including me, particularly when I told him the real reason for my going. 'You agree to me going with you, then?' I said to make sure I'd got it straight.

'Let's not hedge, Adams.' He aimed the stem of his pipe at me. 'If you don't go, your sister might make it difficult enough to stop Howard going. I don't want that to happen, so I back down. I don't like being forced into a course of action like this, but I'm too much of a pragmatist to throw the whole thing away on a point of honour.' The hard line of his mouth softened slightly and he leaned back. 'Besides, I think Howard might very well need someone to keep a check on him. We also need a bit more muscle and expertise which I think you can contribute, and although you may not agree with what I'll tell you about my contentions concerning the history of Antarctica, I think you've brains and interest enough to grasp what I'm talking about. Which is more than can be said for anyone else on this expedition who has so far joined us. Aside from that, the fact that you are a writer may be a great advantage if we are successful. A first-hand account by a professional author would help enormously to ram the truth into that lot of thick-headed old women who call themselves archæologists.'

Grampion's eyes gleamed at the thought and he held out his hand. 'You see, however you might have become involved with us, I intend to see that I make the most out of your talents.'

I shook his hand. I could understand Jenny not liking the man because of his crusty English manner – traits that don't sit easily with most New Zealanders – but as far as I was concerned, he called a spade by its right name and, weird theories aside, I thought we would get along very well.

'Just remember,' he said, 'you may make suggestions about this expedition. I make the decisions.'

Chapter 4

We talked for about half an hour, Grampion outlining the make-up of the expedition to me. With me, there would be eight men in all, each with a specific area of responsibility aside from the myriad general duties that everyone would be expected to perform. Grampion would, of course, be leader; Howard would act as guide, but a man named Stan Dawson, an American, would do the actual navigation; a Finn called Ari Kokko was their mechanic; a French Canadian, Gus LaFlette, their dog-handler; another American, Charly Train, was a geologist; and a New Zealander with the unlikely name of 'Plum' Pitt was to be their cinematographer. Train and LaFlette weren't expected from overseas until next week and Pitt was only required occasionally at the moment, when his particular equipment needed sorting out; the other two, Dawson and Kokko, were living in the house with Grampion and Bannister. My task on the trip was to be radio operator. Dawson had been assigned, but I persuaded Grampion that I understood the equipment they were going to use well enough to relieve him of the extra task.

The archæologist seemed pleased. 'You could well turn out to be more a help than a hindrance after all. Dawson will have plenty on his plate without the worry of the radio.'

'What about Bannister? What's his job on the trip?'

'Silas?' Grampion's lip curled into a smile around his pipe-stem. 'I'm afraid you wouldn't get Silas any farther into the wilderness than somebody's country estate. No, Silas helps me organize my jaunts, then he looks after my affairs when I'm gadding about. If I had to do it all myself, I'd never get into the field.'

He stood up and looked over his meerschaum at me. 'Let's go and introduce you to Dawson and Kokko. They're in the garage packing up sledge rations.'

We left the maelstrom in the study and Grampion led me down a short passage which opened into a large, well-equipped kitchen presided over by a huge Maori woman with a bright floral apron and a wide smile. Grampion introduced her as Mary, their cook and housekeeper.

'Belongs to the people who let me use the house,' Grampion explained. 'Mary, this is Mr Adams, who is joining our expedition.'

Mary put the fourteen-inch cast-iron frying pan down as lightly as if it had been made of aluminium, wiped her strong brown hand on her apron and held it out. 'Don't belong to no one but my old man,' she boomed good-naturedly, 'and that only as long as he keeps me well-loved and well-fed. You staying for lunch? I'll put on a couple more chops.'

I laughed to myself as she pumped my hand. By the look on Grampion's solid face, I could see that he wasn't used to having the hired help anything but deferential.

'Not today, thanks, Mary. I'll look forward to it another time.'

We left her clattering happily, and Grampion showed me through another door in the kitchen that opened directly into a three-car garage connected to the house. There was only one car in it at the moment, a four-door Datsun 1600. The rest of the space was taken up by stacks of food supplies being broken up into individual packs. Silas Bannister was checking off items on a list while two other men arranged them in piles comprising twenty man-day rations – a food pack containing such items as chocolate, porridge oats, biscuits, sugar, butter, bacon, pemmican, milk powder, potato powder, cheese, sultanas, egg and soup powders and even some dried onion for taste; all, except the onions, extremely high calorie food which is essential to operate efficiently in low temperatures. Each food pack would supply 4800 calories per day for twenty days. But I found all this out later when I did my own stint at packing. At the moment I was more interested in the two men with Bannister.

One of them stood literally head and shoulders above the other. He was at least six foot five and massive, with that thick torso that denotes power rather than agility. Growing out of a neck like a strong man's thigh was a shiny round head with a shiny red face. A thin shock of sparse dirty blond hair and a straggly Zapata moustache tried to hide the impression that the head was really the shape of a battered baseball. What there were of eyebrows perched on mounds of scar tissue that pressed down over two small, humourless, bloodshot, light blue eyes. He looked like a wrestler whose favourite method of attack was to batter his opponents unconscious with his head.

The other man was shorter but still solidly built. He looked compact and quick and very sure of himself. His thin mouth seemed to have a slight sneer twisted permanently into it and his eyes were dark and watching. He noticed us first and one eyebrow cocked quizzically towards Bannister. The tall Englishman looked up and for just an instant surprise widened his eyes, but it was quickly covered with a lazy smile. I got the distinct impression he thought I would have been long gone, summarily dismissed by his boss. Evidently he didn't know the details of Howard's argument for my accompanying them and thought that Grampion would soon have been rid of me.

'Showing Mr Adams around before he leaves, Mr Grampion?' he said with what I thought to be a hopeful note.

Grampion didn't appear to notice. 'Mr Adams is going to join us on the expedition.'

Bannister's practised suavity covered his surprise and he said, 'Welcome aboard, then, Mr Adams. I can't say I'd go out of my way to spend months living in the snow, but then I'm not really the outdoor type.'

Grampion introduced me to the shorter of the other two. 'This is Stan Dawson. He's the man with the most polar experience and is acting as my second-in-command.'

'Logan Adams,' I said, and he shook my hand perfunctorily.

'Since I am supposed to be second-in-command,' he said to Grampion, 'how come I don't have some say in any new additions to our group?'

Grampion bristled. 'Second-in-command means you are in charge of the safety and outfitting of the party. That's how Silas outlined your job when you were hired. I am the man, and the only man, who says who is in the party.'

Dawson's expression never wavered. 'Sure,' he said. 'I was just wondering what Mr Adams was supposed to do on the expedition. All the jobs have been allocated.'

'He'll look after the radio,' Grampion stated.

Dawson's eyes narrowed thoughtfully. 'I was looking after that part of it.'

'You'll have plenty to do without that.'

I felt that the American was put out because he hadn't been consulted so I tried to smooth the path. There'd be enough problems surviving in the Antarctic without getting off on the wrong foot to start with. 'I know the equipment, Stan,' I said, 'and I've had quite a bit of Arctic experience. I think you'll find I'll pull my weight.'

He looked at me and smiled, but his eyes were distant. 'Sure,' he clapped me on the shoulder. 'We'll get along all right.'

'And this is Ari Kokko – ' Bannister took up the introductions – 'the man with the mechanical mind.' The way he said it, it wasn't a compliment, but the big man didn't seem to notice. He moved towards me quickly and I was forced to reassess my opinion about his agility as he engulfed my hand in his.

'Glad to know you,' he said in barely recognizable English.

I thought he was being friendly until I felt the pressure

increase on my hand and caught the malevolent glint in those watery blue eyes. He was strong! I tried to resist the crushing force of those steel-tendoned fingers, but I could feel his hand closing around mine, squeezing the bones together as easily as it would a child's. He looked down at me, his small mouth parted in a half smile and the smell of fish on his breath pungently close. He wasn't kidding! He was going to break my hand!

Instinctively I took the thumb of my right hand, the hand he was trying to pulp, into my left and ground my knuckles into the nerve on the back of his hand. He gave a small gasp and his hand sprang open involuntarily. He stepped back slightly bewildered, looking at his hand, amazed that he had been made to let go. The whole incredible incident had only taken a few seconds, and glancing around I could see that neither Bannister nor Grampion had noticed anything amiss. Dawson, who was standing in a better position to see, had a somewhat amused but thoughtful expression.

'I can see we're going to be just one big happy family,' I said, making an effort not to give the big Finn even the satisfaction of seeing me rub my hand.

'Don't mind Ari,' Dawson said, giving me a supercilious smile. 'He's always playing his little jokes. Keeps us all in stitches.'

Grampion didn't know what we were talking about, so he ignored it and said, 'Right, Logan, we'd better leave these men to their work. They've got a tremendous amount to get set up in the next few weeks. The sooner you can pitch in, the better. When do you think that will be?'

'I have one or two things to get sorted out.' I mentioned the book promotion. 'But I should be free by the beginning of the week.'

'You'll be staying here?' It was more a statement than a question.

There was no reason not to, but the thought of being cooped up with this crew suddenly didn't seem very appetizing.

'I'll stay on at my hotel until I clear up my other business.'

'Fine. I suppose we'll be seeing enough of each other once we're in Antarctica.'

They were my sentiments exactly.

I left the house in St Helliers with no sense of pleasure. Of the four men I'd so far met who were going on the polar expedition, only Grampion seemed in any way amenable. Howard's attitude I could understand, but Stan Dawson had no real cause to resent me, and that gorilla, Kokko, needed to be kept in a cage. I hoped the three others would be easier to like or it was going to be a thoroughly unpleasant trip.

I headed the car towards Parnell and Jenny and Howard's house. She would be wondering how I'd managed. I navigated the long curving driveway and pulled up behind their Holden. If Howard was home, so much the better – we now had to come to some sort of working arrangement and the sooner the better.

Jenny had heard the car and opened the door as I reached it. She sounded a lot brighter. 'Come in, Logan. I've just put the coffee-pot on.'

'Howard home?'

'No, he's still got lectures to give at the university.'

'I thought you said he was quitting?'

'He'll see the term out, or most of it anyway.' Some of the brightness went out of her voice. 'It's not easy for him.'

We sat in a little breakfast nook in the kitchen and Jenny poured out two large mugs of coffee. 'Well, how did you get on with Lord Grampion?'

'Careful, Jen, your Kiwi Pom prejudice is showing.'

She laughed and mixed a heaped teaspoonful of sugar into her coffee. 'I guess I do put him down unjustly. I suppose I blame him for Howard being able to go back to Antarctica. But he can be awfully pompous and pushy.'

'Whatever he is, he seems to be well organized. And better than that, well supplied with money. Aside from dog teams, we're taking a Weasel full-track vehicle and two Sno-cats.

That kind of equipment doesn't come cheaply.'

'I understand he's extremely wealthy. I don't know where it comes from – businesses, I think – but it makes him completely independent when it comes to setting up expensive archæological expeditions.' She sipped her coffee. 'I take it you've been accepted on the team?'

'I'm going if not quite accepted.'

'They believed Howard's story, then?'

'I only spoke to Grampion, and whatever you think of him, he's no fool. I had to tell him the truth.'

'Oh,' she said resignedly, 'that will make it hard for Howard.'

I had thought of that when Grampion and I had discussed it. 'There's no need to say anything about it to Howard. As far as he's concerned, Grampion accepted his reasons at face value.'

Jenny was obviously relieved. She knew how much it was hurting her husband to be forced to have me along.

'Besides Warden Grampion,' I asked, 'what do you think of the rest of the crew?'

Jenny's generous mouth curled. 'I only met them once, when they first arrived. We had dinner at the house in St Helliers. I've spoken to Silas Bannister many times on the phone since, but I don't really know him.'

'What was your impression?'

'Of Silas Bannister? All smarm and charm. I suppose he does his job well.'

'And the others?'

'Stan Dawson?' She shrugged her shoulders. 'A rather caricatured loud-mouthed American, and that Finn – what's his name? Kokko – he gives me the creeps. He just sat through the whole dinner stuffing his face and looking at me as if he thought I was going to be dessert.' She laughed. 'I sound quite the xenophobe, don't I? But don't believe it. Some of my best friends are foreigners.'

'What about "Plum" Pitt?'

'I haven't met him yet – ' she poked fun at herself – 'but since he's a New Zealander he should be all right.'

'I wonder how Grampion came across them? They don't seem the types he would normally know.'

'No, he's got no experience in Arctic or Antarctic exploration. Most of his digs have been in South and Central America and in the Middle East. Howard says Bannister found Stan Dawson, and he brought in Kokko. I don't know about the other two, the dog-handler and the geologist. I think they were suggested to Grampion by people in some geographic society, but I'm not sure. Pitt evidently heard about the expedition on his own private grapevine and offered his services to Grampion. He's apparently fairly well known as a mountaineer and also for making movies in all sorts of out-of-the-way places all over the world.'

'What are you going to do now?' she went on. 'Do you have to arrange with anybody to go off like this?'

I could almost hear D'arcy Maginnes, my publisher, screaming already. 'I was supposed to go from Australia to the States on promotion tours. I'll have to cancel that,' I said.

Jenny reached for my hand, chagrined. 'Oh, Logan, I have dropped you in it.'

'I don't think so. Book promotion tours aren't my favourite way of spending time. And if I can't get a novel out of a trip to Antarctica, I've been calling myself an author under false pretences. Who knows, we might even find Grampion's lost city.'

She smiled wanly. There was only one thing Jenny was interested in – her husband's return.

Chapter 5

D'arcy Maginnes didn't like the idea of my cutting his promotion tour short. 'Antarctica!' like a small explosion was blown back around the world to me. 'But what about the States? Australia was just a warm-up and that's only half done!' His voice crackled on over the long-distance line from Toronto.

'Look, D'arcy,' I said when he'd run down a little, 'I'm the man who puts the words on the paper. And to do that I need to have something to say. Would you rather have me huckstering around the world something that's selling pretty well anyway or getting together first-class material for the next?'

There was a pause from the other side of the world. D'arcy was weighing up the pros and cons on the little gold balance in his head. I represented an asset that he didn't actually own but was nevertheless a source of profit. How could I or would I be used to best maximize that profit was ticking through his mind. The result popped out like a computer card. 'Okay, Logan,' he said, 'do the Antarctica bit. I'll even throw in a five-thousand-dollar advance on the book if you live to write it.'

I laughed to myself. It might sound as if D'arcy Maginnes was being generous with his money, but I knew that he was really just pinning me down to actually producing something for him out of the trip. 'Right, D'arcy, you'll get your book even if I have to make it up.'

I called Grampion next and told him that I had sorted out my commitments and would be able to join them any time.

'The sooner the better,' he said. 'What about Sunday? I'll be out of town with Stan and Ari, but Silas can get you settled in.'

'Sounds fine.'

'Good. With Train and LaFlette arriving, that means everyone will be here by Tuesday.'

I took David to the museum next day as I'd promised, but I didn't see Howard when I picked him up. I gathered from Jenny that he was still smarting and wasn't too enthusiastic about my company. I couldn't really blame him, but it wasn't going to help anybody, especially him, if he continued in his coolness. But I didn't have much time to dwell on it as David and I took in every exhibit on every floor, and I was a weary man when I returned to my hotel.

I unlocked the door to my room, took a few steps inside and stopped. The room wasn't as I'd left it. I had arranged some papers concerning the promotion tour on a small table by the bed and had placed a military brush set in a leather case on top of them. The brush set was still there but in a slightly different position and one of the snaps on it that had been damaged at one time and needed a tricky twist to make it close properly was now open.

Someone had been in there. Not the maid. She'd cleaned up before I left.

I slammed open the bathroom door but the room was empty. Nevertheless, I could see that my toilet gear had had the once-over also. I went back to the bedroom and opened my large flight bag. Everything was there: travellers' cheques, passport, even about fifty dollars in cash in one of the pockets. Whoever had gone through my things, robbery obviously wasn't the motive. I tried the sliding doors that led out to the patio but they were still locked. Not that that meant anything: if you can get in through a locked door, you can get out again leaving it locked.

I checked everything over once again and then poured myself two ounces of whisky from my flask, fished a fresh pipe from my bag, settled into the room's only comfortable chair and tried to make some sense out of it. The man had been a pro. If it hadn't been for the snap on the brush case and my own awareness of how I'd left everything, I would never have noticed anything amiss. Nothing had been stolen, and in any case thieves don't carefully replace everything they touch in the same spot that it came from. Someone just wanted to know about me!

Ridiculous. But maybe not all that ridiculous. In the past I had used some pretty touchy political information in my books, and perhaps someone thought I was mixed up in something similar in New Zealand. Somehow the thought of any international intrigue in such a quiet backwater struck me as humorous, and by the time I'd had dinner that evening I'd put the incident to the back of my mind.

The last few nights I'd got into the habit of taking a walk through a small park that backs on to the hotel and after dinner I wandered out as usual. The ground drops away steeply from the park down to a public swimming bath below and a small estuary called Judge's Bay. The Tamaki Drive sweeps along beside all this on reclaimed land along the waterfront. There are steep steps down the cliff face and then a pedestrian overpass that spans the baths and the drive.

I stopped on a small viewing platform at the top of the steps and looked out at the harbour as I lit my pipe. There was a cruise ship just entering the Rangitoto channel on its way to the open sea, all blazing lights and farewell whistles. While I watched, a man passed me and went down the steps to the overpass. I didn't pay him much attention; a heavy-set man, a Maori or Islander, I thought.

I followed a moment or two later in a pleasant, ruminative mood and it wasn't until I was in the middle of the bridge that I noticed that the man was coming back towards me and that two others were quickly descending the cliff stairs behind me. They too appeared to be Polynesians, roughly dressed in old denim jackets and jeans. One was carrying a beer bottle by the neck and the other a thick batten.

Toughs fresh from the pub, I thought, looking for an easy mugging to replenish their wallets, and I was trapped on a narrow footbridge thirty feet above a roadway busy with late-night traffic.

The two from the park side were closest, but the bridge was too narrow for both to walk abreast. I stuck my pipe in my pocket and sprinted towards them.

It caught them by surprise. The man in front hardly had time to raise his bottle before I leaped up and caught him in the chest and stomach with a crunching double kick made more powerful because he stepped right into it. He smashed back into his companion and they went down in a tumble as I cracked down heavily on one knee. Before I could regain my feet the third man was over me, swinging a beer bottle.

'This'll take the crap outa ya, Adams!' he yelled as he brought the bottle down with enough force to squash my skull.

I threw myself under the blow and the bottle thumped into my back, thankfully not breaking. I was still low, but now I had my feet under me. I thrust my arm between his legs and heaved up. He was a thick, heavy-set man, more fat than muscle, and if it hadn't been for his own momentum, I don't think I could have got him up so easily or so high. As he went up in the air, I gave his body a shove sideways and he sailed over the safety rail of the bridge and dropped screaming to the road below. I heard the squeal of brakes and the dull thunk-thunk as wheels passed over flesh.

The other two saw him go and it cooled any fight left in them. They turned and ran, one painfully, back the way they'd come. I started after them but the bang I'd taken on the knee slowed me to a hobble. By the time I climbed the stairs back to the park they were long gone.

When I limped into the lighted lobby of the Heron I realized that my pants leg was torn open and a bloody scraped knee was poking out. The girl behind the desk raised a polite eyebrow.

'The last time I was in Auckland, you could walk down the

street at night without worrying about being mugged,' I said testily.

She was all solicitude now that she realized that I wasn't just a drunk who'd fallen down. 'Is there anything we can do?'

I could hear the police and ambulance sirens cutting through the still night air as they converged on the Tamaki Drive. 'You might phone the police,' I said, 'and tell them that I might be able to assist them with their enquiries concerning the man who fell off the Parnell overpass. Adams in 103.' I began to limp across the lobby.

'Are you all right?' she asked anxiously.

'Yes, nothing serious,' I said, and fingered the tattered cloth of my trouser leg. 'Not much can be done for the pants, though. I'm afraid we'll have to declare them dead on arrival.'

By the time I'd had a shower to try to take some of the soreness out of the spot on my back where the bottle had caught me, a sergeant and a constable arrived. I spent the next three hours at the central city watch house having my injuries recorded by a police doctor and making a written statement for a very understanding detective-lieutenant. It was a straight robbery attempt as far as he was concerned. They thanked me for my co-operation, apologized for the attack and for the inconvenience, and after mentioning that I might be asked in to have a look at a line-up if they picked up anybody that fitted the descriptions I'd given, laid on a patrol car to return me to the hotel.

It wasn't until I was back in my room and climbing wearily into bed that I remembered. The man who went over the rail had called me Adams.

Chapter 6

The next morning I checked out and headed over to the house in St Helliers. When I drove under the Parnell overpass, there was no sign of last night's litter of cars, body, blood and broken beer bottle. Police, ambulance and wrecking truck, the social dustmen, had cleared the mess so that no early-morning motorist would ever know that violent death had occurred a few short hours before.

'Good to see you again, Logan,' Silas Bannister said, and took my bag from me at the door. 'Mr Grampion said you'd be along some time this weekend. I think he told you that he and Stan would be away in Wellington for a few days seeing about berthing facilities for our boat?'

'He said it would be all right to get settled in.'

'Certainly, certainly,' he said effusively. 'Come, I'll show you your room first and then we can have lunch when you've got yourself arranged.'

The house was built on two levels, with a bedroom wing to one side of the main living area and the kitchen and garage, which I'd seen on my first visit, on the other side, with more bedrooms upstairs. He showed me into a small room that I presumed was once a child's room. 'The other bedroom is bigger,' Bannister explained, 'but we'll have to put two in there. I thought you'd prefer to be on your own.'

'Thanks,' I said. 'This will do perfectly.'

'Will you be doing a book about the expedition?' He sat down in a comfortable chair and took out a slim silver cigarette case.

I opened my bag and began hanging my meagre wardrobe

in the closet. 'If I don't, my publisher is going to be very unhappy.'

'I read *Assassination*. Enjoyed it very much. Very authentic. It seems much of it is based on actual experience; if so, your connection with the world's various espionage agencies is fascinating.'

'I've met a few odd people over the years,' I said non-committally, 'but I write fiction, not fact.'

'This expedition is fact.'

'You'd never believe it.' I laughed.

'True,' he replied, not smiling. 'I sometimes wonder if it's not just a bad dream.'

It was a strange thing to say and I waited for him to explain further.

'I mean it's one of the most complicated and difficult expeditions I've ever helped Grampion put together,' he continued smoothly. 'It's been an absolute nightmare. I make no secret of the fact that I'll be glad when it's under way.' He glanced at a chunky gold watch with an intricate and very expensive chain-mesh strap. 'What do you say to an apéritif before our Mary the Maori clangs the dinner bell?' It was said with an attempt at light-heartedness, but I detected a note of disapproval. It seemed that the housekeeper didn't fit his conception of the proper servant any more than she did Grampion's.

We went back to the lounge in the central section of the house and Bannister poured us two large whiskies from a small, well-stocked bar.

'Seems quiet here this morning. Where is everybody?'

'The calm before the storm, I'm afraid.' He handed me a glass. 'As I said, Warden and Stan are in Wellington arranging the berth for our ship and also meeting LaFlette, who's flying in today from Canada with twenty Labrador huskies. Kokko is in Christchurch checking over the two Sno-cats and the Weasel. The idea is to sail down the coast and pick them up there. Pitt, the cameraman, isn't needed yet; Train arrives tomorrow and I hope you won't mind meeting him as I have literally a thousand things to organize, and Howard is at home in the bosom of his family. However, Warden, Stan, Gus LaFlette and Kokko will be back by Tuesday and everyone else will be here for dinner that night. The first general assembly, so to speak, so make the most of the peace while it lasts.'

Over lunch we talked about the planning for the expedition and Bannister filled me in on what had been done and what was still to be done. He seemed to have it all well in hand.

I held up my glass of nicely chilled hock in a small toast. 'For an expedition headed into the rigours of the frozen south, you don't appear to believe in any preliminary toughening-up period.'

Bannister smiled and returned the toast. 'I think the rest would get by with beer and chips if I didn't arrange things on a little higher plane.'

'Warden said you were an expert organizer. You keep an eye on his business interests, too, don't you, while he's off digging up lost cities?'

'If having complete *de facto* control and with it the responsibility of several million pounds' investments and numerous large businesses is what Warden considers "keeping an eye", then yes, that is correct,' he said with his usual urbane smile. 'But my doings are really all rather on the dull side.' He changed the subject. 'Now, you seem a man who would have many exciting adventures to relate.'

'If you call being mugged exciting,' I answered by way of conversation and told him about the attack on the overpass. 'The funny thing is,' I continued, 'I'm almost sure the man who died called me by name.'

I glanced up and was surprised to find Bannister with his fork stalled half-way to his mouth and his face ashen.

'You all right?'

He put the fork down untouched. 'What do you mean – he called you by name?'

'Adams. I think he called me Adams while he tried to take

my head off with a beer bottle.'

'But you're not sure?'

I shrugged. 'If it made a bit more sense, I might find it easier to believe.'

'Yes, it does sound incredible. You probably misheard whatever was said in the heat of the moment. Hard enough to understand this New Zealand accent even when you've got time to listen.' He began to eat again, but his appetite seemed to have deserted him, and when I asked him what needed to be done first, his mind was clearly on other things. 'Not much really, today. I expect the radio equipment early next week and naturally you'll want to check all that out. Warden will be arranging specific jobs once everyone's here, but until then you're pretty much on your own.'

'You mentioned meeting the geologist chap tomorrow.'

'If you wouldn't mind. He'll be in on Flight 504 Air New Zealand at ten-fifty tomorrow morning.' He stood up, took a key from his pocket and handed it to me. 'For the front door. I have to go into town to arrange some details of our move to Wellington. I'll have to leave you to settle in.'

As I went back to my room to finish unpacking, it occurred to me that I'd probably never have a better opportunity to poke through the house on my own. Save for Mary in the kitchen, where I was sure she'd remain, the place was empty.

I bypassed my door and looked into the bedroom next to it. It was the larger room Bannister had referred to with two single beds; the room destined for Train and LaFlette. Like mine, it had a sliding glass door which opened on to a large flagstone patio. I left it and moved to the last room in the hallway.

I eased the door open and stepped in. It was more or less identical to the room next door but occupied. One of the beds had been neatly made but the other had just had the covers pulled up. On it was strewn a welter of discarded clothes that by size were plainly Ari Kokko's. On the table beside it were several well-thumbed Scandinavian porno magazines and the half-eaten remains of a chocolate bar. In the bureau, the clothing had been stuffed into the drawers. That area of the room was a mess. Oddly, the other side had a military neatness. I assumed this to be Dawson's corner. I had a quick look in the bureaux and the closet but found nothing that told me anything about the two men. The absence of personal items seemed odd. Here were two men far from home in a strange country about to go to an even stranger country and there wasn't a letter, a photo, a single thing that related them to anyone else in the world. Even their clothes were relatively new and unremarkable. And two such different men. Dawson with his shoes and boots carefully ordered and cleaned, his bed tightly made, the drawers in his bureau enough to make a Dutch housewife proud; and Kokko, a sloven in mind and body. I wondered why they shared. They could easily have taken separate rooms and let the rest of us fit in as we came.

My bedroom and the others I'd checked were in a ground-floor wing. The master bedrooms, or rather, the master and mistress bedrooms, I found in the central portion of the house on a second floor reached by a clever little stairway from the main entrance hall that I hadn't realized was there because it had a door to it. There was a landing that overlooked the drive in front of the house and the bedrooms, facing the rear of the house, led off this. Neither was locked and a large bathroom and toilet joined them. Grampion had appropriated the more masculine of the two and I went into it first.

It offered no surprises. Disorderly, but the kind of disorder in which you knew that its creator could put his hand on anything he wanted without a search. I thumbed through several archæological treatises from different learned societies beside the bed, but there was nothing else of note.

I went through the bathroom, all bright colours and non-absorbent shag-pile carpet, the kind of bathroom that makes you want to get up in the morning, and on into Bannister's room.

There was nothing particularly remarkable about his room

either, except for a closet full of Savile Row suits, jackets and slacks, and drawers overstocked with expensive shirts. Grampion must pay him very well, I thought. And then something white on the floor of the closet caught my eye. It was a piece of folded paper, and I had smoothed it out instinctively before I realized I was probably not meant to read it. It was a big, solid gambling debt at Borriges, a very posh, very select club in London, marked 'Paid in full'. Just under £30,000 paid off over the last ten months! I wondered how he managed to lose so much and live so well at the same time. It was a trick I could well utilize.

I refolded the receipt, returned it to the closet floor, and went downstairs to Grampion's study. It was still jammed with equipment, more even than the first time I'd seen it. I came upon three well-read and annotated copies of Immanuel Velikovsky's books, *Worlds in Collision*, *Ages in Chaos* and *Earth in Upheaval*, on Grampion's desk, and it was apparent that they were part of the base on which he built his theory of Antarctic civilization. I took them back to the lounge, hoping I could get at least a grounding in the archæologist's thought processes from the books.

Bannister returned about four-thirty and went out again shortly after. I hardly noticed. I was immersed in a detailed, blow-by-blow description about how not so long ago the world ended.

Chapter 7

I read most of the night and put down *Worlds in Collision* not long before the first birds shook themselves awake. The other two books were a further historical and geological grounding for the main theory put forward in *Worlds in Collision*, and I put them aside until I found out about the idea in general.

Velikovsky, I read, believes Venus to have once been a comet which had some very near misses with Earth and Mars until it settled into a planetary orbit. The main conjunctions came in the fourteenth and seventh centuries BC and, particularly in the initial meetings, the earth took a fearful pounding. So bad, in fact, that it was knocked completely out of its orbit and the poles shifted.

It was an incredible idea and one that nobody would take seriously if it were not for the immense amount of verification, historical, archæological and geological, that the author had amassed in a lifetime of work. The step-by-step picture of the earth passing through the tail of this great comet that was to become a planet, the seas heaving themselves on to the land, whole regions sinking, the ground ripped open, clouds of gases darkening the sky for years, climates changing drastically almost overnight, most of the human race perishing and the survivors having to find a new calendar to replace the old because the earth now took five days longer to circle the sun; this was just the surface of the cosmic disaster that Velikovsky explained in painstaking detail.

And Antarctica? Apparently a sub-tropical land that suddenly found itself in the polar regions when the earth toppled from its place in the heavens, more or less instantly frozen like the woolly mammoth found embedded in the ice in the Siberian tundra, the meat still edible and grassy food between its teeth. I could see Grampion extrapolating the theory from there. If Antarctica was a sub-tropical or temperate land in fairly recent times, why should there not be a civilization built on it and why could not some of it have been preserved?

The magnitude of such a find would further verify Velikovsky and completely upturn all the established theories about the history of the world. It was an achievement that would ensure a prime place in posterity or at least until the next cataclysm. I began to understand why Warden Grampion could spend so much and risk so much on Howard's story, even though he didn't entirely believe it. The prize was so great it justified everything.

I turned out the light finally and slept for the few hours left before I was due to go out to the airport and meet the geologist, Charly Train. As I drifted off I thought: he must know quite a bit about the geological aspects of the Velikovsky theory. It would be something to learn.

Bannister was up and away before I emerged and it wasn't long until I was out on the road speeding along to the airport. I had slept until the last minute, and only very rapid moving would get me to the terminal on time. Mary had been keeping my breakfast and she wasn't very pleased when I left it. I wasn't very pleased either and hoped I could get something not too ghastly at the airport.

I hurried into the bustle of the main concourse right on the dot and made a beeline for the Air New Zealand information desk. I had no idea what Charly Train looked like and, unless he was carrying a rock hammer, I didn't think his being a geologist would help much in identification.

The passengers from Flight 504 were just checking through Customs and I asked the girl behind the desk if she would put out a call for Charles Train on that flight to come to the information desk. Her voice boomed hollowly over the loudspeakers, and if you half knew what to expect I supposed you might possibly understand it. Once again the call went out unintelligibly, but at least the name Train stood out fairly well and I presumed the geologist would be looking out for some message for him. I waited by the desk watching the people moving to and fro and wondering which one Charly Train would turn out to be. A chunky individual with big hands and a battered suitcase shouldered his way up to the desk, although there was no one to shoulder against, and stood behind a slim, dark woman who'd popped in just ahead of him.

Must be him, I thought. I'd seen no one else emerge from Customs who looked remotely like a geologist experienced in Arctic conditions as Train was supposed to be. I was looking him up and down trying to make a first-sight assessment when the woman ahead of him turned and stepped over to me.

'Are you from the Grampion Antarctic Expedition?' she asked.

She had the friendly, aggressive look of a news reporter and my mind fumbled for a moment trying to shift into the proper gear. 'That's right,' I said, wondering how she'd picked me.

She held out a strong hand. 'Charly Train,' she said.

There was no doubt she expected the dumb look on my face. 'Charly's for Charlotte, not for Charles,' she repeated like a litany said a thousand times before. 'I take it you were expecting someone else?' She smiled. She had a big square mouth that showed a lot of teeth. Great if they're good and hers were perfect.

'Somekind else.' I was beginning to recover from the initial shock and I could see she was enjoying the upset she'd caused. 'I take it you realized I'd be looking for a man.'

'Something between Paul Bunyan and an Eskimo.' Her wide-set, dark eyes lost their twinkle. 'And that's just what you're going to get, besides a damned good scientist.'

'I'm not the man to convince, I'm afraid.'

'Aren't you Silas Bannister?'

'Silas was pretty busy so he asked me to meet you. Logan Adams.'

She looked at me directly, then her gaze shifted inward and I could almost see the card index riffling behind her big eyes. 'The writer?' she said definitely, the question behind it being, 'What's your connection with this outfit?'

'My fame is world-wide.'

'I've heard of you.'

Did I detect a faint put-down? Perhaps she didn't like adventure novels. 'I'm going to be one of your companions on this jaunt,' I said. 'Do you have any luggage?'

She pointed. 'I left it over there. No one mentioned you were coming with us,' she continued, striding along beside me.

'No one mentioned to me you were a woman.' I picked up the bags and headed towards the exit. 'But I suppose nobody knew that.'

'I don't know why.' She laughed. 'Do you think it's because I sign everything "Charly" and they just assume I'm a man?'

I shook my head. Charlotte Train was very self-possessed, but Warden Grampion didn't strike me as the kind of man who would welcome a woman on his expedition, no matter what her qualifications.

When we had settled in the car I said, 'Look, there's no one at the house today, they're spread over the country organizing like crazy. I missed breakfast and I'm starving. How about stopping in town for lunch?'

'I could eat a wolf if it had wine to go with it.'

She had a definite air about her, not a person who said maybe. I glanced at her as we drove out of the airport. A strong jaw, high cheek-bones, alert and competent, a person to be reckoned with. It would be interesting to see how she handled Grampion.

'How do you fit into this?' she asked as we sped along in the light Sunday traffic. 'Ghost-writing the memoirs?'

'I always put my own name to anything I write.' I told her that Howard Turbott was my brother-in-law and he had invited me along.

I headed downtown to the Intercontinental, or the Big 'I' as it is known locally. By international standards it's just another hotel, but it does boast a restaurant on its top floor that gives a superb view of the city's vast and impressive harbour.

'It's beautiful,' she said as we took our seats by the large windows. The day was crisp, and the buildings along the quay, the freighters and container ships riding at the many piers behind them, even the high span of the Auckland harbour bridge and the houses on the North Shore, stood out with hard clarity in the clean air.

The waiter delivered two menus and left us to our deliberations. 'I don't know about the wolverine,' I said, 'but a small steak wouldn't do me any harm.'

She turned from the window. 'Hmm, sounds good to me.' She took the wine list from its holder and looked it up and down. 'I don't know these local wines. What are they like?'

'Good. I'd never order anything else. Anyway, it irks me to have to pay double or triple the price for an overseas wine that has nothing to recommend it except the distance it's travelled to get here.'

She laughed. A genuine, full-throated laugh. 'Your Scottish ancestry is showing. But I'm quite willing to bow to your judgement.'

The waiter returned and we gave our orders. Just that: I gave mine and she gave hers, but she graciously allowed me to pick the wine. Here was a woman who was well used to operating as an equal in the world of men but hadn't lost the ability to be charming. She might not have as much trouble with Grampion as I first imagined.

'You seem to know more about me than I do about you.'

'As you said, your fame is world-wide. Anyway, with a name like Logan Adams, I didn't expect you to be a Bulgarian.'

The waiter brought our steaks and I poured us each a glass of Bakano, a very dry red that I like. I took a sip and said,

'How did you get involved with this expedition anyway, seeing that it's quite obvious nobody knows you personally?'

'Warden Grampion is well known to the Geographic Society in New York, and he asked them to put him in touch with a top geologist who was experienced in Arctic or Antarctic work. Since I've spent most of my career in Alaska, Labrador and the North-West Territories doing field-work for various mining companies, my name was one of the first to be recommended.'

'Without mentioning the fact that you're a woman.'

'Raymond Strenger at the Society is a friend of mine, and he knows that I sometimes have trouble with that sort of nonsense.' She smiled and took a mouthful of steak. 'Since it never seems necessary to point out that a man is a man, he sees no need to point out that a woman is a woman. Very unchauvinistic, Raymond.'

'Not much point if you come all this way and then get turned down.'

Her dark eyes looked straight into mine, hard and clear. 'I don't think that will happen,' she stated matter-of-factly.

We finished lunch and headed out to the house in St Helliers. It had been more than pleasant. We'd chatted about places we both knew, told stories about our adventures and misadventures, laughed and enjoyed ourselves.

She glanced at me across the front seat of the car. 'You look happily pensive, Logan.'

'I was just thinking that so far the cast of characters for this expedition ranges from the guilt-ridden through thick-headed sadist to unfriendly and fanatic. Your presence is going to make life a lot more bearable.'

'You don't mind a woman along on such a long, cold trek?' There was a flash of humour in her eyes.

'I'll give you my full support for what it's worth, seeing that I'm rather a Johnny-come-lately myself.'

'You and Howard must be close?'

'Great buddies.'

'Well, if he'll take you, he should take me. He really needs me.'

Which was true. It was her ace. And she played it well enough when the time came.

Chapter 8

No one was at the house but Mary when we arrived. When I introduced her to Charly, she was stunned.

'You little bit of a girl going to the South Pole with all these men?' Her big face was a round, brown world of consternation. When Charly said she was, Mary looked more worried but she merely said, 'Well . . .' and went slowly back into her kitchen, all her bounce gone for the moment.

'I think you shook her up a bit,' I said, and we both chuckled. I picked up her bags. 'Come on, I'll show you your room.'

The way we were set up at the moment, she would have had to share with LaFlette when he arrived, so I said I'd move into the double room and let her have my single.

'I don't want to start off by asking favours,' she objected. 'We'll all have to share on the ice.'

'True, but the first thing is to be allowed to go,' I pointed out. 'No use causing a stir for nothing.'

When Silas turned up later in the afternoon, he took the transformation of Charly Train into a woman with barely the lift of an eyebrow. 'This *is* a surprise.' He took her hands in both of his. 'We had expected . . .'

'A man,' Charly filled in. 'Logan explained that you'd been under some misapprehension.'

'So it would seem, but I assure you I have nothing against your being a woman.' He held her hands a moment too long for a friendly hallo and gave her his most winning smile. 'Unfortunately, Warden Grampion tends to a male chauvinist view of the world and I can't quite see him taking a woman to Antarctica.' He held his long-fingered hands palm up as if to show they were clean. 'However, since he hired you, I'm afraid we'll have to wait to speak to him about it.' He really seemed rather pleased with the change and I think it tickled him to see his boss make a mistake.

It was about ten the next morning when we heard the purr of the Jensen in the driveway. We had just finished a late, rather subdued breakfast. Silas looked at his watch. 'That will be him. He left the car at the airport.'

The front door banged and Silas stood as Grampion stumped into the room, followed by Dawson and a great bear of a man who I surmised was Gus LaFlette, the French Canadian dog-handler. He wasn't as tall as Kokko but that didn't make him short. He looked shorter still because across the chest and shoulders he made two of me. He had a big cedar block of a face, a bushy black moustache with a broad nose mashed over it, hair all over the place and eyes that twinkled even when he wasn't smiling.

'Hallo, Silas. All settled in, Logan?' Grampion greeted us amiably, then frowned as he noticed Charly rise from the table. I guess he thought she was a leftover from a dirty weekend we'd been having while he was away.

Before any of us could introduce her, Gus LaFlette boomed, 'Charly!' He moved forward quick as a cougar for such a big man, lifted her up in front of him by her elbows and looked at her with undisguised affection. 'By God,' he said in a harsh French-Canadian accent that would have made a Parisian wince, 'I didn't know you'd be on this trip with us! By God, that's good!'

'I won't be if you break my arms, Gus.' She laughed deep and full.

'I think maybe it would take more than me to do that, eh?' He winked.

'Warden,' I said, 'this is Charly Train, your geologist.'

Charly moved forward, hand outstretched. 'Glad to meet you, Mr Grampion,' she said, as if nothing at all was out of place.

Grampion took his meerschaum out of his mouth with one hand and automatically took her hand in the other. 'Charly Train?' he said.

'That's right. Short for Charlotte.'

'You're a woman!' his voice grated.

A flick of annoyance swept her face but she kept her smile. 'It's not hard to miss.'

He dropped her hand as if it were red hot and said pompously, 'I think there's been some mistake. I understood you to be a man.'

'Why was that?' Charly asked blandly.

'In our correspondence, you never mentioned . . .' he fumbled.

'That I'm a female. Does everyone who writes to you have to declare their sex?'

'The Society was particularly asked to supply the names of . . .'

'Competent geologists with experience in Arctic conditions. Well, I'm the best.' Her voice was hard and I realized how many times she must have run this gauntlet trying to establish her position in a job traditionally male.

'By God, she is right,' Gus put in. 'And she can run a dog team nearly as good as me.'

'There are other factors, I'm afraid.' Grampion was trying to regain his composure.

I could see the anger flow up into Charly's face but Silas cut her off. 'Perhaps if we sat down and had a cup of coffee, everyone would be more comfortable.' He called for Mary to bring in a fresh pot, and, from the way she appeared, she'd been close enough to the door not to miss anything.

Dawson swaggered over to the table and sat down. 'Yeah, I could do with a coffee.' He looked at Charly. 'Stan Dawson, honey.'

Silas stepped in smoothly. 'I'm terribly sorry. Our introductions got off to a bad start. Stan Dawson, the party's second-in-command, so to speak – Charly Train.'

Charly's lips were still tight but she smiled, said 'Hi' to Dawson and sat down. The pressure subsided for a moment and we all shuffled to seats at the big table as if it was a meeting of the board. Grampion sat at the head and I could see by the way he was calmly stoking up his pipe while the others poured their coffees that he was over his first shock. His eyes flicked out through the smoke screen he was raising assessing and cataloguing. When we'd settled he said quietly between puffs, 'Miss Train, we seem to have got off somewhat on the wrong foot.' Charly's face started to relax at what appeared to be the beginning of an apology. She soon found out the word wasn't in Grampion's lexicon. 'And I have no doubt the fault lies entirely with you.'

'What fault?'

'Come now. You can't make me believe that in all our correspondence it was pure chance you never used a "miss" or even a "ms", that it never occurred to you, when I outlined an expedition to the Antarctic with a small party of men, that I might be interested to know you were a woman, or that you didn't think I would assume you to be a man when you always signed C. Train or Charly Train but never Charlotte Train. There was no misunderstanding on my part, only deceit on yours.'

Charly's expression didn't change. 'And if I'd told you I was a woman?'

'I would have looked for someone else.'

'Exactly.' Her voice was bitter-edged. 'I have all the qualifications you want, but you'd rather take a man even if he rated lower.'

'Quite right, and you very well know why. I'm sure it's

already been a problem in your work in isolated areas. A woman, particularly an attractive woman, on a trip where she would have to live closely with several men is bound to cause tension. It has nothing to do with her ability to do her job.'

'I can look after myself.'

'She sure right there,' Gus spoke up. 'I see her once flatten a drunken oil rigger with a whisky bottle.'

'Which is exactly the point,' Grampion answered. 'Considering her survival in what must be a very tough business even for a man, I have little doubt that she is well able to handle such situations. But it is her presence that causes them in the first place. I prefer that no such situations be allowed to develop and for that reason I don't want a woman on this expedition.'

Charly looked down into her coffee, saying nothing for the moment. Grampion had her on the ropes because what he said was true.

'Don't you think that perhaps Miss Train's disruptive influence has been overstressed,' Silas put in, 'and that the men might be able to control their libidos for a month or two with the help of the cold and the work?'

Grampion didn't like the taint of sarcasm in Bannister's tone, but it was Dawson who answered. 'Not if it was you out there, Si. You'd be chasing her all over the glaciers.' He turned towards me as Bannister reddened. 'And I'll bet our intrepid author wouldn't be far behind.' He said it like a joke but it was meant to stir.

'I break in half anyone who make trouble for Charly.' Gus half rose from his seat and the twinkle was gone from his eye.

Dawson sneered at him. 'You would, would you? Not everybody breaks that easy.'

Some leader of men, I thought. In the few dozen words he'd spoken since he came in he had managed to anger three of us.

Gus was about to make some retort but Charly cut in. 'Knock it off!' she snapped and turned to Grampion, who was watching the scene speculatively. 'Mr Grampion, as you can see, your assessment of the situation is absolutely correct.' She glared around the table. 'Controllable, but correct. What do you propose to do about it?'

'I'm afraid I'll have to look for someone to replace you.'

'That might not be too easy. Men with my experience and qualifications mostly work for oil or mining companies on contract. You leave for Wellington in two weeks and ship out in three. Hardly time for anyone to break a contract, get here and have their gear in order. And who'd want to leave a solid job under the cloud of a broken contract for a few months at the South Pole? You may not want me but I've got more hard, practical experience in Arctic conditions than you, Logan, Howard Turbott and probably everybody else except Gus, and I'm expert in field geology and surveying. I think you might have a lot of trouble finding anyone, man or woman, to take my place.'

Grampion hid his face in the business of relighting his pipe. When it finally emerged, from between his big, meaty hands, he said flatly, 'It's a good point, Miss Train, and I fear you are probably correct.'

'God, Mr Grampion, we can't take a woman with us!' Dawson barked. 'Surely Silas can find us another geologist. If the money's right you can get anybody.'

Bannister gave him an enigmatic smile. 'Not everyone can be bought, and I would think that the only person here who would know anything about the availability of geologists is Char . . . Miss Train herself.'

'Exactly.' Grampion cut the discussion short.

'Does that mean I can go?' Charly asked calmly.

Grampion gestured around the table. 'As you can see, there is some difference of opinion whether you should. Normally, I would make the decision myself, but this is a case that touches each man on the expedition, so what I propose to do is this. Tonight at dinner for the first time we shall have together our entire expeditionary force. I will explain the situation to them and we'll take a vote.'

'Jesus Christ!' expostulated Dawson. 'First Adams and now

a woman! I'm supposed to be second-in-command on this trip, but nobody takes a damn bit of notice of anything I say.'

Grampion rose. 'Perhaps if you said something to heal the breaches instead of opening them, you might have more success. Excuse me, please, gentlemen, Miss Train.'

'I guess I'm just not cut out to be a leader of men.' Dawson gave Charly a long leering look. 'Or women.'

I could see Gus LaFlette's thick neck suffuse to a deeper mahogany so I stood up and held out my hand. 'We haven't been introduced yet. I'm Logan Adams.'

He forgot about Dawson and wrapped his hand around mine. 'Auguste LaFlette, but Gus she will do.' He beamed. 'Say, you sound like Canadian?'

'I'm a New Zealander but I've lived in Canada for a lot of years.'

'He's the Logan Adams who writes those books you like so much,' Charly said.

Gus sat back, the chair creaking in protest. 'By God, you write all that stuff?'

'If it has my name on it.'

His eyes twinkled around that big flattened nose. 'Maybe if you make the book about this adventure we are going to have – ' he inclined his big head towards Dawson – 'you won't have far to look for the bad guy?'

It was so apropos that the laughs were spontaneous. From everyone barring Dawson, that is. His perpetual sardonic smirk disappeared and his face went black. He didn't like it when we laughed at him, and when he got up and stomped out we laughed even more.

'Still want to join our big happy family, Charly?' I asked, and she turned her eyes to heaven in mock despair.

Chapter 9

Gus and I spent the day arranging and packing equipment into large crates, making absolutely sure we had a complete inventory of what went into the boxes and that they were appropriately marked. We were taking a lot of gear and food with us and we had to know just what was in what.

I tightened the metal straps around the last case for the time being and stood back. 'That'll do me for the moment, Gus. What do you say we clean up for the big dinner?'

He boomed out his agreement and we headed back into the house from the garage where we'd been working. I was feeling good. Handling the gear we were to take with us had started a trickle of excitement that I knew would swell to full spate as we got more into the adventure.

'You look loaded down with thinking, Logan,' Gus laughed. 'Watch out, she's not good for the health.'

'Just thinking about the trip.'

'Hey, by God, she going to be one hell of a time.' He punched my arm enthusiastically. 'Maybe we even find Grampion's lost city for him, eh?'

'What do you think about this lost city?'

He gave an eloquent Gallic shrug which shifted about a hundred pounds of shoulder on each side. 'Funny people go to funny places for funny reasons.'

That, I thought, was the most succinct description I'd yet heard of our expedition.

Gus and I had a shower and shave and changed our clothes. Kokko had evidently returned earlier in the day because I heard him and Dawson go down the hall, early birds to the festivities.

Shortly after, Charly's door slammed with an unladylike whack.

'Sounds like Charly punctuating her introduction to Ari Kokko,' I observed.

Gus's big hands fumbled with a florid tie that matched his shirt only in the fact that they were both loudly patterned. 'He Dawson's buddy?'

'They seem to have some sort of relationship.'

Gus cocked an eye at me in the mirror. 'Stan, he don't seem to like anybody. What's Kokko like?'

'Only met him once.' I gave my shoes a dust over. 'I get the impression he does what Dawson tells him.'

'Then he better tell him to lay off Charly.'

'I thought you said she could look after herself?'

'Everybody needs a little help some time, eh?'

'Known Charly long?'

He finished his tie to his satisfaction and slipped into a sports jacket that would have warmed a cold horse if it could have stood the colour.

'I meet her first in 'sixty-nine in Labrador. That was her first field job where it is really rough and cold. It was a big party doing a survey for a mining company and having a first go over the area to see if anything interesting turn up. I was guide.' He chuckled at the recollection. 'All the guys treat her either like she is a baby or something to warm their sleeping-bag. But she leave them gasping. She work longer, harder and better, and they try like hell to keep up till their knees shake like a cornered doe!'

'What about the sleeping-bags?'

His laugh rolled out. 'Haw, by the time they finished every day, they're too tired to think about that.'

When we were ready we stopped to pick up Charly. She answered the knock immediately. She looked beautiful. The long blue kaftan she wore covered her completely with just a hint of figure showing when the cloth clung to her body as she moved. Her hair fell long and black and simply to her shoulders, accentuating her clear-cut features.

'You don't look much like a fearless explorer,' I said.

'I suppose that's a compliment. I didn't know whether to dress in mucklucks and a woollen shirt to show them what a toughy I am, or to doll up and make them want to take me along for my decorative value.'

'I imagine even the mucklucks and the woollen shirt could have achieved that.'

'The author ever ready with a well-phrased line.' She said it like a joke but she was pleased nevertheless.

We were the last to arrive in the lounge for the pre-dinner drinks. Howard was there, talking to Grampion. Kokko was sitting by himself with a glass of vodka enveloped in one hand and the other in a bowl of crisps which he methodically jammed into his mouth. Silas and Dawson were talking to a red-haired man in a resplendent outfit, the very latest in style, that more than rivalled Gus's for colour except that all his matched.

Naturally everyone looked at us as we entered, but it was Charly they saw. Silas swept over, with Grampion not far behind.

'You look lovely, Charly.' Silas took her arm.

'Miss Train, Gus.' Grampion acknowledged us with a nod. 'I don't think you've met everyone yet.' He turned to the others. 'Miss Train, Charly Train,' he announced, 'is the geologist we've been expecting.' I could tell by the lack of surprise in the newcomers that they'd already been filled in on the 'problem'. 'Gus LaFlette is to be our dog-handler and cook; Logan Adams our radio operator and official recorder.'

Howard and Pitt moved forward and Kokko stood wiping his paw on his pants.

'This is Howard Turbott, the man who I hope knows where we're going.' Grampion forced a laugh to show that he meant it as a quip. 'And "Plum" Pitt, our photographer.'

Howard shook hands with Gus and Charly. Pitt said with a grin, 'My real name is Cecil. I guess my parents must have hated me. Anything's better than Ces Pitt, I figured, and grabbed the first handle anyone hung on me. I suppose the

"Plum" comes from my plumage.' He gestured to his colourful attire and we smiled in acknowledgement. He wasn't a big man but he moved easily and looked tough and wiry. The blue eyes under the pale red eyebrows were friendly but assessing.

'And this is Ari Kokko, our mechanic,' Grampion continued.

'We've already been introduced,' Charly said coolly.

There was a bit of chip stuck on Kokko's moustache and he picked it off, poked it into his mouth and leered at her. Gus stepped forward, hand outstretched. 'Gus LaFlette,' he said.

The Finn turned on him slowly. He was taller than Gus but I didn't think there was much in it. Those little pig eyes folded into gristle and scar tissue peered out at the French Canadian without warmth. 'Ari Kokko,' he replied as if it was a challenge and slapped his hand around LaFlette's.

Gus wasn't expecting Kokko's little hand-squeezing trick. A surprised look came into his eyes as the Finn slammed on the pressure. Kokko wasn't going to kid around; he could see as well as anyone that Gus was strong and he wanted to get an early advantage.

The surprised look left Gus's face and a tight smile replaced it. '*Mais oui*,' he mutttered, 'we have a strong one here, eh?' His big shoulders hunched and his jaw muscles knotted as he countered the pressure. Kokko's thick neck swelled with the strain as his face got even redder.

'What are you two playing at?' Grampion snapped as we were all drawn to watch the still and silent struggle. When Gus said more or less normally, 'A little game, Mr Grampion', I knew he had the Finn's measure.

Kokko's face went from crimson to purple and his eyes squeezed back out of sight with effort, but it was no use. Gus had his hand close in to his own body now where he could bring an even greater pressure to bear.

'Stop this nonsense!' Grampion's voice was harsh with anger.

'Kokko!' Dawson's command was clear and sharp.

But it wasn't up to Kokko now whether he let go or not.

I could almost hear the bones in the Finn's hand grind one on the other. Suddenly he grabbed Gus's wrist with his other hand and wrenched free, cursing volubly. It was in Finnish, but that it was cursing was unmistakable. Gus laughed and turned to the others. 'A little fun, just like Indian wrestling we do back home.' He patted Grampion on the shoulder. 'We just like schoolboys, eh, Mr Grampion?'

Grampion had been in enough all-male camps in different parts of the world to recognize the trials of strength that isolated men amuse themselves with. It's normal until some sort of pecking order is established. But he still had a worried pucker between his bushy brows as he and Silas tried to get the evening back on a more friendly tack. I don't suppose he'd ever seen anything quite so determined or filled with suppressed violence among his more academic colleagues.

Kokko backed off to where he'd left his drink and I noticed he was holding it in his left hand, the other jammed in his pocket. Dawson quietly gave him hell as the Finn sullenly tipped the vodka down his throat.

'That's not your best trick, Ari,' I commented pleasantly as I passed. 'Two tries, two losses.'

His face swelled with anger, but then subsided like a hot bubble in a mud pool. Dawson looked at me, his contemptuous smile at the ready. 'It's just a game, Adams.'

I left them, Dawson to his whispered admonitions and Kokko to breathing vodka, got myself a Scotch and joined Howard. It was about time we made some sort of show of being old friends and brothers-in-law.

'How's Jen?' I said.

'Fine.' Coolly.

'David?'

The tone warmed slightly and a softer look came into his eyes. 'Okay.'

'Look, Howard,' I said quietly, 'if you want to have the rest think that you invited me on this trip because we're big buddies, you're going to have to try a little harder.' He just looked at me, saying nothing. 'I don't get it.' I shook my head. 'I can understand you being angry because Jenny forced me on to you, but other than that, you don't even know me. I'd just as soon be friends and enjoy the trip.'

'I know you, Logan.' He said it tightly, constricted. He was trying to contain it but the pressure was too much; it shot out like a jet of hot steam. 'I know you. For years I've heard nothing else. The great Logan this, wonderful Logan that, Logan could show you how to get that done, isn't it too bad Logan isn't here to help you write your theses, Logan would go skiing with me if he were here. And now, Logan will keep you safe when you go away! I don't need it and I don't want it and I don't give a damn now what the others think about you and me.' His voice trailed down to a soft choke. 'If I didn't love your damn sister so much, I would have told you to go to hell.'

He turned and walked stiffly over to the drinks cupboard while I tried to recover from the unexpected venom in his attack. Angrily I drank some of the Scotch. To hell with it! This whole screwed-up expedition was getting more and more sour. I wondered if I shouldn't just chuck the lot and let my sister work out her own marital problems. But I knew I wouldn't and that made me more angry.

Having flushed all that through my mind, I felt better. It wasn't all bad. There was still Charly. Her presence could offset a lot of unfriendliness from Dawson, Kokko and Howard. That is, if Grampion hired her. I wondered when he'd hold the vote. Surely he wouldn't let it drag over till after dinner.

He didn't. After we'd all had a couple of drinks, Grampion came to the middle of the big room and gave a calling-to-order cough. 'You all have met Miss Train and you all know that I was under the impression she was a man when I engaged her.' There was a rustle of humour at the idea of anyone making so blatant an error, but Grampion was all business. 'I won't go into whose fault it was or if there was a fault. The fact remains that, although Miss Train is a highly qualified geologist and a trained surveyor and also has a great deal of experience in the type of conditions we'll be meeting, she is, as it were, odd woman out in an otherwise all-male expedition. We'll be living very closely and it could set up a difficult situation.'

'I've been on plenty of climbs with mixed parties,' 'Plum' Pitt put in. 'It's never been a problem. Jesus, leave Victoriana to the antique dealers.'

'We'll be taking one four-man tent and two two-man tents,' Dawson said. 'Who's she going to sleep with?'

'Oh, for God's sake!' Charly said.

'She can come in with me.' Kokko almost slobbered at the thought.

Grampion gazed at him distastefully, and I thought maybe Charly's going wasn't such a good idea. With the type of mind Kokko obviously had tucked somewhere in that thick skull, he was sure to cause trouble.

She just eyed him as if he was something unpleasant that she'd scraped off her shoe. 'I'm afraid that even if in some remote aberration of mind and body Mr Kokko did succeed in arousing my passion,' she said flatly, 'he'd be unable to come up to the task of satisfying it.'

It took a minute before Kokko realized what Charly had told him. When it finally sank in, and he saw that most of the men in the room were quietly laughing to themselves at Charly's put-down, he blushed right to the top of his lumpy head. It just wasn't Kokko's day.

'I think we can assume that most of us can control our ravening desires, Dawson,' I said. 'If you find not, I'm sure Ari won't mind sharing a tent with you.'

'This is just what I'm talking about, Mr Grampion,' Dawson complained. 'These guys are already fighting with each other about the broad.'

'Right,' Grampion cracked with parade-ground firmness. 'I don't think any further discussion will be particularly edifying. As I said, we'll vote on it, and we'll vote on it now.' He took out a small notebook and tore out several pages. 'A secret vote, I think, is best so's not to embarrass anyone. Naturally neither

Miss Train nor Silas will vote and I will hold my opinion in reserve in case of an even split.'

It looked fair enough. Gus and I would vote for her and most likely Pitt, too. If Howard put his name to it, and I could see no reason why he shouldn't, she'd be a shoo-in.

Then I saw Dawson speaking quickly to Howard in a corner while the rest of us marked our ballots on a small desk and handed them folded to Grampion. Howard nodded his head and Stan Dawson clapped him on the back and smiled. Maybe it wouldn't be so easy, I thought.

Kokko, Howard and then Dawson marked their papers and Grampion began to unfold them. If it was a split, odds were that Grampion would put the final no to it. I glanced over towards Charly and gave her a wink. She looked calm and winked back.

Grampion separated the pieces of paper into two piles and gave us the result. 'Four for Miss Train going; two against.'

There was a small cheering and a palpable easing of tension. Except from Dawson. The sardonic sneer vanished and his eyes were bullet hard as he turned towards Howard. Howard shrugged and shook his head all but imperceptibly. Then Dawson swung to Kokko. The big Finn's ears went vermilion and he looked away sullenly. Plainly, Stan Dawson had thought he knew how Ari would vote and had put all his attention on Howard to make a split and probably win with Grampion as tie-breaker. Howard had come across, but the Finn had let him down. Clearly Kokko wanted his own back on Charly, and he couldn't get it unless she was on the expedition. I almost regretted she'd won.

But Dawson wasn't finished. 'Just a minute,' he called out. 'I think Ari made a mistake. He doesn't speak the language very well. He really wanted to vote no.' He looked towards the Finn, his face like a dark rock. 'Isn't that right, Ari?'

Grampion spoke before Ari could make a reply. 'It doesn't really matter, Stan. I would have voted for Miss Train going anyway.'

This shook everybody into silence. 'I couldn't just force a decision on you in a matter like this. If the majority had been against her going, I would have had to look for someone else. But, as Miss Train said, that wouldn't have been easy and might have been impossible. Rather than jeopardize the expedition in this way, I'm quite prepared for Miss Train to go with us.' His voice tightened. 'And I'm sure grown men with the kind of self-control needed to travel in the type of country we're headed to, can exercise the little bit more that might now be needed.' He turned to Charly and gave her his arm. 'I think we might go in to dinner now.'

I laughed to myself. Grampion, ever the pragmatist, wouldn't care if Charly got raped three times a night so long as she was fit for work during the day. I went into the dining-room with an exuberant Gus, wondering how this odd-ball outfit could ever survive as a unit long enough to get to Wellington, let alone Antarctica.

Chapter 10

The next day we picked up the radio equipment from Customs and I spent the following week pulling it apart and putting it back together again to make sure that every diode, resistor and transistor was operating properly. We were using an Earnest Turner TR 11.H transceiver in one Sno-cat capable of high or low transmitter power of either 40 or 10 watts, and the smaller Pye C 12's in the Weasel and other Sno-cat. They weren't the latest word in radio transceivers, but they'd been tested in conditions very similar to the kind we'd be facing and had performed excellently. I wasn't unhappy with them at all.

Pitt and I were packing his movie film into watertight metal boxes when Grampion came in and asked me to go to Hamilton in the morning to collect some special rope he'd had made for the trip.

'Extra strong for its weight, but elastic enough to take up the strain without a heavy jerk if a vehicle goes into a crevasse,' he explained. 'Take the Jensen. There'll be too much rope to get into that little car of yours.'

The next morning, bright and early, I slipped behind the Jensen's wheel. I was looking forward to the trip. It had been a long time since I'd enjoyed the feel of a really first-class car on the open highway. I lazed it through the morning traffic towards the Southern Motorway out of Auckland.

I was doing a little over sixty on the inside lane with very few other cars out-bound from the city to worry about. The incoming traffic on the other side of the wide grass median strip was still fairly thick, although the bulk of the workers who had been on their way to jobs in the city already had their heads down over their desks. The Jensen was a dream. The genuine leather bucket seat moulded comfortably into my back, exuding that rich leather odour that vinyl can never achieve. Only the slight whisper of tyres and an almost imperceptible purr of engine was audible. The car wasn't even trying at that speed.

I caught up with a slower-moving diesel tractor-trailer and pulled out to pass in the outside lane. My speed had crept up and I was touching seventy. I pulled out, but when I tried to straighten up there was no response. The wheel turned freely!

No steering, doing seventy, headed across the median strip towards a stream of cars and trucks speeding in the opposite direction. And beyond them, a heavy concrete buttress of an overbridge ready to stop me cold. Adrenalin poured into my system and for a few seconds everything outside slowed so that I seemed to have time enough to contemplate the entire situation. The car hurled itself through the heavy, viscous air of slow time, I braked, double declutched into a lower gear and wondered if I could jump before I slammed into something. But it's not so easy to step out of a Jensen, and in a detached way I watched a huge concrete-truck, its big bucket turning slowly, carve out a collision course. I could see the driver's wide-eyed face as he applied the airbrakes, and I gave the accelerator a touch to try and get by. Rather the stationary buttress than twenty tons doing fifty miles an hour.

I didn't quite make it. The concrete-truck whacked my left rear fender and I spun around, sliding back-first towards the huge pillar holding up the road above. A car flashed in front of me and then I saw open space. There was nothing to do but tread hard on the gas to try and offset the slide. It was enough to cushion the impact and I ricocheted off the buttress and shot back across the northbound lane towards the median, and the Jensen, now slowed to about fifty, ripped into the metal and wire restrainer along the edge. I watched curiously as the left side of the car peeled off like a banana skin.

Then it was still. The restrainer had soaked up my momentum and brought me to a halt. I snapped off my safety-belt and stepped out of what was left of the car. I slammed the door and it closed with a soft click. What a well-made automobile, I thought, and then my knees buckled as I flipped back into real time.

It took me half an hour to stop shaking. I'd lived a long stretch of my life in about fifteen seconds and my body was letting me know it couldn't do that very often. I didn't even notice the traffic policeman putting a blanket around me or the equally shaken concrete-truck driver blabbering how he never even saw me coming.

The only damage was to Grampion's beautiful Jensen. The truck's heavy steel bumper hardly had its paint scratched, but the Jensen looked as if it had been battered by both the sharp and the blunt ends of a giant axe. The police took a statement from the truck driver and sent him on his way, kept the rubberneckers moving on the motorway to try and prevent more accidents caused by people not watching where they were going, and organized a breakdown truck to tow away the remains. I explained about the steering and the skinny sergeant wrote it down noncommittally in his notebook and gave me a breath test. His eyes were emotionless, a man who'd seen so much idiocy on the roads that he just naturally doubted any driver's word.

'We'll check up with the insurance adjuster,' he said.

'Is it a police matter? No one else was hurt, no other damage?'

He snapped his notebook shut and smiled professionally without warmth. 'If there's any problem with the claim the owner might want to hold you liable.'

He offered me a lift back to town, but I declined and went instead with the breakdown wagon. I was more interested than he in why the steering had failed. I explained to the garage foreman about it and asked how long it would take to find out what had happened. He looked at the broken car and thought maybe they could get at it in the afternoon. If I came back about four o'clock they'd probably be able to give me some idea.

I hired another car, continued my journey to Hamilton to pick up our rope, and was back at the garage by four. The foreman took me over to the Jensen jacked up on a hoist.

'It was the steering all right,' he said.

'I know that. What I want to know is why.'

He directed a powerful light underneath the front end. 'See that assembly there held together by bolts? Supposed to be all locked up, you know, very secure. They don't make a car like this so that it falls apart on the first bounce.' He stood up, rummaging in his grease-streaked coat, and extracted the heads with part of the shank of three bolts and one complete bolt. The three were sheared off. 'This is all we could find of them.'

I looked at them blankly. 'They broke?'

'I suppose so,' he said dubiously. 'Must have been the crash.'

'The steering went before the crash.'

'Yeah, well . . .'

'Well?' I prodded.

He juggled the broken bolts in his hand. 'Only way I could see the steering going before the crash is if these were loose. You know, enough to make things come apart inside. Then the crash sheared them.'

'Surely they wouldn't all loosen at the same time.'

'I wouldn't have thought so myself – ' he scratched a greasy finger into his ear – 'specially on a quality machine like that. Still, funny things happen with cars. I could tell you a thousand stories.' He didn't sound very convinced.

'You said they were all locked up.'

'Supposed to be,' he said. 'Split pins through the nut and the shank of the bolt; but there's nothing much left of the shanks except this one.' He held up the one whole bolt. 'And there was no sign of any pin with it.'

I thanked him and told him I would have the owner of the Jensen get in touch with him regarding the insurance. He held up his thumb in a salute as I climbed into my rental car. 'Watch your back, mate,' he said without a smile.

As I drove back to the house, I pondered the mechanic's remark. Maybe it was better advice than he knew. In the last two weeks somebody had gone through my hotel room very carefully, I'd been assaulted, and today I'd nearly been killed. Perhaps my 'author's imagination' was working overtime, but I intended to take the mechanic's advice seriously.

By the time I turned into the driveway it was dark. I opened the heavy front door and went in just as Bannister came down through the stairway door leading to the upper-level bedrooms.

'Ah, there you are,' he said. 'Didn't think it would take you all day to go to Hamilton.' He moved towards the lounge door. 'The rest are at dinner. Perhaps we'd best go in.'

'I had a bit of an accident.'

He stopped and turned back, his eyebrows arched in question.

'I lost control of the car on the motorway and ran into a concrete buttress among other things.'

'My God! Are you all right?'

'Not a scratch. But I'm afraid Warden's Jensen is a write-off.'

'What happened?'

'According to the mechanic who looked the wreck over, the bolts holding the steering assembly were loose, not even any retaining pins that he could find. I think Warden had better have a hard word with the people who service his car.'

Silas's long face seemed to drain of blood and his voice squeezed out of a dry throat. 'Ari looks after all the cars.'

I hadn't thought of that. 'Well, I guess the man to talk to about it is just in the next room.' I opened the lounge door. 'Coming?'

'Logan . . .'

I turned back to him and was surprised to find that he looked even worse. 'What's the matter, Silas?'

'There's something . . .' He seemed about to say something but just couldn't find the words. He wiped his sweat-sheened face with a handkerchief. 'I guess hearing about the accident has upset me,' he said finally. 'Perhaps we'd better go in to dinner.'

We went through the lounge into the dining-room. Everyone was there except Pitt and Howard who were still living out.

'What's the matter with you, Silas?' Grampion asked. 'Not feeling well?'

'Adams has had an accident,' he said by way of explanation.

All eyes turned to me as I sat down. 'The Jensen was completely wrecked,' I told Grampion.

'How?'

'Steering assembly came apart and I lost control.'

There was a babble of questions from Charly, Gus and Grampion but neither Kokko nor Dawson said much. I told them about the steering bolts and turned to Kokko. 'You service the cars, Ari; what do you think happened to that assembly? Had you had cause to do any work on the steering lately?'

'What's that supposed to mean, Adams?' Dawson cut in sharply.

'It means that I'm asking our friendly Finn here if he did any work on the Jensen steering lately. Or don't you understand English?'

'It sounds to me as if you're accusing Ari of sabotaging the car. He never even touched it.'

'How the hell do you know?' I felt really mad now. 'And what's it got to do with you anyway?'

Grampion rolled out his pompous voice. 'Ari has never done anything but service the Jensen since it's been in the country.'

Silas pushed his chair back and stood up. 'I'm afraid I'm not feeling too well,' he said. 'If you'll excuse me, I think I might go outside for a bit and get some air.'

Dawson got up and went to Bannister's side. 'Yeah, you don't look too good, buddy,' he said solicitously. 'Do you want a hand?'

Bannister shrugged away. 'No,' he said shortly and walked out.

'Englishmen,' Dawson spat, making it sound a filthy word. 'Come on, Ari.'

Kokko jammed another forkful of potato into his mouth and lumbered out after the American. Not much later Grampion and Gus finished their dinner and excused themselves, and Charly, the last at the table, asked if I'd be too lonely by myself as she had a good bit of technical reading to do. I assured her that bachelors got very used to eating alone.

'I'm glad you weren't hurt,' she said as she walked to the door. 'Silas was pretty taken aback too by what happened. He looked more like the one who'd had the accident.'

When she left, I worked through my dinner methodically, going over what had happened, hardly tasting the food. What she had said about Bannister was true – and odd. And I realized as I went over it in my mind that he hadn't really reacted over-strongly until I mentioned the loose steering. It made me remember his reaction to the mugging. There again he hadn't seemed to take much notice until I mentioned that I thought one of the thugs had known my name.

Silas Bannister, I thought as I finished my dinner, it's time we had a little private talk.

Chapter 11

When I re-entered the lounge, only Charly was there reading.

'What's the matter?' she asked, putting aside a heavy textbook. 'You look ready to eat somebody for dessert.'

'Just doing some thinking. Have you seen Silas?'

'Not since dinner. He said he was going for a walk.'

I started for the door.

'*Is* something the matter, Logan?' she said, rising. 'Is it the accident? You really weren't hurt, were you?'

She was genuinely concerned. 'No,' I said, 'but I'm beginning to think that might not please everyone as much as you.'

She gave me an enquiring look, so I briefly related what had happened to me in the past two weeks and how I was beginning to think the events might be related.

She didn't seem overly convinced. 'And what has Silas got to do with it?'

'If I knew that, I wouldn't need to talk to him. It's just an impression, an over-reaction on his part, a feeling that he wanted to say something more, but didn't.' I shrugged my shoulders. 'Male intuition? Who knows?' I left her and went out of the front door on to the drive.

The moon was up and nearly full and it took no time at all for my eyes to adjust. I walked along the drive to the road and looked up and down. Nothing. Probably walked around the back way to the cliff, I thought, and retraced my steps around the house. The lights were on in Dawson's and Kokko's room and I could see them moving about as I passed.

The grounds of the house were fairly extensive and I was beginning to think that, moon or no, Bannister might not be that easy to find, when I saw a figure in the trees ahead.

'Silas!' I called, but he turned at my voice and disappeared into the trees.

I went as quickly as I could. The bush wasn't dense but in the dark it was difficult to get through without flattening your nose or falling over a branch. Then I heard the sea running and slowed down. There was no beach here, I remembered, just a soft sandstone cliff about forty feet high that abrasive waves had gradually undercut over the years until an edge had formed with a clear drop to jumbled rock and swirling water below. Out of the trees, it was easily enough seen in the moonlight, but there was no sign of Bannister. I quartered back and forth along the edge for a moment or two and had just about decided that he'd gone around some way and back to the house when I saw him.

He lay face down in a slowly heaving swell, curling and grinding itself into the base of the cliff.

The rock face was treacherous, little more than compacted mud and sand, but I slid and scrambled and clutched my way to the bottom and into the rolling water and broken rock at the base. It was hard enough to keep my own feet, but I finally managed to grab Silas and haul him up to a little ledge a few inches out of the water. I couldn't see well with the cold sea water dripping into my eyes, but the feel of the loose, depressed bone at the back of his skull left little doubt. I tried mouth to mouth, but it was useless. At last I had to leave him and climb back to the top.

The police were there within minutes of my call with all their bell-ringing, siren-blaring confrères from fire and ambulance. Lights glared into a circle by the cliff and with a minimum of talk and a maximum of speed they had ropes over the side, men down them and Silas Bannister's body hauled to the top.

I stood shivering wet under a blanket with the rest of our group, standing in the harsh light and shadow, staring at the canvas bundle that had once been a not unlikeable Englishman. He must have wanted to keep away from me an awful lot, I thought, to stumble over a cliff he knew was there in bright moonlight. What questions did he have such blinding answers to?

After questioning all of us, the police were satisfied that Silas had felt ill after dinner, gone out for a walk and had probably fainted and fallen over the cliff. They left and we sat quietly in the lounge nursing our individual thoughts. Pitt and Howard were contacted and arrived subdued and quiet. I told them what happened and then there was nothing much else to say. Mary brought coffee, moving like a wraith, without a sound. Silas would have appreciated that, I thought.

Of all of us, Grampion was the most stricken. His pipe drooped from a slack mouth and his years showed in the sag of his face.

Gus put his coffee down and poured himself a whisky instead. 'Altogether – ' he knocked the shot straight back – 'she has been one bad day. First Logan and now Silas.'

Pitt and Howard looked questioning and I realized that they hadn't been told about the crash. The tragedy of Silas had paled it into insignificance. I gave them the details and looked over to Ari Kokko slumped in a chair, picking at his ear.

'That discussion ended,' I said, 'when I asked Ari what he knew about Jensen steering assemblies.'

'This is a hell of a time to start accusing Ari again, Adams!' Dawson was straight in.

Howard looked at me as if I was deliberately trying to make trouble. 'What are you saying?' he almost cried.

'I'm not saying anything. I'm trying to ask King Kong a simple question and Dawson keeps answering!' I wasn't feeling in the mood to walk softly.

'Well, I'm damn well sick of it.' Dawson kept talking. 'This guy causes trouble every time he opens his mouth . . .'

'There seems to be only one man around here whose open mouth causes trouble,' Charly interjected, 'and it isn't Logan.'

'Okay, honey, I guess we know whose bed you'd like to warm,' Dawson sneered, and turned to Grampion, who was hardly listening. 'Warden, this whole business stinks. How can we go to the Antarctic with a guy like that?'

Grampion's solid, aggressive body seemed fallen in, his forcefulness dissipated. He looked at us for a moment, trying to gather himself together, but the fire was almost out. 'Perhaps it would be best just to call the whole thing off,' he faltered. Bannister's death had obviously hurt him more deeply than any of us thought.

'Call it off?' Howard was stunned. So, obviously, was Dawson.

Grampion gestured weakly around the room. 'There's animosity everywhere . . .'

'We could get rid of that,' Dawson put in, but no one took any notice.

'And now with Silas . . .' Grampion's voice trailed off.

'But Silas wasn't going with us,' Howard argued. 'He was just organizing, and most of that's done now in any case.'

'I think also,' Charly said to take a little of the callousness out of Howard's remark, 'that if anyone would hate to see all this organization wasted, it would be Silas.'

The fire began to flicker again in Grampion's eyes. 'He'd want that, wouldn't he?' You could almost see his body bulk out again as he pulled himself straight. 'It would be somewhat of a memorial.'

I didn't think Silas would care quite that much, but in a moment Grampion burst back into flame, using the rationalization that it would be what Silas would have wanted to stoke the blaze. Howard and the rest heaped on the enthusiasm and even Dawson and Ari said how much they thought of Silas and they wouldn't let him down. The expedition was all go again.

After that, except for the funeral at the weekend, we all worked full time towards our departure to Wellington, and from there, our ship to the Antarctic.

Chapter 12

'What would you like?'

'Rye and ginger,' Charly said.

The waiter took our order and balanced himself down the slightly swaying aisle of the dining-car. We were having a before-dinner drink on the overnight train to Wellington.

The others had already arrived there and presumably were hard at work loading the *Gotha Dan*, a 1000-ton Norwegian motor vessel that would take us to McMurdo Sound and Scott Base. I had stayed over to collect our four dog sledges which Gus had asked to have slightly modified with mileometers that would enable us to measure distance travelled over the ice and snow. They were simple bicycle-wheel affairs that trailed the sledges but gave a reasonably accurate log. Gus said he didn't trust all the fancy surveying instruments that needed expert precision work to repair if anything happened to them; the wheels needed no more than a screwdriver. I'd volunteered to collect them because he had to see to the dogs and, happily, Charly had also stayed behind to check up on some facts about the geology of Antarctica at the University of Auckland.

'What do you think of Grampion's idea of a lost civilization?' I asked when the drinks came. I wanted to hear what a geologist thought about it.

'It's not as crazy as it sounds,' she said. 'There's no doubt that Antarctica was once a land capable of sustaining forests and all that that implies: animals, birds, possibly people.'

'But that was millions of years ago!'

'Was it?'

I shrugged. 'So I've been taught.'

She laughed, not deprecatingly but delightfully, as if the whole thing was a joke. 'Scientists,' she said, 'gather up facts and try to fit them into an overall theory – most often a theory shot through with anomalies – then they expound the theory as gospel and the uninitiated accept it as proven. It very seldom is and, as you can see with only a cursory glance at the history of any branch of science, theories are continually being modified or discarded. I'll bet you were taught in school that the atom was indivisible?'

'I'm not quite that old.'

'Well, it wasn't long before –' her eyes twinkled – 'and in any case, it was still being taught long after it was known not to be true. People don't like discarding ideas they've grown up with; not even scientists.'

'But that ice cap on Antarctica has been there for millions of years. Maybe it once was the Garden of Eden but not so recently as to have cities there.'

'I agree with you, but the evidence is not so clear-cut as all that.' She paused, looking for some place to start as I waited.

'What do you know about the Ice Ages?' she asked.

'Only that they came periodically and the last one receded about twenty-five thousand years ago.'

'Yes, that's what has been taught in schools, but is it true?'

The question was rhetorical and I waited for her to enlighten me, and in fact quite enjoyed being lectured to by this beautiful woman. Whatever she was, Charlotte Train wasn't one-dimensional.

'The figure of twenty-five thousand years or more,' she began, 'got its start with a scientist named De Geer. He noticed that in the coastal lakes and rivers of Sweden there are varves, annual bands of silt and clay deposited as the glacial sheet melted. By counting the varves in over fifteen hundred lakes and rivers stretching from the coast to where the glaciers are now in that country, he estimated it took five thousand years for them to melt that far. Naturally he had to guess many times which varve in one lake corresponded to a varve in another lake. Then he made an even greater surmise: that in an area where no varves are found it took the ice an additional four thousand years to melt. He then surmised even further that the glaciers stopped melting at the beginning of the Neolithic period, and he thought that started maybe five thousand years ago. A total time since the ice began to melt of fourteen thousand years.'

'Mostly guesswork.'

'Almost completely.' She rolled her eyes heavenward. 'And then other scientists freely interpreted this already weak data and came up with a figure of twenty-five to forty thousand years ago when the European ice cover began melting.'

'Not very convincing, but is it wrong?'

'I think it is,' she said earnestly, 'and I could explain some of the more modern methods of estimating time like radio-carbon dating and the use of ancient pollen to do some of the finer estimations, but I think the story of Lake Agassiz better puts the whole thing into perspective.'

The name sounded familiar but I couldn't put a place to it exactly. 'Is it in Canada?' I guessed.

'Was,' Charly explained. 'Lake Winnipeg, Lake Manitoba and a number of other lakes in Canada and the North Central States of the US are remnants of it. It was the largest glacial lake in North America and it was formed when the ice melted after the last ice age.' She stopped a moment and lit a cigarette, then looked at me steadily. 'Now listen to this. This lake, exceeding in area the aggregate of the Great Lakes, was formed, lived and dried up in less than one thousand years.'

That was really jetting along as far as geologic time was concerned, but I couldn't really see what this had to do with cities in Antarctica, and I guess my expression said as much.

'Don't you see?' Charly punched it home. 'The whole of that giant lake, a sea really, was made up entirely of melt water from the North American ice cap and it seems it took that ice under a thousand years to disappear. Do you realize the catastrophic amount of energy, heat, needed to melt that amount of ice that quickly?'

'It would have to be a world cataclysm.'

'Exactly, and according to erosion estimates of what were the shores of the lake and the wonderfully preserved glacial striation of the rocks – and I've studied it – the whole thing only happened a few thousand years ago, four at the outside.'

'About the time Egypt was having all those plagues and problems,' I said.

Her eyes widened slightly. 'You've read Velikovsky?'

I nodded. 'Grampion has copies of his books. Do you believe his theory that the earth had a near miss with the planet Venus before it was trapped into its orbit?'

She ran a hand through her long dark hair. The blinkered scientific establishment would crucify anyone who touted such heresy; they'd done a fairly good job on Velikovsky himself, but she said, 'There's a lot to support the collision theory, but whether or not it's true, I think there's little doubt there was a world cataclysm of immense proportions after man had long established quite high systems of civilization.'

'And because the earth was knocked end over tip off its axis, the ice melted in some places and formed in others?' I finished my whisky while I thought about it. 'Places like Antarctica. Temperate one moment, polar the next. Bang! Civilization there is snowed under.'

'In a simplified way, yes. The collision shifts the world on to a new axis, the poles change. What were once the polar ice caps are now not only in a more temperate zone but the heat generated by the collision speeds their melting. All that moisture in the air now falls as snow year after year in the new polar region until a new ice cap is formed.'

'The Icelandic tradition of the Fimbul-winter, a winter that lasts for years.'

'Right. That's the theory Warden is working on, anyway. It would certainly put him in the history books if he could prove it.'

The next morning the train, the *Silver Star*, threaded its way along the coast, the only reasonably flat stretch, into the hilly city. With all that fantastic scenery to start with, you'd think Wellington would be a gem, set as it is in a rim of soft hills around a large natural harbour, but it turned out cramped and ugly and without imagination.

It was just eight o'clock when we pulled into the station and saw Gus waiting for us on the platform. He gave Charly a swing, me a friendly punch on the shoulder and informed us that the expedition members were already aboard the *Gotha Dan.* We collected the sledges, loaded them along with our own bags into the back of the panel van Gus was driving and squeezed in the front with the big French Canadian.

'Grampion wants to sail as soon as we finish loading,' Gus informed us. 'We got to pick up the Sno-cats and the Weasel in Christchurch and the more time for that the better, eh?'

'Everything going all right with the loading?' I asked.

'You bet.' Gus steered the truck through the early-morning traffic. 'We all pitch in and help the captain and his crew. Soon everything stowed *magnifique*!'

Chapter 13

The command to let go the stern line was passed by the first officer on the bridge to the men on the after deck, and as the heavy mooring line snaked aboard I could feel the big diesels below increase their beat. The *Gotha Dan*'s stern swung slowly away from the pier, and at just the right moment the bow line was heaved free of the receding dock and quickly hauled in. We backed clear and then, in a neat manœuvre, the captain brought the ship around, starboard propeller ahead, port reversed, so that the vessel almost turned in its own length, and we began to thread our way out through the crowded harbour towards Cook Strait.

It was ship handling that filled a passenger with confidence, especially when you thought of the perilous seas we were bound to meet below the 60th parallel. Gunnar Borge, the Norwegian captain, was a seaman who would have filled you with confidence had his ship been made from 45-gallon drums with a packing-case deck instead of the sturdy red-hulled, blunt-bowed freighter specially reinforced for work in ice-filled seas which he now commanded. He and his crew formed a happy, tight-knit group that revelled in sailing in the worst waters in the world. I only wished we could say the same of our own group.

Not that anything untoward had occurred in the last few days of loading or that on the surface much had seemed amiss, but there were many unhappy crosscurrents. Howard hardly spoke to me and generally kept himself isolated from the rest. Grampion, although back to his old commanding self, had lost a leavening of humour since the death of Bannister. Even the garrulous Pitt seemed subdued, sensing the ill will washing back and forth.

I stayed on deck watching Wellington fade in the light mist – a much more attractive city from a distance – and enjoying the chill spring breeze whipping through the funnel of the strait. The *Gotha Dan* slowed and the pilot climbed down to his gently heaving cutter and left us to the open seas ahead. As the twin diesels picked up again, driving us through the green swells, I made my way below with a curious mixture of exhilaration and apprehension. We were bound for a fascinating adventure, but there seemed to be too many unknowns.

We headed first towards Christchurch, a city about half-way down the east coast of New Zealand's South Island, where, at the port of Lyttleton, the two Sno-cats and the Weasel were loaded, to be carried lashed to the broad foredeck of the *Gotha Dan* until we disembarked at Scott Base. After that, our course was due south to Antarctica, the strange continent which, except for a few dry valleys and the occasional strip of barren, rocky coast, was completely covered with a mantle of ice thousands of feet thick.

The weather held good as we plunged on into the Southern Sea and shipboard life settled into a routine. The captain insisted, gallantly, that Charly have a separate cabin, but the rest of us doubled up: Gus and I in one cabin, Howard and 'Plum' Pitt in another, Dawson and Kokko again left to themselves and Grampion taking a spare bunk in Borge's stateroom.

There wasn't much to do; Gus had to see to the dogs in their kennels on deck and I was glad to give him a hand, not only to keep myself busy but to get to know the animals as well. I felt they could well be our best means of survival on the ice. Machinery, no matter how well designed, has a disconcerting habit of packing in when subjected to cold that drops to fifty and sixty degrees below zero.

The sky was cold blue, the sea foam-streaked but relatively calm, and the big huskies yapping and barking in expectation of the meat I was bringing them when Howard, bundled in a thick turtleneck sweater and heavy jacket, closed a steel door and came out to the kennels. He hesitated when he saw me, then continued out. He stopped at one of the kennels and made friends with the magnificent beast inside. The dog, hungry as it was, wagged its tail and bumbled playfully around.

'That's Brand,' I said. 'Gus says he's the leader of the lot. A Greenland/Labrador cross.'

I had thought maybe Howard had come up on deck to make some kind of friendly overture, but his voice was the same temperature as the sea creaming round our bows when he said, 'You're causing a lot of trouble on this expedition, Logan – making insinuating remarks about Ari, doing everything you can to break things up, but it's not going to work.'

I was dumbfounded. 'Why would I want to break things up?'

He gave me a pitying look. 'Come now, Logan, I'm not stupid. Jenny doesn't want me to go back to Antarctica, so she got her brother to try and make it impossible. Even Stan and Ari can see that.'

'And what do they know about it?'

'I have been working with them for some time. We're not exactly enemies.'

All I could say was, 'If you think Jenny would do that to you, you're crazy.'

The muscles of his jaws bunched and he hissed through clenched teeth, 'I've had years of you and I've just about had enough! Keep out of my way, Logan; I'm warning you!'

He lurched away over the gently rolling deck and disappeared back into the ship, leaving me with twenty yelping dogs wanting to be fed. At least they seemed to like me.

A few days later, with Campbell Island, New Zealand's last southern outpost, well astern, the first mate called us all up to the bridge. Captain Borge took us out on to the small starboard wing. The weather was clear and we were quartering into a long sea swell, but they were just huge rolling mounds of water with no breaking. 'We are about to cross the Antarctic convergence,' he said, 'where the warmer waters of the Pacific meet the cold Southern Sea.'

Interesting, I thought, but what could we possibly see; cold or warm, water looks much the same. But I was wrong. When I looked out I could see stretching from horizon to horizon a long bright green line, a very definite change of colour in the water.

'The green colouring is sometimes as much as fifteen miles across and is formed where the two bodies of water meet,' Howard explained. 'The warm water contains dissolved mineral salts, and the cold water is high in oxygen. Where they meet, the conditions are just right for phytoplankton: very, very tiny plants, and their chlorophyll stains the water that vivid green colour. It's the beginning of one of the earth's largest food chains.'

Kokko looked for a moment, then spat over the rail and went back below, but the rest of us watched fascinated as we steamed through the discoloured water until finally we emerged into the clear cobalt blue of the Antarctic Sea.

Not long after it began to live up to its reputation as the stormiest ocean in the world. The wind rose to a screaming whine and the sea piled up on itself in its hurry to try to smash the *Gotha Dan* down. For two days we drove at quarter speed into the maw of the gale, each thundering wave almost stopping us, shuddering under an incredible weight of water, but the *Gotha Dan* powerfully shouldered the sea aside and plunged on.

Gus and I, encased in foul-weather gear, our harnesses snapped on to safety ropes, braved the foredeck to feed the dogs huddled in their kennels. I was worried about how they were faring in the icy spray that periodically slashed into their boxes, but Gus said that the little bit of cold wouldn't worry them, and when Brand even gave us a happy bark and a wag of his tail, it was evident they weren't bothered much at all. The more I saw of these solid, powerful animals with their thick, heavy coats, the more I appreciated them.

On the third day the wind dropped, leaving a heaving, frustrated sea that could do nothing but make us uncomfortable, and I awoke to a distant thundering. Gus and I quickly dressed and hurried on deck to find out the cause of the deep rumbling booms. We were the last out, and the others spared us not a glance, so absorbed were they in the spectacle spread across the green swirled sea. As far as you could see lay hundreds of icebergs. Not the jagged pinnacles of ice that form the Arctic bergs, but huge flat cakes a third of a mile long and 200 feet high; the tabular bergs of the Antarctic calved from the giant ice shelves that push out to sea from the continent.

I moved up beside Charly as the *Gotha Dan* picked her way carefully between the ice islands. She was enthralled. 'They're magnificent,' she whispered. 'Some are like ruined cities with palaces and castles.'

And so they were. The ice, tinted in many subtle pastels, had been carved by sea and wind into something seen in children's story-books; alabaster abbeys, winding streets, brilliant spires that snapped back the sun's rays, with flights of snow petrels and shearwaters flickering in and out of the myriad caves, caves that boomed and thundered as the sea rushed in and out. And in the water, sleek black shapes of a pack of killer whales hunting the Crabeater and Weddel seals that used the icebergs as a resting place.

'The trip would be worth it just for this,' I said.

All that day we threaded through the bergs, Pitt filming as much as he dared, not wanting to miss any of the spectacle but aware he must husband his film for the trip ahead. The captain handled his ship expertly, but as the long day dimmed into night and we were still among the giant ice masses, I realized that darkness would put us in real danger. Even with light we had once scraped ominously along the chiselled side of a towering berg; at night we stood a good chance of running smack into one.

We didn't see the captain at dinner that night. He remained

on the bridge. Talk was desultory; we were all listening to the thunder echoing around us from the icebergs. Kokko, who was looking apprehensively out the thick porthole of the wardroom, suddenly said, 'God! We're surrounded!' and sprang to the door, the rest of us following quickly into the frigid night.

Rising perpendicularly only yards away from the port side, a mountain of ice glinted in the starlight. It lowered over the ship, dwarfing it in its immensity. Even more terrifying, another berg lay to starboard not much farther away and, as I watched, I could see that the two were going to meet. There was nothing sudden to it; just the majestic, ponderous brushing of two massive ice islands at the bottom of the world. It must have happened thousands of times, tens of thousands. But this time our little ship was in the narrow passage between those giant ice molars and, when they closed, they would chew us up as easily as we would crush a grape, leaving nothing but a few pips of twisted metal.

There was absolutely nothing we could do except hope that the *Gotha Dan* could make it through before it was caught and ground to bits and then dropped to the bottom of the sea. Captain Borge had the engines at full speed plus, and the ship pounded through the ever-closing passage towards the opening, barely visible as a dark patch against the faintly luminous ice. Behind, the ice closed and the din of smashing mountains reverberated into a smothering roar, echoing and re-echoing between the shining cliffs to each side of us. The very noise was enough to shake us to pieces.

Charly gripped my arm as she and I and all of us watched helplessly as the jaws closed astern, coming fast upon us. I felt the ship rise as the water in the passage was squeezed up and ahead. We rose like an elevator, the ice cliffs so close I could have touched them, so close the steel sides of the ship screeched in passing. And then like a melon seed we popped out on the wave, the ice chomping monstrously but lazily behind us as if so insignificant a titbit as a 1000-ton ship was too minor to notice.

There was a communal sigh as we released long-held breath, relaxed tensed muscles, realized it was well below freezing and slowly clambered inside to the warm. But even inside we could still hear the bergs grinding in the night. I don't know about the others, but it was a long time before I could get to sleep and forget those massive ice cliffs crunching in on us like the walls in a Poe horror story.

The next day was bleak and cold and the *Gotha Dan* ploughed through acres of brash ice that barely slowed her. The beautiful, dangerous bergs were behind and we were making good time southward. For two days we encountered nothing apart from soft brash, but on the third it became a more formidable barrier of pack ice. It was sparse at first and the *Gotha Dan* was able to maintain a reasonable course and speed, but by noon the heavy broken ice exceeded open sea and we were reduced to dead slow as we ferreted about looking for open leads that would allow us through this ice maze. Several times the lead we were following pinched off and we would reverse carefully and try another way. Sometimes, ominously, the ice would close behind us and gently take us in its frigid grip, and I remembered Shackleton's ship, *Endurance*, trapped for ten months in the pack ice of the Weddel Sea on the other side of Antarctica. They drifted nearly 600 miles before the ice, tired of the game, crushed the ship and left the men to try to survive on the ice.

But Captain Borge was well aware of the dangers. When the pack ice closed in, it was every spare man over the side with long poles to pry the clutching ice from the ship's sides while Borge manœuvred the *Gotha Dan* back and forth to make a little room. It gave me an eerie feeling at first to be standing away from the ship on ice only a few feet thick hundreds of miles from land. How much we relied on that fragile shell of steel and wood for our survival.

But by the second day it seemed not at all odd to climb down the side of the ship in the middle of the ocean and walk away. And perhaps that over-confidence was why I very nearly didn't make it to Antarctica. The ice had closed in on us once again, not badly, but enough to stop us breaking through to a large open lead only fifty yards away, and we all clambered over the side to try to free a large chunk of ice that was jammed under the boat, fouling the starboard screw. With that out of the way we hoped we could barge ourselves free. I positioned myself between Gus and 'Plum' Pitt with Dawson, Kokko, Howard, Grampion and several crewmen ranged on either side of us. Even Charly manned a pole and pulled her weight with the rest. Borge hadn't liked the idea of her working off the ship at first, but Charly had insisted and proved she could hold her own no matter how hard the task.

We all pried and heaved at the huge ice cake. Freezing sea water swirled up from the stern of the freighter as Borge worked the ship on the port propeller. Suddenly the block broke free and reared up leaving a strip of black water between us and the ship. The floe I was standing on had a sharp downward slope to the gap that was opening and I started to back up quickly. A sharp blow struck me across the shoulders and, unable to stop myself, I plunged head first into the sea.

The water surged into my heavy clothing and gripped hard, an icy clamp across my chest that made my muscles seize and rammed the breath from my body with the shock. I came up gasping against the side plates of the *Gotha Dan*. I could feel the weight of frigid water in my boots pulling me down, but I pushed away from the freighter's side and thrashed back to the ice. For a moment I caught the tableau of figures ranged on the ice above me, their poles like lances held by ancient knights, but then my whole attention was absorbed in trying to get a hold on the sloping edge of ice and haul myself out.

My fingers were too numb and I could feel my leaden body like a thing apart dragging me down.

'The ship!' I heard Charly's voice like a whisper from another world.

I saw it then as I clutched frantically at the ice, consciousness fast ebbing, the heat of thought draining into the cold.

The *Gotha Dan* was swinging back towards me! Dimly I wondered if my cold-anæsthetized body would even feel it when that thousand tons of steel squelched me against the pack.

A pole slammed in over me, wedged from ice to ship, and Gus's face appeared almost next to mine. His great hand grasped me by the collar and the last thing I remembered was being flung sprawling on to the ice and hearing the pole snap with a crack like a brittle bone.

Chapter 14

When I came to, I was stripped of wet clothes, swaddled in heavy woollen blankets and lying in my bunk in a warm cabin, but I was still cold. Captain Borge was standing over me, his fingers round my wrist, taking my pulse. He saw my eyes open and scowled.

'You are lucky you are a fit man,' he growled. 'But I suggest you save your swimming for another voyage.' He turned and I saw that Charly was behind him holding a large steaming mug, with Gus and Grampion also wedged into the small cabin. 'Give him some of that soup,' the captain told Charly.

I tried to hold the cup myself but my hands were shaking too much so Charly spooned the thick broth into my mouth like a mother with a baby.

'Don't expect this kind of treatment too often,' she said gruffly, but the soft look in her eyes did more to warm me than even the hot soup.

The captain stood back and put his peaked cap over his thick hair in a square, no-nonsense attitude. 'Well, I think you'll live,' he said, 'and you can thank your friend, LaFlette, for that. No one could get down that slope of ice to help you without slipping in themselves. Another moment and if the water didn't get you, the ship would have. At first I thought he was trying to hold the ship away by wedging that twig of a pole against it and the ice, but it was just for something to brace himself on so that he could grab you. Bloody quick thinking.'

I looked over at the burly French Canadian. 'Thanks, Gus.'

He shrugged his big shoulders. '*Mon ami*,' he said, 'without you, I would have no more exciting books to read, eh?'

Grampion came over. 'Damned glad to see you're all right, Logan. I'll go and tell Pitt there's nothing to worry about. He's worried sick about you.'

'Pitt?' I said.

'It was Pitt who knocked you in,' Grampion explained. 'When the ice cake broke free, he turned to move away and his pole hit you in the back. Just an accident, but he feels he's to blame.'

'Tell him that for a mountaineer he's bloody clumsy,' I said, and returned to enjoying Charly's ministrations.

The long lead we were trying to reach when I took my ducking proved to be a direct road into the open water that forms in the warmer months between the ice pack and the continent proper. The prevailing south-westerly wind pushes the ice away from the land and it is this fact that allows explorers to reach Antarctica provided they can find a way through the ice barrier first. Two days later we got our first sighting of the continent as we passed the ice cliffs of Cape Adare to the westward and sailed through the Ross Sea towards McMurdo Sound.

I was completely recovered now. They had all been very solicitous of my well-being, popping in every so often to see if there was anything they could do. Even Dawson and Kokko in tandem had made a token visit; Howard had seemed genuinely worried and 'Plum' Pitt had fallen over himself in apology.

'Jesus, Logan,' he'd said, 'I just turned and whack, away you went, a perfect swan into the briny.' I told him to forget it, no harm done. And there wasn't. When we got our first sight of Ross Island, I was on deck with the rest.

We steamed down the rugged, mountainous coast of Victoria Land under the lee of ice cliffs that rose perpendicularly out of the cold blue sea. The air was full of shearwaters and albatross, and small Adelie penguins frolicked all around, sometimes leaping ten feet straight up to the safety of a berg or an ice ledge as we passed.

But it was the sight of the volcanoes, Erebus and Terror, on Ross Island that brought everyone out on deck. Named after the two ships of the explorer, Sir James Clark Ross, Mount Terror was extinct but Mount Erebus, rising over 13,000 feet, trailed a plume of smoke another 2000 feet into the still air. One side was jet black, the other caught the low afternoon sun in brilliant tints of yellow and scarlet, and the sight of this volcanic furnace rising out of the heavy ice of the continent made me realize that many strange things might be found in this enigmatic land – perhaps even Grampion's lost city.

His mind on the same track, Grampion said, 'This continent has allowed only a handful of men to probe into it. Who knows what it could be hiding.'

We spent our last night aboard the *Gotha Dan* enjoying a small farewell party with Captain Borge and his crew, and the next morning steamed around a long finger jutting out from Ross Island to Pram Point and Scott Base. Scott Base and the American McMurdo Base near by are both located on Ross Island, but the island is connected to the mainland by the Ross ice shelf, a permanent ice cover over the sea that is as large as France. Expeditions find no difficulty crossing this to the continent itself. In fact, it is usually the easiest part of the journey since it is relatively flat. There is even an airstrip on it, I was to learn.

The weather remained good, and Captain Borge nestled the *Gotha Dan* against the ice shelf near to the Base, and with the willing help of the small wintering-over party that maintains the facilities over the stark and bitter months until the major influx of scientists arrives in the summer, we soon had the ship unloaded. Borge didn't want to waste time. It was still early in the season and the weather even at the best of times could deteriorate rapidly. By evening Kokko, Dawson and I, driving the Sno-cats and the Weasel, had hauled most of our supplies and equipment over the pressure ridge of ice and exposed rock where the ice shelf grinds into the island, and up to the string of low, flat buildings that comprise Scott Base. Whatever I might have thought of those two, they handled the big lumbering Sno-cats with the ease and aplomb of a London cabby on Oxford Street at rush hour. The dogs were ecstatic at being off the rolling ship and on to real snow once again, but Gus got them finally quietened and bedded down out of the wind in the dog enclosure with the Base's own twenty animals. The rest slogged along loading the sledges for the vehicles to pull up to the Base. By the time the day was out and we had waved the *Gotha Dan* farewell, we were all looking forward to a hot meal and an early night.

The hot meal we got, the early night no. I suppose it was to be expected that eleven men who had just spent many months cooped up in ten huts interconnected by corrugated iron tunnels, most of the time unable even to set foot outside into the howling brutal winter weather, would want to make the most of some new company. But when they realized that one member of our party was a woman, they absolutely outdid themselves as hosts, and it was easy to forget our weariness and get caught up in the spirit of the thing. We were the first party to arrive that season, something Silas had arranged with the Antarctic Division of the DSIR in New Zealand, so that we would be on our way inland by the time the regular contingent of scientists flocked in to take advantage of the short summer spell, and the Scott Base men made us more than welcome. Charly they treated like a queen.

It hadn't occurred to me until then, but she was probably one of the first women to visit Antarctica. If not, she would certainly be the first to go into the interior on an expedition. But the men from the Base weren't interested in history, they just wanted to talk to a real live woman. The officer in charge finally had to point out to his staff that Miss Train was no doubt very tired and that she would still be at the Base the next day. Apologetically, they showed us to our sleeping quarters in the hut opposite the main entrance and I was surprised to find that we would enjoy individual cubicles.

'A happy state of affairs that will end when the thundering herd begins to arrive in the next few weeks,' the radio officer informed me and then promised to acquaint me with his equipment the next day. I shucked off my heavy woollen trousers and shirt. I tried not to think of Charly. After a bit, I stopped trying and thought of her until I was asleep.

In those high latitudes with summer approaching, the night was non-existent. The sun still shone at midnight and we looked forward to a very long day. By the end of the week we had our equipment unpacked and sorted out and only awaited a break in the weather, which had degenerated into a whining rip of wind that scooped up the snow into opaque fog and drifted it into every conceivable cranny. Even so, we all practised with the dogs under Gus's expert teaching and everyone, barring Kokko, became reasonably adept at handling the awkward fan hitch in which all nine dogs are individually harnessed to the sledge in a spread formation. It was evident that the big Finn didn't like dogs – he didn't really appear to like anything – and the animals reciprocated by tying their traces in knots and dumping him unceremoniously into the snow. He didn't see the joke and slogged off towards the Base, angry at our laughter.

That evening after dinner, when we had all gathered to plan our route up to the plateau, Gus chided him. 'Hey, Ari,' he boomed across the table, 'I tell the dogs not to be so nasty to you, and Brand, he say he sorry, they won't do it again long as you nice to them.'

Kokko gripped the edge of the table. 'You stupid Canuck,

I'll run you and your goddam dogs down you ever get in front of me!'

'Shut up, Ari!' Dawson barked, and the Finn lapsed into sullen silence.

Gus just laughed and ignored him, but I was sure he hadn't heard the last from Kokko.

Grampion looked speculatively over his pipe at the brooding giant, a slight pucker between his eyes the only indication of his thoughts, and then spread a detailed map on the table so that we could all see.

'As you know,' he said, 'Howard isn't sure exactly where he saw the city, but he is sure where his party was operating before – ' he paused slightly – 'his companions disappeared.'

Howard gave no reaction, just kept looking down at the map. Since he had arrived at Scott Base, he had been more than usually withdrawn. Even Charly, with whom he'd seemed to be able to relax to a degree, hadn't been able to get through to him. I suspected it was the attitude of the men at the Base. When they had found out who he was, they had perceptibly cooled and their manner turned from friendly to formal. As far as they were concerned, he was a man who had left two friends to die in the wastes of the polar plateau.

Grampion continued, pointing to the map. 'They had been surveying this area along the George V Coast west of the Arctic Institute Range in Victoria Land. As you can see, they were operating very near to the South Magnetic Pole and all their navigating had to be done by sextant, sun compass and dead reckoning. They were still near the coast when the accident occurred, relatively so at any rate, wouldn't you say, Howard?'

'Yes, we had decided to cut across the plateau on the trip back.' He indicated the route on the map. 'It can be a brute of a place at that point. There's nothing to stop the wind as it sweeps down from the Pole. It's been known to reach two hundred miles an hour in the winter.'

Two hundred miles per hour! I could only just visualize the frigid air of the South Pole building up more and more speed as it howled across thousands of miles of featureless snow plain.

'But we hadn't yet climbed up to it when we were separated,' Howard continued. 'We would still have been quite close to the coast near the Mawson Peninsula.'

He put his finger on the map and Dawson shook his head. 'That's a helluva big piece of snow under your finger. Can you give us a closer position?'

'I wasn't navigating. You know that. I can tell you the general area and that's all.' Howard had been through it all before and sounded a little exasperated.

'But you'd know the place once you got there?' Pitt asked.

'Yes. Particularly the nunatak that I climbed to look for Bill and Steven. It was very distinctive in shape. If I saw it, I'd know it.'

'A dry valley with a city in it might be hard to miss, too,' Dawson said.

'Quite true.' Grampion smiled, knowing full well that only he and Howard had any great faith in the existence of the city. The rest of us were just paid hands of one kind or another.

Howard missed the nuance of sarcasm in Dawson's remark. 'On the contrary,' he said in his best classroom voice, 'it could be very hard to find. The valley is narrow and fairly deep. The glacial ice surrounding it makes it deeper still. Unless you walked up to the edge, you could easily miss it. The nunatak, on the other hand, can be seen for miles.'

So it was find the nunatak, a mountain summit poking up through the continental ice cover. And Grampion's method of doing this was eminently simple. We would go to the place in which Howard was reasonably sure the valley lay, an area bigger than Northern Ireland, and simply spread out and look for it. I suppose it wasn't as silly as it first sounded: Howard did have a good idea of the area and once there would be able to veto most of the more unpromising spots, but at the time the plan didn't fill me with confidence. And we had to get there first!

Howard outlined the route. We would cross the Ross ice shelf past Black and White Islands and Minna Bluff poking a long finger out from the mainland, and then go up the Skelton Glacier to the polar plateau, 8000 feet up and 300 miles from Scott Base. From there we would turn north, more or less following the curve of the Prince Albert Mountains through Victoria Land, and thence into Wilkes Land and our destination near the Mawson Peninsula.

The names made it sound rather civilized but they all stemmed from man's penchant for sticking a flag into any piece of real estate that seems to be empty or inadequately defended and claiming it for some king, queen or country. The reality was a desolate land of ice and bare rock, with very little of the latter. On the plateau itself, nothing lived. On the coasts only seals, penguins and birds existed, and their real home was the sea. As far as man was concerned, these ten wind-racked huts we were in, hanging grimly on to the shirt tail of the continent, were, with a few other such establishments, the paltry sum of the little dominance he had over the huge, implacable continent. Nevertheless, every area, mountain, valley, every conceivable thing that could be named had been named; the graffiti on the walls of history.

We were ready to go, we had a place to head for, and the weather reports were getting better. The next day we tidied up any last-minute problems, and the radio officer and I checked out what frequency we would use to contact Scott Base and set up a daily schedule. We would call in at five o'clock each day, and if that time was missed, seven o'clock. 'But don't be surprised if you can't get through,' he said laconically. 'We have a hell of a time making contact in that area. Auroral activity near the magnetic pole's probably the cause, but no one knows for sure. I can raise New Zealand easier than get through up there.'

'Oh, great.'

'You're the ones who want to go,' he pointed out. 'Nobody's forcing you.'

Only too true, I thought, and I also knew that he would do a very competent best to keep a radio link open. 'Well, at least you won't worry too much if you can't raise us.'

He shrugged. 'Depends for how long. But if we don't know where you are, there's not a hell of a lot we can do anyway.'

'Just keep an ear out,' I said.

The wind began to drop later in the day and, about four, a four-wheel-drive Land-Rover slogged its way into the camp along the track from McMurdo, the American base two miles away on the other side of the point. Two men emerged and bundled themselves towards the entrance.

'Looks like the Americans have landed,' I remarked, turning from the window of the mess.

Dawson, who had been going over the route with Grampion at the table, stood up, had a look out the window and said, 'Just remembered, Warden, I told Ari I'd give him a hand fixing those tow ropes on the vehicles. He'll go off his nut again if I don't show up.' With that he was away and gone.

A moment later the officer in charge of Scott Base came in with the two men from the Land-Rover now divested of their heavy outdoor clothing. The first was tall and spare, in his late forties, and had the crinkled eyes and weathered skin of a man who'd spent the better part of his life outdoors. The other, although younger, had the same general build but was obviously a man of the city. Even his too new, heavy cord trousers and thick wool sweater looked out of place on him. You could see that he would have felt better in a dark grey suit and well-polished shoes stepping out of a taxi rather than in mucklucks and a parka stepping out of a Land-Rover.

Only Warden, Pitt and I were left in the mess as the Scott Base OC introduced the strangers.

'Guy Poulson – ' he indicated the older man – 'the base leader at McMurdo and . . .' He groped a moment for the other man's name.

'Barry Goodenough,' he supplied.

'Barry's doing an article for a magazine about McMurdo,'

Poulson explained. 'Going to stay with us about a month or so over on the Riviera, but I thought he should rough it for once and see what it's like over here where it's really cold.'

He was referring to the standing joke between the two Bases that McMurdo was warmer, which was true because Scott was more exposed to southerly blizzards on their side of the point, and we spent the next few minutes saying our hallos and working that gag into a friendly lather.

Pitt, who had previously been doing some minor repairs to his Nikon, loaded it with film and jumped up on a chair. 'Got to record this international meeting for posterity,' he said, lining up the two base chiefs and Grampion. He took a couple of quick shots and then jumped down for a new angle. Barry Goodenough tried to move out of range but the room was small, and when he saw that he was going to be in Pitt's picture, he hastily covered his face with his hand.

'Hell,' Pitt said. 'You look like a Congressman caught coming out of a brothel. Let me get another shot.'

'You don't want me in it,' Goodenough protested.

'Why not? You can use it in your magazine article. You know, King Whatsit as seen with author. Better than name-dropping.' He had his eye in the view-finder all this while, juggling to get another shot while Goodenough, trying to laugh it off but anger souring his smile, backed away.

It was an extraordinary performance and I wondered why this American was so adamant about not having his picture taken. Lots of people are camera shy, still they usually end up with their mouths in an 'Oh no' circle on somebody's slide projector, but Goodenough really made sure that Pitt couldn't take him.

It only lasted a few seconds, though, because Charly came in and new introductions had to be made. After that it was all small talk as one after the other all our crew and base personnel wandered in and out of the mess. Even Kokko and Howard made a brief appearance, though Kokko, who kept looking at his watch, and Howard, who obviously felt ill at ease with anyone from the Antarctic Bases, soon left. Only Dawson never showed at all.

But what interested me more was the extra-friendly way in which Charly and Goodenough were getting along. I noticed them several times, heads together in the corner in seemingly serious conversation, and once, although they left separately, I got the impression that they had arranged to meet outside the mess. I tried to kid myself at first that I was just keeping an interested eye on her. I just liked her. More than liked her, I realized abruptly. And, typically male, felt possessive. Not something she would appreciate. Nevertheless, I regarded her interest in the out-of-place American through a slight wash of jealousy.

That evening, after Poulson and Goodenough, wishing us all well, had climbed back into their Land-Rover and disappeared over the hill to McMurdo, I had that feeling of jealousy somewhat assuaged.

'You alone?' she asked after I'd opened the door of my cubicle to a light knock.

'Hard not to be in a room this size.' She came in and sat on the edge of the cot while I closed the door. I offered her a Scotch from the flask I dug out of my gear and stoked up my pipe while she sipped pensively.

'You and Goodenough seemed to hit it off,' I said.

She looked up at me, her dark eyes a-sparkle. 'Is that a green-eyed dragon I hear?'

I laughed. 'Possibly.'

'Barry was just interviewing me for the piece he's doing. It's not every day that a woman goes on an expedition into Antarctica.' She reached out and touched my hand. 'But it's nice to know you noticed. I was beginning to think you thought I was just one of the boys.'

'Watch out or Dawson will be running to Warden saying you're stirring up my lustful passions.'

She became pensive again. 'That's why I came to see you.'

My eyebrows rose, but she had something else on her mind.

'Didn't it seem strange to you that Dawson didn't turn up all day?' she said seriously. 'Not easy in a place like this. He didn't surface till Guy Poulson and Barry had left.'

Now that she mentioned it, it did appear odd. 'Seems like he didn't want to be seen by the Americans,' I mused.

'Well, I thought that might be it, too,' Charly said, 'so when Barry and I were talking I showed him some of the photos Pitt took of the group in Auckland and asked him if he recognized Dawson.'

'And?'

'Barry's done quite a bit of writing about what's going on out here in Antarctica. It's rather his speciality.' She paused and I waited. 'He wasn't sure, but he thought Stan looked like a man who was attached to a Russian scientific party who were at McMurdo a few years ago on one of those mutual exchanges.'

'A Russian scientist? Stan?' I was incredulous.

'Not exactly. Barry thinks he was some kind of enforcer to keep the real scientists in line.'

That sounded more like it; Stan Dawson didn't fit my stereotype of a scientist.

'And his name was Stanislaus Dyrsin,' Charly added.

'Well, well,' I said as I tried to make some sense out of this strange piece of information.

'Do you think it has any connection with what happened to you in Auckland?'

'I was under the impression that you needed a lot of salt with those stories.'

She didn't smile. 'I think something strange *is* going on.'

'I just wish I knew.' I puffed on the thought for a moment. 'I certainly can't front him with it. Goodenough's got no actual proof, and we're leaving tomorrow. They'd just say I was crazy and drop me from the expedition.'

Charly did smile now. 'And the real reason you want to let things ride is curiosity. You want to find out for yourself what's behind it.'

Even though I tried to hold it back, I could feel the smile push through. 'You're getting to know me awfully well.'

'Are you complaining?' she said, mock innocently.

'Let me wipe that smile from your face,' I said with equally mock severity. I leaned over and kissed her.

It started as a light kiss, a brushing of lips, but in a moment we were standing, bodies pressed together, our arms tight around each other. How much, I realized, I had wanted to hold this woman.

'You're a slow starter, Logan.' Charly looked up at me. 'I practically had to throw myself at another man to get you moving.'

'And brazenly come to my room in the middle of the night.'

'Nonsense,' she said, turning her head to the bright frost-encrusted window, 'the sun's still up.'

'And will be for many more weeks. I hope you're not one of those prudes who'll have nothing to do with love in the afternoon.'

She ran her fingers through my hair and pulled my face down to hers. 'I'd better not be,' she said softly. 'It won't be night again till we get back.'

Chapter 15

By nine the next morning we had lost sight of the line of small buildings, scientific huts and myriad aerials that comprised Scott Base as our tiny convoy headed slowly out through the pressure ridges on to the Ross ice shelf. There was little wind but the temperature had dropped to forty degrees below zero and McMurdo Sound, which had been relatively ice free when we arrived, had frozen solidly to a depth of about six inches.

Tissue paper to an ice-breaker and no real barrier even to a ship as small as the *Gotha Dan*, but impressive all the same.

The Sound was too far behind to see now and a slight haze of snow blowing off the great plain of ice in front of us had blotted out most of Ross Island, although the peaks of Erebus and Terror could still be seen rising into the clear blue air above the drift. We were headed at the moment almost in the opposite direction of our preliminary destination, the Skelton Glacier, because we had to make a long detour around Black Island and White Island and the long narrow rocky protrusion of Minna Bluff. The ice near this land would be heavily crevassed as the shelf pushed slowly by, grinding and piling up on the solid obstructions. Although the thickness of the ice in the shelf could measure hundreds of feet, some of the crevasses could conceivably swallow an entire Sno-cat and plunge it down to the sea below. Not that you had to fall that far to be in a lot of trouble. But for the moment the ice was flat with a thin snow crust and it offered us perfect driving conditions.

Gus was forging ahead with one of the dog teams marking a route; not absolutely necessary with such good conditions but more to give the animals a workout without too much pressure on them. Charly and I led the vehicles in the Weasel, towing one sledge loaded mostly with barrels of fuel. Dawson, Grampion and Howard were in the Sno-cat behind, and Kokko and Pitt behind that in the other, both with two heavily laden sledges following in their wakes. Fuel accounted for most of what we carried, with food coming a distant second. It takes a lot more to keep a big machine going than it does a man.

'We're making good time,' Charly said, looking back at the plume of snow tailing up from our clattering tracks. I glanced over at her and smiled at her bright, enthusiastic face. We were making seven miles per hour, just about our top cruising speed hauling the two-and-a-half-ton sledge.

'Even at this rate it will be three or four days for us even to cross the ice shelf,' I said. 'And that's the easy part.'

But for the moment we were going well; visibility was

reasonable and the Weasel's straight-six Studebaker engine sounded healthy. I'd had a fair amount of experience driving full-tracked vehicles in the army and it hadn't taken too long to get the feel again of steering by regulating track speed. The Sno-cats were even easier. They had two separate tracked platforms, front and rear, which were actuated by a conventional steering wheel. They also had a further advantage on a turn in that the front platform turned one way while the rear moved the other, both forming tangents to the arc of the vehicle's swing and allowing full power to be delivered constantly. The Weasel, on the other hand, had a tendency to bog down in soft snow on the turn because its skidding track would dig a trough for itself. However, I'd had little trouble so far and that first day's run of just over forty miles pleased everyone.

Towards the end of the day we found Gus waiting for us by the trail, the dogs already staked out and a small tent erected. It looked so meagre on that vast ice plain with the distant frozen mountains as a backdrop; a few specks of animals, a rag of cloth, a light sledge and a man so small in the immensity around him. I shut down the engine and was at once surrounded by an almost palpable silence. Even the yapping of the dogs and the voices of the others climbing wearily from the Sno-cats dissipated thinly in the huge quiet.

Another small tent and our larger four-man tent were quickly set up while I contacted Scott Base with the Turner transceiver mounted in one of the Sno-cats. By the time I had completed the short report on our progress, Charly had the Primus going and she and Gus were busily preparing some kind of hash. Everyone was squeezed into the larger tent eagerly awaiting whatever came out of the pot; even Kokko was more convivial than usual and actually smiled when Charly handed him a bowl of food.

Once we had washed down the calorie-rich hash with hot soup, fed the dogs their pemmican and checked to make sure everything was secure outside, Grampion unfolded our main map and pointed to our position.

'It doesn't look much, but for the Antarctic it's damnably good,' he said, looking pleased and turning to Howard. 'Wouldn't you say, Howard?'

Howard looked more relaxed now that we were actually on our way, more confident. 'Early days yet, but it's a good start. We'll have to make sure we give Minna Bluff a wide berth, though.'

'It would be a damn sight quicker if we could cut in close around it,' Dawson put in.

'Not if we lose days picking our way through crevasses,' Howard pointed out. 'We'll have enough trouble with that, Stan, getting up the glacier.'

'They're not as bad as all that,' Dawson said.

'They may have got worse since you were last here,' I said.

Grampion gave me a dour look, thinking I was being sarcastic, but Dawson wasn't quite sure. He clamped his mouth shut and eyed me speculatively.

There wasn't much more to discuss and we soon broke up; Gus and Howard taking one small tent, Dawson and Kokko the other, and Pitt, Grampion, Charly and I the big tent. We removed our heavy outer clothing and gratefully scrambled into the thick sleeping-bags. I looked unhappily at Charly in the bag beside me, thinking that it would be a long time until we could sleep as we had the night before.

The following day was bitter; cold air rolling down from the polar plateau plummeting the temperature and whipping the snow crystals into stinging needles. It took thirteen miserable hours, driving steadily towards the great peaks of the Western Mountains, before we were able to skirt the huge crevasse areas that guard the approaches to the glacier and come up under the rocky cliffs of Teale Island which stand to its south side. The midnight sun threw long shadows accentuating the wind-sculpted sastrugi around us as we wearily pitched camp at the base of the glacier and climbed thankfully into our sleeping-bags. The easy part was over. Now we had to climb the Skelton Glacier up to the polar plateau.

Next morning Howard pointed at the map. 'The glacier rises in two steps with a relatively flat space in the middle. It's called the Lower and Upper Staircase and the Landing. The first part of the Lower Staircase isn't too bad but it gets steeper after the initial twenty-five miles. We'll have to keep to the middle too because there's a hell of a lot of crevassing where the glacier scrapes down the valley sides.'

'What about farther up?' I asked. 'Can we miss the crevassing altogether?'

Howard barely looked at me. Even though he'd come out of his shell a good deal since we'd begun the journey, he still made it a point to ignore me as much as possible. 'I doubt it,' he said. 'We'll just have to work our way through as best we can.'

We finished our breakfast, still a little tired from the long drive the day before, refuelled the vehicles and struck camp. The temperature had risen somewhat, but to compensate, a thick mist was rolling down the glacier. Grampion decided to push on nevertheless. Gus hitched up the dog team and set out. An hour later, after clearing the drift snow from the engines of the Sno-cats, we revved up and followed his trail.

Like ticks on a great ice beast we crawled all day up the broad sweep of the glacier. It was slow going in the mist even though Gus marked the trail with flags. We were going up now and the Weasel and the Sno-cats with their heavy loads couldn't maintain the pace they'd sustained on the flat.

As Howard had said, the first twenty-five miles was crevasse-free but the slippery ice made the sledges slew round and it took constant attention to keep them lined up and at the same time not to lose the faint track Gus had left. Time and again I had to stop and cast around on foot to pick it up. In the mist, the mountains to our right and left obliterated, it was our only lead.

The last time I had to circle the hard ice looking for the runner marks, Kokko climbed out of his cab and yelled, 'God damn, why don't you keep your eyes open?'

I didn't say anything, but when I'd found the trail I pointed it out to him and directed Charly to swing the Weasel in behind the two Sno-cats. Let Kokko worry about it for a while. He didn't have any better luck following than Charly and I, and when Gus and the team appeared out of the mist late in the day, it was a very disgruntled Finn who pulled up beside him.

'Lots of cracks up ahead,' Gus informed us later in the tent. 'Only two, maybe three feet wide, but we'll have to be careful.'

'I think tomorrow we'd better rope the vehicles together,' Grampion ordered, 'and you'll have to take the lead in the Weasel again, Logan. It's lighter and better able to test any snow bridges we'll have to cross.'

I nodded and Gus laughed. 'Better a dog team, eh, Logan? Even lighter than the Weasel.'

I couldn't help but agree. It was bound to be a tense business feeling across snow spans that bridged crevasses God knows how deep. I went out to the Sno-cat to make our daily radio contact with Scott Base.

The mist had lifted somewhat by the time I returned and an increasing breeze and dropping temperatures had dissipated it entirely by morning. The glacier was starting to narrow at this point and, looking up at that great river of flowing ice, I could see that many of the cracks and crevasses, formed as the ice inexorably ground its way along the valley sides, had spread all the way to the middle. We would have to work around or find snow bridges. Not only that, the glacier was noticeably steeper; it would be a tough haul for the vehicles with their heavy sledges. I only hoped we didn't meet soft drift snow to hamper us further.

Using sixty-foot lengths of heavy three-inch Terylene rope, we strung the vehicles together mountaineering fashion and set out slowly into a freshening wind that was now driving straight down the glacier.

There is nowhere on earth with winds like the Antarctic. They spin off the South Pole, pick up speed across thousands of miles of virtually flat polar plateau and scream into the

Southern Ocean headed for the lower latitudes. We'd been lucky so far not to have encountered much high wind but we couldn't hope for that happy state to continue for very long. By noon it was blowing fifty knots, and outside the vehicles, unless you hung on to something, you were bowled over and sent skidding along the ice. We pressed on into the whirling drift for another hour, using the occasional glimpse of Mount Huggins to guide us, but the wind continued to rise and finally we were forced to stop and pitch our tents in the lee of the Sno-cats. As it was, even with them acting as a windbreak, it took us nearly an hour and a half to pin down the tents. We were hungry, tired and numb with cold when we at last crawled into them. The dogs hunkered down in what shelter there was outside, their backs to the wind and their thick coats gradually filling with snow, quite happy once they'd been fed.

All that day and the next the wind whined and howled and screeched around our tents, ice demons that plucked and tore at the thin material, all that was between us and death in the open. Wrapped in my sleeping-bag, I watched the sheer cloth snap and billow violently in the ripping wind and wondered how it could possibly go on standing the strain.

We didn't talk; the continual keening wind and flapping tent precluded all but the barest conversation and, surprisingly, I didn't think much. Not, at least, in any controlled, logical way. And looking at the tired, blank faces around me, their minds hammered into quiescence by the interminable noise, I knew my companions felt exactly the same.

But the wind dropped at last, flattening into quiet, and happy to be released from the tiny confines of the tents, we wasted no time in shovelling the drift snow from the vehicles and getting under way. It was slow going. Roped together like that, you are either in danger of dragging everybody along or overrunning the tow-rope and cutting it under a track. As I was in the lead, I didn't have to worry about that; my worry was falling into one of the many crevasses we had to cross.

Gus, leading in the dog sledge, had tried to circumvent the

larger cracks – the smaller ones, two or three feet across, we had no trouble with – but many times, to make headway at all, we had to cross snow bridges that might or might not hold the weight of a vehicle. There was no way of knowing in advance. Besides, the lighter Weasel might make it but the heavier Sno-cats behind could break through. Several times Charly and I felt the Weasel lurch sickeningly as the snow gave way beneath us. Either we would manage to scramble across or the crevasse would prove to be fairly shallow and we could drive out after we'd unhitched the sledge which then had to be winched up after us. By the end of the day we had made only ten miles, but Gus informed us, after having ranged ahead to scout the way, that we seemed to have got through the worst for the time being. The rest of the Lower Staircase up the Skelton Glacier was relatively free of crevassing although considerably steeper.

And so it was. So much so that the next day the vehicles, which were gradually losing their efficiency as we climbed higher, couldn't cope on the steeper slopes with the weight they were hauling, and although we cast about for easier gradients, many times we had to relay the loads laboriously to the top.

But we did it and finally we jubilantly levelled off on the Landing 2680 feet above the ice shelf. The day was crackling bright and the majestic escarpment of Mount Huggins, glaring white in its snow cover, rose to our right and ahead 12,100 feet into a cold, cloudless, cobalt blue sky.

I had never seen anything so austerely beautiful. Pitt got his Bolex into action and, slowly turning, tried to capture the panorama of ice and snow, peaks and plains, acres upon acres of wind-carved sastrugi, blues and purples and reflectant whites, but no camera could contain it in its splendid totality.

Grampion came up to me and we both stood silently for a moment, looking, absorbing. 'Can it be captured,' he said at last, 'on film, on paper?'

I shook my head. I had never seen him so subdued. Awed. There could be no arrogance in a place like that. Unless it was the arrogance of a mind devoid of imagination. 'What you all standing about for?' Kokko grumbled. 'I'm hungry.' And so were we all. Even grandeur can't be contemplated long on an empty stomach. Shortly – we were becoming very expert by now – we had our camp set up and the Primus burning hotly.

'If the weather stays good,' Howard said after dinner, 'we should be able to get up the Upper Staircase to the névé tomorrow and to the plateau itself the next day.'

'Not if we have as much trouble with crevasses as we've had the last couple of days,' Dawson grumbled.

'Actually, Stan, we've really been lucky so far,' Howard said. 'They haven't been too wide or too deep for the most part and we've been able to get across fairly easily.'

Dawson grunted his disagreement, and in this case I couldn't help but agree with him.

Howard was serious. 'I'm afraid we've yet to meet any really bad crevassing. The last time I was here, we had to cross holes that could easily have engulfed a London bus.'

He had the attention of everyone now. We hoped his statement was the exaggeration of a traveller's tale. But Howard wasn't a man given to hyperbole. He meant it.

'At least we shouldn't have any trouble seeing anything that big,' Pitt said, his hands encased in a black sack as he reloaded the Bolex film magazine by touch.

Howard was looking at his maps and didn't seem to notice everyone's eyes on him worriedly as he said, 'On the contrary, most of them have a cap of snow hiding them. Almost impossible to see until they fall away. We'll have to be careful. If we do run into that type of crevassing, we'll have to probe ahead with poles to test the snow before attempting to drive across.'

'It's a damn long way to the top of the glacier if we have to walk,' I said.

It was bitterly cold the next day but not much wind. The way ahead was more or less flat across the Landing if you didn't count the pitching caused by wave after wave of semi-hard sastrugi about four feet high. Not too bad for the Sno-cats with their individually articulated tracks, but the Weasel tipped up and forward like a small boat in a short sea.

'If this keeps up I'll be wishing for seasick pills,' Charly grumbled, holding tight to try to keep herself from bouncing off the windshield.

Later in the morning, after we'd finished jouncing over the snow ridges and had begun the ascent of the Upper Staircase, Gus waved us down beside the trail. 'More crevasses,' he said. 'Only these a little bigger than before.'

An understatement. When we edged the vehicles up to a small hole in the snow and climbed out to have a look, the small hole turned out to be a tiny cave-in in the snow cover that opened into a vast luminous green chasm below.

'How do we get across that?' Dawson asked.

'We just have to find where the snow's thick enough to support the vehicles,' Howard said matter-of-factly, and went back to his Sno-cat to get the probing poles.

I had to admire Howard's sanguine attitude, the easy acceptance of hardship and difficulty that he'd shown since we'd arrived in Antarctica. Jenny should see him now, I thought; truly the intrepid explorer. I was beginning to respect him more and more as we went along, and I was also finding it more difficult to believe he'd panicked and left his two companions to die in the snow.

He took one of the poles and began to probe along what appeared to be the edge of the crevasse. About fifty yards down he yelled that it seemed thick enough there to carry the weight of the vehicles.

'How do you know?' Grampion said worriedly.

'There's at least seven or eight feet of snow bridging the crevasse at this point. More than enough.'

Kokko looked at the smooth, inscrutable snow that was supposed to keep us from plunging into that thirty-foot-wide crack in the ice. 'Not for me!' he said and walked away.

For a moment this straight-out refusal to go on had us stumped, but Gus yelled out, 'What are you afraid of, eh, Kokko? Charly and Logan got to cross first. They make sure it's safe for you.'

Kokko didn't turn but his body stiffened under the lash of Gus's words.

'If you are still scared,' Gus continued to lay on, 'Charly will come back and drive your Sno-cat.'

Kokko still didn't move.

'I guess Charly she is right.' Gus turned to the rest of us. 'No balls!'

Kokko turned slowly, his face an ugly cameo in the frame of his parka hood. He didn't speak but the malevolence in his little squeezed-up eyes left no doubt of his feelings. Finally he walked over to his Sno-cat and climbed up into the cab.

'He won't forget that,' Charly said to me with a shiver.

'Gus can take care of himself.'

'I don't think Kokko would care who he took it out on.'

I agreed. Ari Kokko was working up enough hate for the lot of us.

'Let's get going, then,' Grampion ordered. 'And don't take any chances, Logan.'

As I started up and tentatively edged forward, I wondered how he thought I was supposed to obey that injunction and still drive a loaded Weasel with a total weight of 6000 pounds over a thirty-foot bridge made of snow. But we crossed without mishap, as did the heavier Sno-cats. From then on two of us went ahead on skis, probing the snow and listening for the telltale boom of a crevasse when its snow cover was thumped. When the two leading got too cold and weary, two others would take their place. Progress was slow and our trail must have looked like a drunkard's walk where we twisted and turned and many times had to backtrack as we wove our way over or around the treacherous crevasses.

Later in the day, Charly and 'Plum' Pitt were working ahead and Gus was warming himself with me in the Weasel. Charly was well off to the right of our line of advance looking for a better route and Pitt was carefully probing the snow in front of us, indicating the path we should take with flags or arrows in the snow. We picked the flags up as we passed them to our right.

We'd had a fairly straight run for the last fifteen minutes and were beginning to hope that we might soon be through the crevasse area. Gus reached out to retrieve a flag just as the Weasel began slowly to tilt backwards.

'*Mon Dieu!*' His face went grey. 'The snow's giving way!'

I tried to gun the Weasel forward but the crust over the crevasse sank out from under us. The Weasel slid backwards and for a moment caught, its rear tank jammed against one wall of the crevasse and its tracks nosed into the other. But not for long. I had no sooner congratulated myself that our sledge and the tow-rope to the Sno-cat behind were stopping us from sliding any farther into the ice pit than, with a grinding crunch, our two-and-a-half-ton sledge crushed into the rear of the Weasel's cab and slid off to one side. Its weight jerked us over on to our side and the Weasel slipped another six feet before it jammed again, barely held by a single front bogie and the rear tow-bar. The sledge swung like a pendulum beneath us, each oscillation threatening to dislodge our precarious hold and plunge us into the deep chasm.

Gus pulled himself back from the open door on his side of the cab which now looked straight down into the abyss. 'The tow-rope . . . broken!' His voice cracked.

I could see it now, snaking into the depths below the swinging sledge. It had parted under the strain, leaving nothing to hold us! Each swing of the sledge threatened to drag us free and down, God knows how far, into the pit. I could already see the tow-bar chipping through the ice from the weight of the vehicle and sledge. I reached up, swung the door back on my side of the cab and yelled: 'Let's get out of here before the whole thing goes!'

Gus gave me a boost out of the door to where I could stand on the side of the Weasel. I reached down and helped haul him out beside me. The top of the crevasse looked a long way up, and by the little graunching movements from the Weasel, we'd soon be headed a long way down.

Grampion, Dawson, Kokko and Howard's heads appeared over the lip of ice, and a moment later Pitt and Charly arrived at the other side.

'For Christ's sake get a rope down to us!' I hollered. 'This thing's going to go in a minute.'

To prove my point, the Weasel gave a lurch and slipped over to a new angle. My feet went from under me. I dropped flat on to the Weasel's body and grabbed at the track to hold on.

'Logan!'

Gus had slipped too but found nothing to grab. Now he was sliding off the canted body of the Weasel into the crevasse. I let go one hand and snatched at him as he desperately scrabbled to find something to stop his slide. I just managed to get a handful of hood, and luckily it was all of a piece with his jacket. The full weight of his big body stretched me out over the metal side of the vehicle like a man on a rack, and I could feel the sharp edge of the track cut through my mitt into my hand. He dangled there, held by the armpits of his parka and my numbing fingers. Bits of ice cracked away from around the Weasel and fell and fell interminably down into the chasm. The Weasel groaned and creaked with the weight of the sledge swinging beneath it, and I could feel by its movement that it wouldn't hold long.

A rope snaked down from above, writhing a few inches from my face. But I couldn't grab it because one hand was holding Gus and the other was holding both of us. Charly's voice snapped across the space above. 'Put the rope down to Gus. Logan can't take it!'

The rope disappeared and I shut my eyes with the strain and prayed that Gus could get it and take up the weight of his body before my shoulders pulled apart. 'Got it!' I heard him say and felt a wonderful reprieve as he relieved me of his 240-pound load. I got my other hand up to the track and pulled myself into a sitting position on the uppermost part of the Weasel.

Gus tied a bowline around his chest and started walking up the side of the Weasel towards me mountaineering fashion, leaning back into the rope and getting traction from the swing of his body.

With a crack the piece of ice that had been jamming the tow-bar snapped away and the Weasel began to slip. Gus saw it going and leaped forward, swinging on the rope end, while I too lunged desperately to try and reach him. I only just caught his ankles under my armpits as the Weasel and sledge plunged thunderously into the crevasse. We hung there twisting in the air like a bad circus trapeze act, listening to the cacophony of grinding metal booming and echoing as it bounced and broke its way to the bottom.

For an instant there was silence. I was momentarily aware of the faces of the rest of the party peering over the rim above us; then the silence was swept away as a dull crump and then another echoed far below and suddenly a rolling wave of heat washed around us as we dangled, two dolls on a string. The drums of gasoline on the sledge must have split as the Weasel crashed down on them; then the hot engine or a spark had set them off.

Hanging by Gus's ankles, I looked down into hell. Flames were bursting up between the narrow walls of the crevasse and, even as I watched, another drum exploded and the blaze leaped higher, licking the glistening green and blue ice with tongues of orange and red and yellow that flickered out from a rising cloud of dirty black smoke.

Gus reached down and hauled me up his swinging body. 'Climb, *mon ami*, or we roast!'

I needed no urging. Each exploding drum surged the flames closer and the smoke swirled hotly around us, blotting out the sky above. I crawled up Gus's body and monkeyed on up the rope. Gus was right behind and willing hands dragged us over the edge as a roar of flame flailed out of the ice chasm.

We stumbled shakily to our feet and I waved at Charly, standing with 'Plum' Pitt on the other side of the crevasse.

They both waved back through the flames and started off to find a solid area where they could cross back to us.

Grampion and Howard fussed around worriedly, asking if we were all right, untying the rope from around Gus's chest, looking for something to do for us. But Kokko said nothing as he gazed at the flames flaring noisily out of the crevasse. No doubt he would have preferred us to go down with the Weasel or fry at the end of the rope.

Charly and Pitt arrived, and after a hug for us both from Charly, we began to set up camp. One vehicle and a fifth of our supplies were cooking in an ice oven a hundred or more feet down and a reassessment of our position was needed before we could go on.

While the others got the tents up and a pot of cocoa on the Primus for a hot drink, I went over to the Sno-cat that had been travelling behind us. Gus ploughed through the snow to come up to me. His face was all grinning teeth, frosty moustache and twinkling eyes.

'Hey, Logan, you bloody well save my life down there!' he called, giving me a staggering thump on the shoulder. 'Even if you did nearly tear my head off.' He pulled the hood of his parka up above his head to show how it caught him under the chin.

I laughed, then bent down and rummaged through the snow.

'What do you lose?' Gus asked.

'Nearly my life and I'd like to know why.' I found what I was looking for and dragged it up out of the snow for him to see: the end of the tow-rope that was supposed to have held us if we broke through into a crevasse.

He took his mitt off and ran a stubby finger over the end of the thick three-inch rope. 'Cut,' he said, 'maybe half-way through.'

I looked at it. Cut, with just enough left to hold together under the normal strain of driving, but break if it had to support an entire vehicle.

'The Sno-cat must have run over it and cut it under a track.'

'Maybe,' I said.

Gus was quiet for a moment. When he spoke, all the humour had gone out of his voice. 'Are you saying it maybe was done on purpose?'

'I think it's a possibility.'

'You think that bastard Kokko cut it because of what I said to him?'

I shrugged.

Gus's face darkened in thought, then he shook his head. 'He couldn't do it since I tell him off this morning anyway. We hardly stop long enough for a pee and anyway either Howard or Grampion was with him all the time.'

'Then it must have been done last night.'

'Last night! But why? That's even crazier than thinking Kokko did it because he don't like me or you.' He looked at me oddly. 'You say a lot of funny things sometimes, Logan.'

'I know it sounds crazy,' I said, 'but the only thing I can think of is that someone is trying to make us give up the expedition.'

Gus smacked his forehead in exasperation. 'Who would do that?'

Dawson, a Russian? Kokko, his lieutenant? But why get rid of me if they wanted to stop the expedition, and not Howard or Grampion? It didn't make sense, and I didn't want the whole thing to fall apart before I found out. I handed Gus the severed tow-rope and pointed to the cleanness of the cut.

'Did a rough cleat on a Sno-cat make that smooth cut?' I asked.

He looked at it a moment and shook his head.

'I've got suspicions, Gus, and it's not hard to guess who they are against. But suspicions aren't proof and a lot of accusations would just give a perfect excuse to pack it in without finding out what it was all about.'

Gus fingered his heavy jaw reflectively. 'We keep quiet, then?'

I nodded. 'For the moment.'

Chapter 16

Even though Gus and I kept our suspicions about the tow-rope to ourselves, there was a strong lobby to call it a day. We had lost a good portion of our supplies, including all Charly's geology and surveying equipment, but most of the sledge load had been gasoline and without the Weasel it wouldn't be too great a hardship. The biggest argument to turn back came, not unexpectedly, from Kokko, with Dawson backing him up. Kokko dourly pointed out that he had been proved right; it was too dangerous to try to cross the extra-wide crevasses and even testing the snow bridges with poles didn't help. I remembered Pitt's red marker flag fluttering down with the snow bridge from beneath the Weasel and found it hard to counter his argument.

'You tested that snow, Plum?' I said, glancing at the subdued cameraman huddled against the tent wall. 'Didn't it look thin to you?'

'Jesus, it looked okay to me. I wouldn't have put a flag on it otherwise. As it is, I feel I almost killed you and Gus.'

'It can easily happen,' Howard said. 'Okay one place, and a few feet to one side, nothing.'

'We'll have to go even more carefully,' Grampion said, undeterred by the loss of a vehicle and some supplies. 'We must make sure to check over a wider front.'

'If we can't even be sure enough of the snow bridges to take a Weasel safely, we sure as hell can't be sure they'll take a Sno-cat which is a couple of thousand pounds heavier,' Dawson objected vehemently. 'Maybe you think little fairy cities are all over this godforsaken lump of ice and maybe Turbott really believes his two buddies could live nearly a year in the snow without supplies, and as far as I'm concerned, if the pay is right, I don't mind holding your hand while you wild-goose chase around . . . but not if it means risking my life falling into a hole in the ice every fifteen minutes!'

Grampion's heavy face went roseate. Howard's face too betrayed his feelings. Dawson had made a big point of seeming to believe his story and making a friend of him; now he heard just what the man really thought.

But it was Charly who had the answer to Dawson. 'Another quarter of a mile and there are no more crevasses,' she said. 'I've skied well up ahead and we're almost through. If we start now, we could reach the top of the Staircase and be on to the névé of the glacier in three hours.'

Dawson and Kokko had no reply to that happy piece of information, but it was a very subdued expedition that climbed into the Sno-cats and threaded its way past the last of the crevasses, leaving behind the pillar of black smoke that marked the accident.

Charly proved right. We reached the Skelton névé, old snow that had been packed down on top of the glacier giving a firm, dense base for the vehicles to move on, in about three hours; and the next day, ploughing into a frigid wind rolling down from the continental mass, we reached the polar plateau itself.

It spread out featureless and forbidding over the entire continent, an ice sheet thousands of feet thick, 95 per cent of all the ice in the world. From the Pole super-frozen air spiralled out, racing over virtually unbroken snowcrust, sometimes reaching intensities that would make a tropical hurricane seem like simple bad weather. In summer it's not so bad, but summer is short in these latitudes and we still had a long way to go – and to get back. I thought of Scott and his men starving to death only eleven miles from a food cache and not much farther to ultimate safety when an early autumn blizzard pinned them down. The Antarctic left no margin even at its best.

At least from now on we would be travelling more or less

on the flat and with a far lighter load. We made a cache of fuel and food to use on the return journey and marked it with a high snow-cairn topped with flags that could be seen from a great distance on the flat terrain if the weather was reasonable. There was no worry about its being covered with snow; it snows very little in Antarctica, where there is probably less precipitation than in the Sahara: the air is too dry and cold to hold moisture. But the snow that does fall stays, and after thousands of years it amounts to a tremendous accumulation that packs down into hard crystals sometimes inches across. From year to year, however, unless wind-driven drift whipped up from the surface finds something to pack against, there is small chance that a spot will be covered; even the tracks of old expeditions have occasionally been found set clearly in the hard windswept crust.

We were now about 300 miles from Scott Base but still on the same latitude. Our course would cross the plateau into Wilkes Land almost directly away from the South Pole but almost directly towards the South Magnetic Pole. Several hundreds of miles separated the two, creating the unique position of heading north along the 150th meridian while our compasses told us we were heading south. As we moved farther out on to the ice cap away from the mountain peaks along the coast, we would be like a small boat venturing into deep sea, and celestial navigation and dead reckoning would be our only method of telling where we were.

We spent three days at the plateau camp, and on the fourth day we fired up the 200-h.p. Chryslers and set our course into the swirling drift that soon obscured the cairn and flags. Gus and I took a team and sledge to scout the way ahead, and the Sno-cats, yellow galleons, the spare dogs yapping in their wake, followed majestically behind.

I preferred the quiet shush of the sledge to the clatter of the Sno-cats and also to the strained atmosphere that had now descended on the expedition. Dawson's outburst hadn't made relationships easier, and any work he and Kokko had had to do subsequently had been done with a bad grace that further exacerbated the situation. Grampion just clamped his pipe harder and Howard ignored them. I think that those two would have gone on alone on foot now they were so close to their goals, each drawn by his respective need to prove himself right, Grampion to the archæological fraternity and Howard to his wife and son and all the others who disbelieved.

We ground on over the plateau for two weeks; sometimes over easy, smooth crust, sometimes over rough and broken ice and high sastrugi, but thankfully we encountered no more crevassing bad enough to slow or endanger us unduly. The temperature never rose higher than twenty below and the wind blew almost continually, making it impossible to spend more than two or three hours at a time on the sledge without being in danger of frostbite. Howard and Charly spelled Gus and me, and even Pitt and Grampion took their turns, but neither was very good with the dogs. Dawson and Kokko never offered and we were content to let them drive.

Christmas Eve and Day were spent huddled in our tents waiting for a particularly vicious blizzard to blow itself out, and even the bottle of whisky that Grampion dug out of his pack failed to lighten the gloom engendered by bad feeling and weariness. Only Howard's saying we would soon be in the area where Claydon and Rourk went missing bolstered our spirits.

At last the blizzard slackened, the tent sides ceased their constant slapping, and we were able to emerge, eight bedraggled animals, blinking owlishly in the glare of sun on snow. Drift had packed up cab high against the Sno-cats and the sledges were covered. It was hard work digging them out, but the relief of moving around outside again stopped complaints. There was cursing when we tried to start the cold motors and it took nearly two hours with the help of a blowtorch to tease them to life. Finally we set off on the last lap, according to Howard.

'Two or three days if the weather stays reasonable,' he said as the Sno-cats lumbered across the featureless snow plain, 'and we should be over this corner of the plateau and at the George V Coast. Once I've picked out a few landmarks there, we can make a more or less permanent camp and split up into individual parties; fan out in a circle to cover as much ground as we can in the shortest time possible.'

Pitt, who sat wedged in the back of the cab with us while Dawson drove, said, 'It doesn't sound easy to me. You'd need an army to really cover any sort of area.'

'I have a good idea where it is. I've spent long enough thinking about it,' Howard answered. 'Don't worry, I'll find it.' Looking at his set mouth and thinking back over the determination he'd shown in the last weeks on the trail and before, I believed him, but Pitt just grunted and turned away.

Later in the afternoon we changed partners and Howard and I relieved Gus and Charly on the dog sledge. He and I hadn't been on our own since landing at Scott Base; now we took it in turns to drive and ride. Howard plainly enjoyed working the team and was good at it. In an hour we had left the Sno-cats far behind, the dogs pulling us effortlessly over a thin layer of soft snow on a flat hard crust below. When Howard pulled the team up so that I could take over I looked at him patting the dogs, a big bundle of heavy clothes encased in parka, wind pants and huge snow boots, his face rosy with cold and his eyes sparkling as he pushed his glare goggles on to his forehead, and said impulsively, 'You really like this, don't you, Howard?'

He rose and lumbered over to me, beating his mittened hands together to restore circulation. 'You do, too,' he said.

I nodded, and suddenly he smiled almost shyly. 'I'm sorry,' he said. 'I've given you a pretty hard time.'

'You haven't made it easy,' I agreed.

He was silent a moment, looking inward in that peculiar way of his. Then he said, 'Before I even met you, Jenny had burnished your silver armour until I was dazzled. I've never had a very overt personality, and when we went to visit you on our honeymoon, I was scared to death.' He laughed ruefully. 'Your fame had gone before you, as they say, and I was desperately afraid you wouldn't like me.'

'And I didn't help.'

'You made me feel I didn't amount to anything.' There was no anger or bitterness in his voice; it was just a statement of fact. 'By the time we left, I wondered what Jenny saw in me.'

'But she loves you regardless of her arrogant brother.'

'Yes!' He sounded surprised. 'And because I loved her so much, our marriage went along quite well.' He paused. 'But I would never do many of the things she wanted. Go tramping or skiing. Get out in the world. Even go fishing with David. I made a fetish of the intellectual, academic life.'

'There's no particular glory attached to the outdoor life.'

'Of course not, I always realized that. The problem with me was that I really wanted to do adventurous things, wanted to look at the wonders of the world first hand. I even studied biology initially because I thought it would lead me into strange places.' He turned his head away.

'And why didn't you do it?' I asked, though I felt I knew the answer.

'Because of you.'

I said nothing.

He went on quietly. 'Jenny idolizes you. David was brought up on your exploits instead of fairy stories.'

'I didn't know,' I said.

'Why should you know? You are what you are. You're not a man to shape your life to what others think. I didn't do the things that I wanted because I was afraid of being compared with you by Jenny and David. So I took the role of the complete academic, the rumpled professor, the thinker who puts together the findings of other men. I did it well, mind you,' he added bitterly. 'I'm very good at my job.'

'Then why Antarctica?'

He shrugged. 'I don't know. My last chance? What I did know was that I really wanted to come out here. I *am* a biologist, and this is a fascinating continent, or, more correctly, its seas are fascinating. A whole world of creatures that live happily in the most cruel environment possible. But you know how that ended.'

'And then Jenny put me on your back to look after you like a baby.'

'Yes. If there was anybody I didn't want along, it was you.'

'But you didn't want to lose Jenny.'

'I was so afraid if she left, she would never come back.'

'She only threatened because she thought *you* would never come back from *here*!'

He nodded ruefully. 'I know. I've spent a lifetime practising being a fool and I reached perfection in the way I handled this.'

'Now you think differently?'

One of the dogs nuzzled up to him and he reached down absent-mindedly to pat it. 'I thought you only wanted to stop me coming out here or, failing that, bring the expedition to an end as quickly as possible. I'm obviously aware that Jenny, you and everyone else thinks I'm mad to believe Claydon and Rourk are still alive, even if you don't think I personally did them in, and that this entire junket is absolutely pointless.' He stopped and looked me hard in the eyes. 'At least, that is what I thought until you and Gus went into the crevasse.'

'That changed your mind?'

'After the accident in the crevasse, you could easily have finished the expedition by siding with Stan and Ari. When you didn't, it made me look at things more clearly. I realized that whatever I thought about you was a product of my own twisted reasoning. You loved your sister and didn't mind risking your life to help her. But more than that, I knew you weren't trying to stop me even if you didn't agree with me.'

We stood there, two small figures in a great vastness of white; we could have been the only two left in existence, but now, instead of two men alone, we were two men together.

'I'm glad it's settled,' I said.

Howard climbed aboard the sledge and I hollered up the team.

Later when the others had caught us up and we'd made camp, I went out to the Sno-cat that housed our big 40-watt Turner TR 11.H radio transceiver to make our daily contact with Scott Base. I hadn't been able to maintain the daily schedule during the entire trip, reception varied between bad to impossible, but I had been able to get through enough to let them know we were still going and approximately where we were. But when I tried to warm the set up, I soon realized that something more than atmospherics was wrong this time. I couldn't get a spark of life out of it. I opened the panel and found a tightly wound coil that was a scabrous green mess of corrosion and I marvelled that it had managed to operate the night before. Looking more closely, I wondered if maybe it had operated the night before because since then someone had applied a liberal portion of battery acid. I couldn't be sure.

Hell, I thought, I would just replace the part. Then I remembered and swore bitterly to myself. All the radio spares were at the bottom of the crevasse with the Weasel.

Doggedly I trudged back to the other Sno-cat and climbed into the cab. We'd only used the smaller Pye C12's for inter-vehicle communication and I didn't think I had a hope of raising Scott Base nearly seven hundred miles away in one of the worst radio reception areas possible to choose. After an hour of fruitless calling with my ears buzzing from the mash of static, I returned to the main tent.

'The radio's finished,' I informed them.

There was a buzz of consternation.

'Can it be fixed?' Grampion asked.

'The spares went with the Weasel.'

'The Pye?'

'Not powerful enough. I just tried.'

'Good goddamn!' Dawson stopped eating for a moment. 'You were supposed to be such a hot shot with the radios.'

I reached over and fingered his parka. 'You want to be careful there, Stan. Looks like you spilled battery acid over yourself.'

'I didn't . . . !' He looked at the parka and saw there was no mark, reddened, then replaced the smirk on his face all in the space of a second or two.

'I can't figure you, Adams. You're always talking in riddles. I hope you write books plainer than that.' He turned to the others. 'If the radio's busted, I think it's pretty stupid to go on.'

He was a trier, I had to say that for him.

'Nonsense.' Grampion cut him short. 'Maybe Scott doesn't know precisely where we are, but we know, and I see no reason to contemplate turning back. You surprise me, Stan. I would have thought with your experience you would have been used to little setbacks like this.'

Dawson didn't reply, but the admonition didn't seem to worry him and he went back to his meal wearing the usual sardonic twist to his lips. One day soon, I promised myself, I would smash that smile into his teeth.

The next day the plateau started to slope down towards the coast still a hundred miles distant and by afternoon Howard recognized some of the features of the now more varied snow-scape. Several nunataks piercing through the ice cover gave him a rough position, and when we camped that evening in the long shadows of the low, unsetting sun, he got out his maps and announced that another thirty miles closer to the coast and we should be able to find the valley fairly easily.

Later, I crawled wearily into my sleeping-bag. Charly snuggled herself into her own bag next to mine and smiled as best she could through frost-cracked lips. She had been pulling more than her fair share of the weight and her normally high cheekbones stood out gauntly in her wind-roughened face. But she was still beautiful. She thrived on this type of life, and although she was as tired as the rest of us, her eyes were alive and bright with inner drive. But there was much more to this expedition than just straight physical hardship, and I wished then that I had voted against her coming.

'I think things are going to hot up a bit now that we're getting close,' I whispered so that Grampion and Pitt on the other side of the tent couldn't hear. I started to try to explain, but she held a finger to her lips.

'I understand,' she mouthed. 'Gus told me about the rope. And I can guess about the radio, too.'

'Just be careful.'

She blew me a small kiss and I went to sleep feeling illogically better.

Chapter 17

'That's it!' Howard said excitedly from the top of a Sno-cat cab where he'd climbed to get a better view. 'I recognize that line of nunataks over there; looks like a lot of women lying in the snow with just their breasts showing.' He stopped, flustered, and looked guiltily down at the rest of us standing below in the snow. 'Sorry, Charly,' he apologized.

Charly just laughed. In some ways Howard was very Victorian.

'Do you think you can locate the valley from there?' Grampion said, not caring if they were called the booby breastworks as long as they helped find his city.

Howard climbed down. 'I think so. We camped there the day before I saw the valley. When Claydon and Rourk went missing, I couldn't risk trying to find it again to orientate myself. It would have taken too long and I wasn't sure of my navigation. My only chance was to press on and try to make it back. But I'm pretty sure I can put us fairly close, using them as a base to work from.'

We rolled on towards the upthrust tips of the ice-buried mountains that really did resemble huge rounded breasts set two by two in a long line. We were quite close to the George V Coast now, and although this coastline didn't have the high ranges that bordered the Ross Sea, it was nevertheless changing from the virtually level polar plateau into a more rugged, undulating configuration. Looking at it, it wasn't hard to believe dry valleys could be hidden there, much like the reasonably well-explored Victoria Coast far to the east. I realized I had no doubt now that Howard had been telling the truth all along. Or what he thought was the truth. He had seen something – something very strange – and something equally strange had happened to his companions.

Later, Grampion began methodically to plan the rest of the operation. 'Howard is fairly sure that the valley lies somewhere in this area,' he said, putting a big square finger on his map. 'We'll leave our big sledges here and break up into four parties of two each. Howard knows the general direction he and the others were travelling when they left here, and each of the parties will take a line at a tangent to it so that we can cover as large a sector as possible. If we don't find it on the first sweep, then the next day we'll shift over and take in another slice. That way we should be able to check the most probable area within a few days.'

'And if we don't find it?' Pitt asked.

'We'll worry about that if and when it happens,' he said, brushing aside the thought.

The next morning Gus and Howard, Charly and I readied the dogs and the other four the Sno-cats. Gus and Howard were to take the first sector to the west, Charly and I the next, then Grampion and Dawson, and last, to the east, Kokko and Pitt with the camera equipment. But Dawson objected, saying it would be better if the orders were reversed. 'It looks an easier go that way for the Sno-cats,' he explained. 'The dog teams can get over the rougher ground better than we can.'

Grampion didn't mind, and Dawson told Kokko to take the westernmost end of the line and he would come next inside him. The terrain to me looked equally undulating, but that's how we went out.

And found nothing.

Charly and I drove the team on hour after hour, hoping always to see over the next rise the pyramid nunatak that Howard had carefully described to us. I continually scanned the broken horizon with my binoculars, but every hopeful projection turned into a disappointment on closer inspection. Only the weather was kind and I was thankful for that as we wearily urged our tired dogs over the last few miles back to camp.

We hoped one of the other teams had had better luck, but one look at the quiet group that met us told the story.

'Nothing, I'm afraid,' Howard said a little defensively.

'Early days.' Grampion put confidence into his voice. 'We'll go out again tomorrow.'

And so we did; and the next day after that, and again the next. Even when the wind rose and the temperatures dropped, we flogged ourselves to carry on because time was running out. It was a long, hard way back to Scott Base and the short Antarctic summer was already on the wane. But it was fruitless and we were a tired, dejected, short-tempered bunch when we finally stumbled in after that last day.

'It's no goddamned good,' Dawson spat. 'I don't think there ever was a valley!'

'It's there. I know it,' Howard insisted.

'Maybe it is and maybe it isn't,' Pitt said, 'but we sure as hell can't find it.'

'Maybe it was stolen away like Turbott's two friends.' Kokko put in his two cents.

'It's there,' Howard repeated tightly.

Dawson's tone was one long sneer. 'Let's stop playing games, Howard. You didn't want to say what really happened to your buddies, so you cooked up this whole lost city crap and Grampion was stupid enough to believe it. God knows why, it's one-hundred-proof fairy-tale.'

'Then why did you come?' Charly snapped.

'The same reason as you, baby: money. I don't mind pissing about in the snow for a couple of months as long as the pay cheque is big enough. But now we've all had our fun and it's time to go home. And Howie here should just count himself lucky that we didn't come across his friends and find out what actually did happen to them.' He turned to Howard. 'Buried too deep, eh, fellah?'

Howard took a swing at him, but it was too cramped to do any damage before Gus wrapped his big arms around him and held him fast. It could easily have turned into a brawl; it would have been like a sackful of dogs and cats in that small tent, but Grampion rapped out, 'That's enough!'

'I'd just like to point out,' he said in the ensuing silence, 'that we have a long journey back, and unless we work together we might not live to enjoy any pay cheques.'

Howard looked at him pleadingly. 'We can't go back yet,' he protested. 'It's near here, I know it! It should have been close to where we looked the first day. I was certain we'd find it first time out.'

'But we didn't, Howard.' Grampion's voice was quieter now.

'You think I made up the valley, too?' Howard asked bitterly, but he already knew the answer. 'You were always playing the long odds on it anyway, weren't you? It was a chance you had to take.'

'Yes, I suppose I was grabbing at a dream,' Grampion said sadly. 'My theories concerning this continent have been laughed at so long I would have given everything to have proved them. I would have come out here on the slimmest of chances, and I guess I did.'

'We still have time.'

Grampion looked around the tent.

'I'm not chasing any more dreams,' Dawson snarled.

Nobody had to ask Kokko what he thought.

Pitt shrugged his shoulders. 'I think we've run the hundred.'

Something was wrong here. We'd covered a huge amount of territory in the last gruelling days, and if Howard's valley wasn't here, then he'd made a bad mistake. But he was so sure we were in the right place and I'd come to respect his judgement more and more concerning the Antarctic. After all, he'd found his way out of this wasteland without instruments and coming back he'd led us exactly to the spot he'd wanted. Even if he wasn't exactly sure where the valley was, our method should have found it fairly easily.

Grampion was obviously beginning to think there was no valley to find, that Howard had made the whole story up. I guess he'd always half believed that anyway. But I didn't because too many people had tried to stop us getting there. And were still trying!

Something else was nagging at my mind; something Howard had said a few moments earlier which had made me remember another thing that I'd previously thought odd.

As I thought about it, Gus said that he would continue the search if Grampion and Howard wanted and Charly said the same. Howard looked gratefully at them and then noticed Charly's haggard face.

'No,' he said, gently touching the back of Charly's raw, chapped hand, 'you've done enough. I appreciate it very much.'

Grampion sighed. 'I guess we should make plans for the trip back, then.'

Some of the pieces that I was trying to put together slipped into place. 'I have an idea,' I said. Dawson looked at me sharply and I went on. 'We could do with a day or two's rest before we head back; we're not pressed for time, we'd planned to spend at least another week or so here if we found anything. How about Howard and I taking a Sno-cat out tomorrow for a last look?'

Howard looked as if a death-row reprieve had just come through from the governor, but Dawson said, 'I don't think we should risk the vehicles any more than we have to.'

'Then we'll take one of the dog teams.'

'But where will you go?' Pitt asked. 'There's not much we haven't covered.'

'Charly and I saw something to the east of us today but it was too far to check out. Isn't that right, Charly?'

She looked at me strangely; we hadn't seen anything; but she nodded and said, 'It could be worth a look.'

'Just a waste of time,' Dawson argued, 'risking equipment on a wild-goose chase. What's the point?'

'The point seems obvious, Stan,' Grampion interjected. 'It's why I spent so much money getting us out here!'

It looked as if we were in for another acrimonious argument, but Pitt said, 'I can't see any reason for them not to have another look. Then everyone should be satisfied,' and Dawson grumbled himself into silence.

Howard and I got an early start in the morning and set off in an easterly direction with me driving. He was excited and had talked himself into believing that what Charly and I were supposed to have seen was the elusive pyramid nunatak, although he was nevertheless puzzled how it could be so far to the east when he had been sure it was more to the west. When we were well out of sight of the camp, I turned the dogs at a right angle and began to drive them across the territory we had covered in the days before.

Howard twisted himself in the sledge and looked at me quizzically. 'Where are you going?'

'I think you were right in the first place. It is to the west.'

'But we looked there!'

'*We* didn't look there,' I pointed out. 'Grampion and Dawson and Pitt and Kokko took the most westerly half of the segment the first day; the rest of us were farther to the east.'

'I know you don't like Dawson or Kokko,' he yelled over the swishing runners, 'but with Warden and Plum with them, they couldn't report not seeing something they had.'

'It's just a hunch, Howard.'

'But what about what you and Charly saw?'

'We didn't see anything. I just didn't want anyone to know where we were actually headed.'

Howard said nothing, and there was really little more I could tell him. It *was* just a hunch, a hunch evolved out of a combination of minor events that by themselves seemed to have no significance. And even taken together, I thought, they didn't add up to much. But the proof was in the seeing. I urged the dogs on.

Once I had moved far enough to the west, I turned north, approximating the course taken by Kokko and Pitt on the first day. It was very cold, at least thirty below, but there was no wind except what we made ourselves as we plumed through a soft layer of new snow covering the hard crust beneath. The air was so clear you felt you could almost touch the horizon. About eleven-thirty, Howard, who was driving now, pulled up the team and shaded his eyes against the glare from the snow.

'I think there's something over there to the left,' he said, trying to suppress the rising excitement in his voice.

I unshipped the binoculars from their case and looked at the dark triangular blob in that world of white. 'Could be. Let's have a look.'

It took us another hour before we were close enough to be sure, but by then Howard was in no doubt.

'It's the nunatak all right! That's it! That's it!' he kept saying over and over as he mushed the dogs to an even quicker pace.

I believed him. Some nunataks are roughly conical, some rounded; they come in a great variety of shapes. But this one had almost the exact form of an Egyptian pyramid, four sides rising at just the right angle to the apex, sides that seemed almost flat from a distance. It was just as Howard had described.

He stopped in the shadow of the steep rock face and I climbed stiffly from the sledge and helped picket the dogs.

'I can't understand how Plum and Ari could have missed it,' Howard exclaimed, overjoyed to re-discover the nunatak. 'The weather was good that day. You could see for miles. Just like today. Maybe they had a breakdown and didn't get this far.'

'Possibly,' I said.

He came down from his high a bit. 'You think Kokko pulled something funny, don't you?'

'What do you think?'

'But Pitt was with him.'

'Makes it even more complicated, doesn't it?'

'You must have some ideas. Why else were you so sure that the nunatak would be where they should have found it the first day?'

'I wasn't sure. It was a hunch, as I said. A lot of little things. You being so certain we should have found it the first time out; Dawson rearranging the order in which we would search when it didn't matter a damn which line the Sno-cats took as far as the terrain was concerned; it just didn't mesh properly.'

'Why didn't you follow his line, then?'

'With Grampion with him?'

Howard was puzzled. 'Surely the same could be said about Pitt?'

I was puzzled too. 'I think we'll have a better idea what's going on when we climb this lump of rock and see if we can spot your lost city,' I said.

'Right!' Howard was excited again, and then he stopped and looked around as if he'd lost something.

'What's the trouble?' I asked.

'The sledge,' he said, kicking at the hard snow crust. 'Claydon and Rourk's sledge. It should have been right here and their gear, too.' He looked up at the nunatak. 'I know this is the place I found it.'

'Wouldn't the snow have covered it?'

He shook his head. 'We're in the lee of the nunatak here and the wind always blows the same way. There's been no drifting here and not enough snow falls in Antarctica to cover something like that in a year.'

'Come on,' I said, turning to the rock. 'The sooner we see what's on the other side, the sooner some of our mysteries might be solved.'

It wasn't a hard climb even in our bulky clothing. From a distance the walls looked flat, but close up they were broken and craggy and afforded plenty of easy foot and hand holds. In less than an hour we had scrambled as high as we needed to get to the other side. And Howard had been right!

There was a narrow valley running away from the nunatak, a deep, dry valley surrounded by glacial ice, a valley that would be almost impossible to find unless you fell into it or flew directly over it. And at its far end was a city. Or was it? At first glance there appeared to be domes and spires but it was hard to tell the scale with nothing to judge by. I took out the binoculars and focused them.

Howard just looked. He was almost crying. 'I told you it was here. I told everybody but they wouldn't believe me. There is a city!'

'Not quite,' I said, and handed him the glasses.

What I had seen was not a city, but it was equally strange in these remote barrens. The domes were geodesic affairs, interconnected and obviously designed to keep out the weather. I didn't think they would have lasted long in the wind on the open plateau, but protected in the valley they were ideal. The spires weren't spires at all, but chimneys.

'What is it?' Howard said.

'Not Grampion's ancient lost city, I'm afraid.'

'There are huge chimneys with smoke coming from them!' Howard continued to peer through the binoculars.

'Steam, I think.'

'Steam?'

I had seen similar stacks with their white billowing clouds at the Wairakei geothermal field in New Zealand, and most likely Howard had also.

'It looks to me like somebody's tapping a geothermal bed, harnessing the underground steam.'

'In Antarctica?'

'You know better than that, Howard. Just because the whole continent's under ice doesn't mean there can't be plenty of volcanic or geothermal activity going on. Look at Mount Erebus on Ross Island; an active volcano for everybody to see.'

He pulled his eyes away from the glasses. 'Yes, of course. It's just hard to think of great amounts of heat under all this ice. That probably accounts for the valley being dry.' He looked back at the domes and stacks in the distance. 'But why?'

'For the same reason we tap the geothermal steam in New Zealand: power.'

Power. It was what kept man's incursions into Antarctica to a minimum. Even in summer it took vast amounts of fuel just to keep from freezing; to travel with vehicles took very much more, and all of it had to be laboriously and expensively shipped in over the most unpredictable and dangerous ocean in the world or flown in equally hazardously. Power was the key to the exploitation of the continent and it looked as if someone had got a secret jump on the rest of us.

'But who?' Howard asked.

'The Russians, of course,' I said. I could see the effect of that statement on Howard's face. 'Dawson's been trying to throw us off the track.'

'On behalf of the Russians?' Howard asked. 'That's his job?'

With the domed base in front of us, it didn't sound so ridiculous.

Howard pondered this a moment and his face went tight. 'I wonder what they did to Claydon and Rourk?'

'Whoever it was, they cleaned up all the bits and pieces after them,' I said.

'You think they removed the abandoned sledge?'

'If they grabbed the men, and I think that's a pretty good guess, they certainly wouldn't leave a sledge around to mark the place.'

'The bastards!' He waved towards the distant domes. 'Let's get down there and see just what all this is about!'

His anger was getting the better of his judgement. 'Don't be bloody naïve, Howard,' I snapped. 'If they were willing to abduct two men to keep what they're doing secret, they're not going to fold up and give in just because we burst in demanding to know what's going on.'

'But Claydon and Rourk are probably down there.'

'And I don't relish joining them on a permanent basis. Use your head.'

Some of the fire went out of him. 'Yes, yes, I see that. But what are we going to do?'

A good question. We couldn't bust into this hidden base like the marines and I didn't see much advantage in returning to our own camp with the news of our find. It was clear now that Dawson and Kokko had been working to keep us from just such a discovery, and once it was in the open, they'd be damned hard to keep under control all the way back to Scott.

'We'll have to pretend we found nothing,' I said.

Howard's eyes widened. 'You're joking?'

'As long as Dawson and Kokko think the expedition has been a failure, they'll cause no trouble. The other alternative is to take them prisoner – not so easy – they might even be armed. In either case we still have to get back to Scott Base. We can't do anything here.'

Howard thought about it. He didn't like the idea. He'd come a long way to prove his story, and he felt somehow that he would be backing off to leave now. But he wasn't stupid either; we really didn't have much choice.

'I guess you're right,' he conceded reluctantly.

After a last long look at the 'lost city', we climbed down the nunatak, unpicketed the dogs and headed back towards our camp. I retraced our path exactly. I wanted to come back from the same direction as we had left. Our story would be that we found nothing and that now even we agreed that the expedition was a failure.

The deception proved too much for Howard.

I fully intended to put Charly and Gus in the picture, but the whole mess blew up before I could speak to them alone. We mushed into camp looking suitably dejected, although Howard's face tended more to the angry. Our tale of failure was accepted at face value. Gus shrugged his big shoulders resignedly and Grampion thanked us for making a final try. Charly looked at me meaningfully; she knew something more had been up than simply just another day's search, but I gave her no indication of the truth with Dawson and Kokko looking on.

However, Dawson wasn't going to let it go. He enjoyed needling and I guess he thought he'd get a last few jabs into Howard while the opportunity existed.

'I just thought,' Dawson said, 'that Howie should put us out of our misery and admit everything he said was a load of crap.'

But it was too much for Howard. He'd heard that refrain too often, believed even his wife and son thought it in secret.

'You Russian pig!' he screamed. 'We found your bloody secret city and it won't be secret much longer!' And then he flailed at Dawson with his fists, mustering whatever strength a year's frustration had given him.

Dawson, surprised by Howard's attack, fell backward in the snow. Then Kokko came to life and slammed Howard with a sledge-hammer backhand. Howard went down, and his body lay there unmoving. Gus rammed a shoulder into the Finn, knocking him down. I grabbed a ski pole from the sledge and held its point to his thick throat.

'Don't move if you don't want a crude tracheotomy,' I hissed as he tried to scramble up.

'And don't you move if you want to continue to live, Logan.'

I looked around. Pitt stood with a cocked ·357 magnum pointed steadily at my chest. He held it expertly, his left hand bracing his right wrist, and I wasn't going to argue. I backed away from Kokko, allowing him to get up.

'Drop the ski pole,' Pitt ordered.

I let it fall to the snow.

'What's the meaning of this, Pitt?' Grampion demanded. 'I certainly didn't authorize any firearms; they're illegal in Antarctica.'

'I suppose I'll be charged with a misdemeanour then.' Pitt laughed. 'Now get over with Logan and Gus before it's a more serious charge. You too, Charly.' He waved the gun and she and Grampion came and stood beside us in a neat little group that Pitt could cover easily. Howard was still lying in the snow, out cold.

Dawson got groggily to his feet spitting blood, his upper lip already beginning to swell. It would be a while before he could sneer well again and I envied Howard his king hit. Kokko was already on his feet, and by the look in his eye as he stalked towards me, he wanted to get a little of his own back.

'Kokko!' Pitt's command brought him to a halt. 'Go to the Sno-cat and radio the base. Tell them that unfortunately our main plan has been fouled up and they'll have to come out and pick us up.'

Kokko gave me a look that said he wouldn't forget as he mumbled, 'Yes, sir,' and lumbered off to the Sno-cat and the Pye C 12. Plenty powerful enough to raise the domes, I thought.

'It's "sir", is it, Pitt?' I said.

'Hail to the leader.' He smiled. 'You don't think we would trust this operation to be run by idiots like Dawson and Kokko?'

'I don't understand,' Grampion said, unsuccessfully trying to grapple with the fast-changing events.

'It really is too bad,' Pitt went on, ignoring Grampion. 'You stuck your beak in just once too often, Logan, and now everyone's going to be in trouble. But for you, we could have all gone home to mother, unsuccessful, but at least alive. What made you take another look where Kokko and I said we saw nothing? I thought you suspected those two, but how come you thought I was in with them?'

'Nobody's perfect,' I said. Let him stew with the thought that somewhere along the line he'd made a mistake. I wasn't going to tell him it was just a hunch and dumb luck.

He shrugged. 'No sweat,' he said, and gestured towards the

tent. 'Let's get inside while we wait for the reinforcements to arrive. The damned wind is coming up again.'

And so it was. Not much, but enough to pick up the drift and swirl it whitely around us, and enough to make his bare hand holding the pistol go numb. I thought about trying to take him, but in heavy clothes and with snow to get through, there wasn't a chance. I headed meekly for the tent with the rest.

'What about Howard?' Charly asked. 'He's hurt.'

Howard was still face down beside our sledge, the dogs eyeing him curiously, wondering if he was supposed to be their dinner. Kokko must have hit him even harder than I thought.

'Get some rope to tie our friends up,' Pitt directed Dawson. 'I can see Logan's itching to have a go at me and I don't want to have to watch him every second while we're waiting. Then drag Howard in.'

We were herded into the tent and Dawson tied our hands tightly behind our backs while Pitt kept his gun cocked and ready.

'What the devil is this all about?' Grampion bellowed.

'I imagine Logan has most of it figured out by now,' Pitt said. 'Ask him.'

Grampion turned to me, looking as if I was responsible for all our problems, and said, 'Well?'

'Howard and I found the nunatak and saw what Howard had thought was a city on his first trip.'

'You found it!' Grampion began to get excited. He was still thinking in terms of lost civilizations. 'Why didn't you say so?'

'Because what it really is is a Russian geothermal project, and our friends here have been going to a lot of trouble to keep us from finding it.'

'A geothermal project?' Charly said.

'Lots of steam to make the wheels go round,' Pitt interjected. 'And we didn't want a bag of nosey people telling the rest of the world about it.'

'You were a bit ham-fisted stopping us,' I said.

We were all safely tied and Pitt began to relax and enjoy himself. 'You miss the point, Logan,' he started to explain. 'We didn't want to stop the expedition. On the contrary, we wanted it to go ahead, take a few turns around the ice, and go back and tell everyone it was all a waste of time. Otherwise some other nutcake like Grampion with half-pot ideas about lost cities might decide to keep looking. Much better if everyone thinks it was a false alarm in the first place. No, Logan, we were trying to stop you.'

'*Merde!*' Gus said under his breath.

I must have looked puzzled, and I was, because Pitt continued: 'Come now, Logan, your secret is safe with us.'

'We know who you're with, smart man,' Dawson managed to squeeze out through lips that now looked like he was practising to be a duck.

'Look, comrade Dyrsin, I don't know what the hell you are talking about. I'm not *with* anyone.'

Pitt smiled. He was about to astound us with his keenness of mind. 'I think your knowing Dawson's real name and that he's a Russian puts the knocker on it. You couldn't know that unless you were with the CIA.'

I almost laughed. 'You've been trying to get rid of me because you think I'm a CIA agent?'

'I'll give you this,' Pitt said, 'you're a hard man to put down. A car crash, a dip in the icy ocean and a drop into a crevasse and you still pop up for more.'

'You cut the tow-rope?' Gus said softly. He was totting up the score.

'I thought that was pretty neat myself.' Pitt allowed himself a smile. 'I sliced the rope about half through the night before when I went out for a piss; then I just waited until I found a good deep crevasse with a thin cover. A couple of marker flags and in you went.' He shook his head. 'Too bad you climbed out of that one, too. I was hoping to get you out of the way and take the steam out of the expedition at the same time.'

'You almost got me out of the way, too,' Gus said.

'Yeah, sorry about that, Gus.'

'What makes you think Logan is with the CIA?' Charly asked.

'You'd be surprised at some of the places we have our own agents. The word was that your side was going to put a man on the expedition. We didn't know who, but it wasn't hard to figure when Logan Adams, whom we already knew from one or two other deals he'd mixed in, turned up with a story about going along to help his brother-in-law and the brother-in-law obviously hated his guts.' He turned to me. 'Surely you could have thought up something better than that, Logan, and you a writer, too.'

'One of my off days,' I said. 'I suppose you were responsible for breaking into my room and the three yobs on the overpass?'

'The mugging was a bit crude, wasn't it? Dyrsin here handled that little fiasco all by himself. When he heard about you, he panicked and decided to enlist the help of some third parties to slow you up.'

'Tough luck,' I said, enjoying Dyrsin's black face.

'Good men are rather thin on the ground,' Pitt went on as if Dyrsin wasn't there. 'His recommendation for this job was an American accent, a talent for stirring, and the fact that he'd once acted as a watchdog over a bunch of scientists who paid a visit to Antarctica a few years back.'

Dyrsin wasn't happy about having his less successful ploys picked over, but I think his mouth was too sore to argue.

'As for breaking into your room,' Pitt continued, 'I did that job myself and I consider I'm quite an expert. What made you guess someone had turned the place over?'

He asked it casually but it was plain he was a man vain of his abilities. It really irked him that I'd known someone had been through my room. 'Didn't seem too expert to me,' I said, hoping to irk him further. There wasn't much else I could do to keep my hand in.

Pitt didn't like it, but it made Dawson, or Dyrsin, brighten up. 'Nobody's perfect,' he muttered and pushed through the tent flap before Pitt had a chance to tick him off.

'Fool,' he snarled, and in that moment the easygoing mask dropped away and the true ruthlessness of the man showed through. 'Plum' Pitt was no light-hearted adventurer always ready with a story or a wisecrack; he was a man who would casually drop you into an icy ocean or a deep crevasse without qualm.

Dawson burst back into the tent.

'He's gone!' he blurted out. 'Howard's taken off with the dog team!'

'What?' Pitt almost screamed.

'He must have been faking, and when we came in here he just piled in and took off. What with the wind picking up we didn't even hear him.'

'What about Kokko?'

'He was busy with the radio.'

'Where's Kokko now?'

'I told him to take the Sno-cat and go after Howard.' Even as Dawson said it, we heard the big Chrysler engine rumble into life.

Pitt stuck his head out of the tent, and from what I could see around him, there was a lot of drift swirling about. It would quickly obliterate Howard's trail and make it difficult to see him even if you were close. I didn't think Kokko had a chance of catching him, and I could see when Pitt pulled his head back into the tent, he didn't think so either.

'It really is amateur hour, isn't it?' I laughed.

Pitt's answer was an angry crack across the side of my head with his pistol. There was a stunning pain, a burst of red that blotted out my vision, then nothing.

Chapter 18

I floated back into semi-consciousness for a moment or two while we were still in the tent. All I remember is a pain like a hot poker in the hinge of my jaw, Charly's lap, and Grampion's voice very distant but very clear.

'Do I take it that you and Dawson and Kokko are some kind of espionage agents?' His tone was incredulous.

There must have been some sort of affirmative answer because he went on, 'But you're a New Zealander!'

Pitt's laugh barked through the tent. 'Where did you grow up, Grampion? Noddy Land? I suppose Kim Philby or Guy Burgess weren't Englishmen. The question is not why is a "Good Kiwi Bloke" working for the Soviets – money, old top, money – but rather why would they want him? New Zealand's not exactly a hotbed of international activity.'

There was a pause and finally Grampion, sounding irritable, said, 'Well, why then?'

'It's beautiful, really,' Pitt said. 'So simple. It's because New Zealand *is* such a backwater in big-time politics, just an overgrown sheep station way down in the armpit of the Pacific. Everybody trusts us. Only the Africans are a bit narked with us for playing rugby with South Africa, and who cares about those nutters anyway. It's perfect. Don't you see, we can go anywhere in the world and get the whole open-arm welcome because we're harmless. How can you take a country seriously when you can't even remember where it is! And who's the most welcome of all? Adventurous types who like to climb mountains and bring along loads of cameras to record the event for posterity. You don't know how easy it is to get into most any country with tons of sophisticated spying specials if you're a New Zealand mountaineer and cinematographer. "Just come right in, Mr Kiwi Friend, and don't worry about Customs with all that equipment you've got. We'll just mark it right through." Not quite as simple as that, but you get the drift. I'm worth my pay.'

I could feel my consciousness sliding back into the deep.

'You're what they call a sleeper?' Charly's voice was near and far at once.

'That's the title, Charly,' Pitt replied. 'Recruited when my face was soft as yours on one of my first climbing trips in Europe. Lots of training over the years and more green than you could count . . .'

He went on, plainly enjoying being able to tell someone what a smart fellow he was, and obviously he didn't think any of us would ever again be in a position to pass on the information. But his words dwindled to a mush of indistinct syllables, then disappeared altogether into the void of my unconsciousness.

When I came to again, I was being half dragged, half carried into a large helicopter by two soldiers with Kalashnikov AK-47 assault rifles slung on their shoulders. The big blades thunked around lazily, spuming up the snow, as the men bundled me inside and strapped me in. Charly, Grampion and Gus were herded in next and buckled themselves into nearby seats under the eye of the two blank-faced soldiers. A third soldier took his place beside the pilot and the machine rose smoothly into the air.

'What's going on?' I whispered to Gus, who was sitting next to me.

'You okay?'

'More or less, I guess. Where are we going?'

'To the lost city or power plant or whatever it is.'

'Howard?'

'They got half the Russian army out looking for him.'

One of the guards said something sharp in Russian. I didn't

understand the words but the meaning was clear: Keep quiet!

It was hard to talk above the engines anyway, so I just turned and smiled lopsidedly at Charly and Grampion to let them know I was in the land of the living. They looked strained and worried as they smiled back.

What had taken Howard and me several hours to traverse earlier in the day, the helicopter accomplished in fifteen minutes. We were soon skimming over the pyramid nunatak and down into the hidden valley. It was late in the evening now, and the sun was low on the horizon, casting long shadows that emphasized every ridge and rise of snow and throwing the deep valley into almost total darkness. I wondered at the lack of light from the domes, but as the helicopter fluttered down to a small pad in their midst, I realized why. They were opaque white so that not the slightest gleam showed through. Their geometrical roundness was also broken up by overstructures that effectively camouflaged them from above. Even the tall stacks were built close to a rock and ice overhang so that the steam rising would drift up the side and be whisked away by the wind on the upper plateau. The plant would be almost impossible to spot from the air unless you knew what you were looking for, and the nunatak at the far end of the valley was the only place where it was visible from the ground. With tens of thousands of square miles of surrounding empty wasteland that not even bacteria could live in, the only surprising thing was that Howard and Claydon and Rourk had ever stumbled on it in the first place.

'So much for your lost city, Warden,' I said as our guards poked us out of the helicopter and marched us towards one of the domes.

He looked up at the cliff of rock surmounted by an incredible cap of striated ice that seemed ready to roll forward and down upon us. 'Only fools would build here anyway.'

'No wonder they paint their domes,' Gus said, tearing his eyes away from the giant overhang. 'Who could live under that if they could see it?'

The domes, we found, simply covered more conventional buildings and maintained a more hospitable temperature within the overall enclosure. The one we were led into contained what looked like barracks and administration buildings. The power generating evidently was handled in the other domes. There were a number of soldiers, some going purposefully about, others obviously off duty. It was above freezing by a good few degrees inside the dome and they were all dressed in normal military uniforms. They regarded us and our heavy clothing with interest as we trudged towards a double-storeyed affair in the centre of the dome.

'I guess they don't get many visitors,' Charly ventured.

'Not women, anyway,' I said.

Once inside, we were turned over to a thick-faced sergeant who ordered two other soldiers to take us into a solidly walled room with no windows. There were two double bunks, a wooden table, a couple of chairs and not much else. The sergeant lumbered in after us while the soldiers stood by the door with their rifles unshipped and ready.

'Take off outside clothes,' he ordered in passably good English.

We did as we were told, piling it in a heap in the centre of the room.

'Now face wall. Put hands on wall, put feet apart.'

I did as instructed and he said, 'That's correct. Everyone do like your friend here. I see this not first time for him.'

The others leaned as I had; it was a position difficult to make a sudden move from, and the sergeant proceeded to run his hands over our bodies, starting with me. He found my pipe and tobacco pouch, had an appreciative smell of the Sobranie, and tucked them back in my pocket. He went over Gus and Grampion in the same way and left Grampion his meerschaum as well. When he came to Charly, he ran his hands slowly over her breasts, down over her hips and the outside of her legs and then started up the inside of her thighs. She heaved away violently, yelling at him to keep his hands to himself. At the same time, Gus and I pushed ourselves upright from the wall, trying to get into a position to help.

The rifles of the two soldiers were aimed right at our heads, stopping us before we could get set. In any case, the sergeant had stepped hurriedly away from Charly. He looked at us and gave an almost Gallic shrug and, laughing, ordered his men to gather up the parkas and thick overpants. Just a soldier, I thought, trying to have a little feel, but not wanting to make an issue out of it.

The sergeant and his men headed for the door.

'What's going to happen to us?' Grampion snapped out, stopping them.

The sergeant turned and shook his head. 'Who knows? Not my worry. Nothing good. Enjoy yourselves while you can,' he said with the perennial philosophy of soldiers everywhere. 'I'll send in some food for you.'

When they'd left and bolted the door we just stood for a moment looking at each other. Gus was still mad and Grampion had ridges of puzzle scarred into his forehead; he still wasn't sure what had happened to his expedition. It was Charly who spoke first.

'Sorry about that. I didn't mean to get you almost killed just because Romeo wanted to see if I was really a girl.'

'You didn't act as if you appreciated his technique,' I pointed out in defence.

'I had to do something to stop him,' she said, unbuckling her woollen trousers and sliding her hand down between her thighs. 'I didn't want him to find this.' She pulled her hand out, holding a ·25 Beretta automatic pistol.

'Christ!' I exclaimed. 'Where did you get that?'

'I had it in my pants pocket back at the tent but everything happened so fast I couldn't get at it under my parka and over-pants, then we were tied up and it was impossible. It wasn't until we were in the helicopter that I managed to get at it.'

I took the gun from her and checked it over. It was fully loaded and ready to go, but it was just a pea-shooter really.

With all the heavy clothing everyone was wearing, I doubted it would stop a man unless you hit him in the head.

'I'm glad you didn't try hijacking the 'copter with this,' I said.

'I'm not stupid, Logan. Especially with you dead to the world. But I was afraid we'd probably be searched so I stuck it into my underpants between my legs. That's why I made such a commotion when I was being searched. Our lusty sergeant was about to feel more than he bargained for.'

Gus grinned. 'She some girl, eh, Logan?'

'What I'd like to know,' Grampion said with asperity, 'is why you had a gun in the first instance?'

It wasn't hard to work that one out. 'I think we now know who the CIA agent is,' I said.

That set both Grampion and Gus back a step and Gus scratched his thick mop and said to me, 'But I thought you were supposed to be him?'

'So our friends surmised.' I turned to Charly. 'Did you know my accident wasn't an accident?'

She looked chagrined. 'I'm really sorry about that; but by the time things started to get that serious, it was too late to do anything about it. What was I supposed to do? Say, "Look, fellas, leave Logan alone. I'm the one you want to get rid of." What good would that have done?'

I shrugged, not liking it.

Grampion sat down dejectedly in one of the chairs. 'Seems as if I'm the only one on this expedition who was legitimately looking for a lost city.'

'And me,' Gus said, giving the older man a friendly thump on the shoulder. 'But now I want to know what we are going to do. Take the guard when they come with the food?'

I shook my head and the movement reminded me forcibly of the long, painful welt along the side of my face. 'And then what?' I said. 'There looked to be half a battalion in this dome alone, and even if we bluffed our way through, where do we go? We woudn't last half an hour outside dressed like this, and if we did manage to grab some equipment, how far do you think we could get?'

'The helicopter?' Grampion suggested.

'Can you fly it?'

He shook his head.

'Well, neither can I.' And to judge from their expressions, neither could Charly or Gus.

'So what do we do, eh?' Gus asked.

'Why don't we ask the person who really knows what all this is about,' I said sarcastically to Charly. I was still annoyed at her leaving me to be the patsy.

We had to defer our bickering as the door bolts rattled and the sergeant entered accompanied by a soldier carrying a large tray of food. I hastily stuffed the Beretta into my pocket, but, just for the moment, entertained Gus's idea of using it to overcome the Russians and trying to make a break. When I saw another soldier with his rifle ready just beyond the door, I quickly forgot about it. The soldier put the tray on the table and went out.

'How long are you going to keep us here?' Grampion wanted to know.

'Base commander decide,' the sergeant answered amiably. 'See you in the morning when finish bring your vehicles here and catch your friend. You all sleep here tonight,' he said, leering at Charly. 'No other rooms, so have good time while you can.'

He left, relocking the door, and we arranged ourselves around the table, two on a bunk and two on the chairs. There was hot stew, tea and bread and we found we were incredibly hungry. In about ten minutes the last splash of gravy had been mopped up and we lit up pipes and cigarettes over our tea. It could have been worse, I thought, feeling better able to cope now that my stomach was full.

I smiled at Charly. 'Sorry to have got on to you before, but if you are with Central Intelligence, they must have some idea what's going on here.'

'Not your fault,' she said, 'but I'm afraid we can't expect much help from outside, not immediately anyway.' She looked apologetic. 'I'm actually not a real CIA agent.'

We looked at her, mystified. 'What the hell does that mean?' I said.

She smiled at Grampion and patted his big meaty hand. 'I really was just a geologist who wanted to go exploring in Antarctica. I'd seen enough evidence in ancient glacial lake beds to give your theory at least the benefit of the doubt, and I was fascinated to come out here and have a look. And I did purposefully not let on I was a woman so you wouldn't just automatically turn me down.'

'The CIA?' I prodded.

'They contacted me in New York after I'd been hired for the expedition,' she continued, 'and told me that they had reason to believe a Russian agent was also a member of the group.'

'Did they know it was Dawson?' I asked.

'Yes, in the sense that they knew he was the man, but they didn't know who he really was; his Russian name or position, you know.'

'What about Kokko?'

'They suspected him, too. He's Finnish, of course, from Oulu on the Gulf of Bothnia, and he was a member of the Finnish People's Democratic League, a Marxist organization with strong Soviet leanings; but, other than that, they knew nothing about him.'

'But it worried them,' I urged, 'possibly two agents infiltrated into an expedition of only seven people, going on what must have seemed a fool's errand?'

'Yes. When they had looked it over from every angle, the only reasonably logical possibility was that maybe Howard *had* seen something. It seemed pretty slim, but they thought they'd better try to keep an eye on what was happening.' She paused a moment, inhaling her cigarette. 'And they asked me to be their eye.'

'It would have been nice if you'd let me know,' I said caustically, 'instead of making sure I was dropped right in it.'

Her dark eyes flickered with anger. 'I was told not to confide in anyone. You weren't even a member of the expedition at the time. And if you remember the night back at Scott Base, I did confirm your suspicions that something was up by telling you about Dawson. I thought you might be thinking you'd been mistaken somehow, and I wanted to make sure you kept your guard up.'

I remembered that night very well, but it was Grampion who answered. 'The point is, I think, can we expect any help from the Americans? Have they been keeping track of you at all or are you just on your own?'

That was the crunch question. Surely they wouldn't just brief her and leave her to her own devices. She wasn't even a trained agent, just a tyro they had to use because they didn't have the time or the inclination to get a pro on to our team. Her answer didn't fill me with hope.

'Of course I had contacts to pass anything I found out to,' she said. 'In New Zealand, I kept in fairly close touch, and even at Scott Base there was Barry Goodenough . . .'

'Of course! No wonder he didn't want to get his picture taken.'

'It was Barry,' she said to me, 'who told me Dawson's real name. But Central Intelligence didn't actually think there was much in it. After all, who would think there would be anything important in the middle of Antarctica? I was just to report anything out of the ordinary when I returned. What else could I do, in any case? It's not exactly a place where you can slip away for a secret meeting in a telephone booth.'

'But they gave you a gun,' I pointed out. 'They must have thought there was some danger?'

'Barry gave it to me at Scott. Just in case,' she said defensively.

Good God, I thought. First they send an amateur, then, as an afterthought, they arm her with a popgun you have to be an expert to use effectively! The CIA wasn't the organization it used to be.

'So Barry Goodenough is just sitting on his bum at McMurdo playing pinocle to pass the time and waiting for you to turn up with a report?' I felt angry. It was so damned inefficient!

'I'm not even sure he was staying,' she said. 'They're a bit short-handed, I understand.'

'So we're left to our own resources.' Grampion put it in a nutshell.

'What about Howard?' Charly asked. 'Do you think he can get back?'

Howard? Of all of us, he had acted the most effectively. But did he have a chance? We turned to the big Canadian.

'What do you think, Gus?' I said. 'Could he make Scott Base?'

'The sledge, she has provisions?'

I nodded. We always kept them supplied whenever we went out. You never knew when the weather would trap you. 'But I don't know if there is enough unless the weather stays perfect.'

'And if the weather stay perfect, the Russians they will have no trouble to pick him up with their helicopters,' he pointed out.

'He did it once before.' I knew I was clutching at straws.

Gus shrugged his massive shoulders. 'He is a man of determination. The dogs are good. Who knows?'

'Even if he did get back,' Grampion said, 'it would take weeks and by then the winter would be closing in. No one could get back here then.'

It was a dispiriting thought. But at least, if he did make it to Scott or McMurdo, someone would listen to him this time. Even if it was too late for us.

'What can we do, then?' Charly asked.

I took the Beretta out of my pocket. 'First we have to get rid of this.'

'Get rid of it?' Gus exclaimed.

'Hide it, I mean.'

'Where?' Charly said. 'If we hide it here –' she gestured around the room – 'they might move us, and then what good would it be?'

'We'll hide it on you.'

'I'm not carrying it around in my pants any more!' she protested.

'Why can't one of us carry it?' Grampion wanted to know.

'Because if they intend to keep us here, they might issue us with some sort of regulation clothing. They must have a lot of workers to operate a place like this, and I doubt that they're volunteers. Why all the soldiers, otherwise? If they do decide to put us in prison stripes on the chain gang, there's just a chance they might let Charly change in private. I don't think they run to female warders here.'

'That sergeant wasn't shy about searching me,' Charly said.

'He was even less shy with the rest of us.' I had another reason for wanting Charly to have the gun, too. I didn't think Kokko had forgotten how she gelded him with words. Of all of us, she probably needed the gun most.

'I can't just carry it around in my pocket.'

'Between your breasts,' I said.

Charly wasn't a woman hamstrung with false modesty. She had her shirt off in an instant and then pulled the thick string vest over her head.

'You haven't got a bra!' I said when she stood bared to the waist. Grampion reddened slightly, but Gus just laughed.

'What you expect in the Antarctic, Logan?' he said. 'It's not good to wear tight clothes.'

'I meant, there's nothing to hold the gun. I was figuring on a bra to keep it in place.'

'Tear off the bottom of your undershirt,' Charly directed me, 'and I'll make a binder.'

I ripped off a wide piece and she folded it into a double strip, open on the top edge and closed on the bottom, and I tied it around her chest. With it folded that way she was able to slip the gun into the fold in such a way that it wouldn't fall out. When she put on her clothes again, the small gun was completely hidden.

'Good,' I said. 'You can't see it at all. In fact, you could pass for a boy.'

'Let's hope that discourages closer inspection,' she said matter-of-factly.

Not long after, two soldiers came and one noncommittally cleared the dishes while the other watched from the door. When they left we stretched out on the bunks more or less fully clothed and pulled the heavy grey blankets around us. There was no way to turn off the one bare bulb in the ceiling, but after about an hour it went out and left us in the dark. I fell asleep almost immediately.

Chapter 19

The next morning we were taken one by one to a small toilet and washroom and then given a breakfast of porridge and tea. We spent the following hour morosely, hardly talking. We'd all had plenty of time to review our situation by then, and no matter how you set it up, it wasn't good.

I wasn't too sanguine about myself, either. They thought I was a CIA agent, and as such I could expect the worst kind of personal attention. I was contemplating this unhappy twist when the door bolts rattled and Dawson came in, flanked by two soldiers with AK-47's. His mouth was still swollen but he managed to put the usual sneer in his voice.

'Time to see the boss,' he said. 'Got to show him what bright and able-bodied workers we've brought him.'

'Lead the way, Stan,' I said, rising.

'Captain Stanislaus Piotr Dyrsin to you,' he said. 'But you knew that already.'

'Yes, but what we couldn't figure out was why your people would let such a small-timer operate on his own.' What the hell, they thought I was CIA anyway; I might as well get in a few shots.

His face reddened. 'I'm asking to question you myself, Adams, then we'll see how long you can keep talking out of that smart mouth of yours.' He gestured angrily. 'All right, let's go.'

We marched along a corridor that seemed to bisect the building and then up a short flight of stairs to the upper storey. There wasn't much to see, a glimpse or two out of the occasional window showed some buildings close by and the wall of the dome beyond, and a hallway bare except for bundles of wire and conduit slung to the ceiling. It looked permanently makeshift. Dawson led us through one of the doors off the upper-level corridor and into a small anteroom presided over by a small, round corporal who, I imagined, had never been able to arrange his wrinkled rotundity into any semblance of military smartness in his entire career. I wondered if Antarctica was used as a posting for the Russian Army's deadbeats and misfits. It would make Siberia look like a holiday resort. When the corporal snapped out an order in Russian which brought our guard to ramrod attention, and then with unhurried efficiency produced four files from his desk and had us neatly marched into the next room, I realized unhappily that we weren't dealing with slackers, shirt-tails out or no.

It was a fairly big room, an office with a conventional desk and metal filing cabinets. Three men waited as the corporal indicated to us to sit in the four chairs arranged in front of the desk. 'Plum' Pitt was the only one I knew, and although he was living up to his name, all turned out in a well-pressed set of beige overalls and a bright neckerchief he'd unearthed somewhere, he didn't look too happy. He was sitting to one side of the desk with an older man in civilian clothes nearly as rumpled as ours, who had a round fleshy face from which faraway eyes contemplated some mystery.

Dawson took a seat next to Pitt while the corporal positioned the guards behind us, took the four folders to the desk, saluted the man behind it and smartly left. The man behind the desk was dressed in a Russian colonel's uniform and I took him to be the base commander. He stayed preternaturally still while the crowd in his office arranged themselves; not even his heavy eyelids moved, nor, it seemed, did the black pupilless eyes. He looked tall and his long, saturnine face and overfull, slightly sensual lips would, I supposed, be considered quite attractive by many women.

He said something quietly in Russian to Dawson, who jumped to attention so fast he almost knocked his chair over. The Russian coloned passed long, narrow fingers over his eyes and said something else with a plain hint of exasperation. Dawson sat down again, red-faced but still trying hard, and turned to us.

'This is Colonel Alexei Karakan,' he said, nodding to the man behind the desk. Evidently Dawson was going to act as interpreter. 'He is commander-in-chief of this base in all military and security terms.' He turned to the civilian. 'And this is Doctor Gasiorowski, the man in charge of the project itself.'

The man's eyes refocused out of his private world and settled on the four of us. Karakan also looked at us intently as Dawson told him our names. The colonel appeared most interested in me, but the doctor began asking questions of Dawson about Grampion and Charly, and finally fiddled through the folders until he had theirs. While he was reading, Karakan questioned Dawson, who in turn questioned me.

'The colonel would like to know who your contact is at Scott Base.'

'Most likely that guy, Goodenough, who came over from McMurdo,' Pitt said, speaking for the first time.

I didn't want to let this line of questioning go on in case

they connected Charly with Goodenough, so I said, 'You've been unnaturally quiet, Pitt. You in the doghouse because Howard escaped?'

'Don't worry about Howard,' he shot back. 'He won't get far. Even if he does slip through somehow, he'll have to make for the cache we left at the top of the Skelton Glacier, and I'll be waiting for him. Then I'll just return to Scott with the story of the terrible disaster that wiped out the expedition on its way back from finding nothing.'

'Do you think anyone will believe that, let alone the CIA?'

'Why not? Your people had their doubts about Dawson and Kokko but I'm a respected New Zealand mountaineer. It's not hard to believe that a whole party could be wiped out in a back-of-beyond place like Antarctica. Of course they'll believe it. In fact, I'll probably end up famous and write a book about it.' He laughed.

The plan he outlined had every chance of succeeding. The Russians could easily drop him near the cache and then he would only have to make his way by dog team down the glacier and say that we had all fallen into a crevasse, or any of a number of perfectly logical stories. Who wouldn't believe him? Even the CIA had only vague suspicions, and none of them were connected with Pitt.

Dawson translated what we'd been saying for Karakan and, smiling sardonically, he made a laconic reply to Pitt. Apparently Pitt didn't speak Russian because Dawson had to translate this too, which he did with some enthusiasm.

'Colonel Karakan,' he said, 'hopes you will be able to accomplish this with fewer mistakes.'

Pitt's mouth tightened but he said nothing.

Gasiorowski, on the other hand, had come to life and was chattering on in a high sibilant voice to Karakan, who finally nodded some kind of affirmative. He said more to Dawson, apparently about Gus and me, and that was the end of the interview. It looked as if Charly and Grampion were of some special interest to him because they went off with him and one soldier while Gus and I went with Dawson and a guard back to our cubicle.

'Where have they taken Charly and Grampion?' Gus wanted to know.

'Old Gasiorowski thought it was Christmas when he found out Charly was a geologist and Grampion has scientific training,' Dawson said. 'He's a bit short-handed in the brain department.'

We tried a few more questions, but it was evident that he knew almost as little of what was going on as we did.

'That's enough from you two,' he said finally. 'No more questions.' He turned to me. 'That is, until I start asking you, Logan. Since I speak English and Russian, Colonel Karakan has agreed to my directing your interrogation.'

'I don't have much to tell.' How true that was if only he'd believe it.

'By the time Kokko and I finish, you'll be begging to spill everything you know.'

'Kokko?'

'He does the bits-that-spatter routine,' he said meaningfully. 'That'll give you something to think about until he gets back from looking for Howard.' With that he went out and locked the door.

Gus gave me a pat on the shoulder. 'I'm afraid, my friend, that they are going to spend a lot of time trying to make you tell them something you don't know.'

I didn't have any answer to that. Even if I blurted out that Charly was the real CIA agent, they wouldn't believe me; which, I reflected gallantly, was one small consolation.

It was late afternoon before Charly and Grampion returned to the cubicle, and the first thing I noticed was that they were wearing coveralls. I held my breath until their guard closed and locked the door behind them.

'The gun?' I hissed.

Charly patted her chest. 'No problem. They just gave us

these coveralls to put on over our own clothes.'

'What have you been doing, eh?' Gus asked.

Grampion sat tiredly in a chair but his face was animated. 'It's amazing!' he said. 'They're building an entire town, a small city, under the ice.'

'It's not a town, it's a military base,' Charly said, 'and it's not under the ice, it's under the ground.'

'What kind of base?'

'A submarine base.'

'Submarine! We're forty to fifty miles from the coast!'

'Let me start at the beginning. Doctor Gasiorowski is so pleased with his project that he was only too glad to tell us the details, and luckily he speaks French. A few years ago the Russians, who'd been doing a lot of research work along the coast from their South Magnetic Pole station, came across a series of huge semi-submerged caverns near the Mawson Peninsula. What was most surprising to them was that the water in the caves didn't freeze over even in the winter. Obviously something was keeping the water warm, so they began a careful study of the currents and almost immediately found that hot underground water was emptying into the sea through fractures in the rock. That would have been just an interesting phenomenon, but further exploration of the caverns showed that they extended for miles and miles under the ground.'

'To this valley?' I said.

'Yes,' Grampion broke in. 'Amazing, isn't it, that they haven't collapsed with the weight of ice on them.'

'From what I saw today,' Charly said, 'I would say that there is considerable instability. In fact, that's why Gasiorowski was so happy to have me turn up. He's without a good geologist and I think he's got some worries about the strength of the rock in some of the galleries. Anyway, much to their delight, at this end of the cave system they found the source of the hot water, a first-class geothermal area.'

'The whole tunnel system is probably the remains of ancient volcanic fumaroles, and the geothermal area's what is left of some quite extensive volcanic activity,' Grampion explained.

'But where do the submarines come in?' Gus asked.

'That's where Gasiorowski turns up,' Charly explained. 'Up to this point the potential usefulness of what had been found hadn't sunk in . . .'

'But naturally they hadn't mentioned their finds to any of the other nations operating in Antarctica,' I said cynically, 'particularly Australia, who, I believe, claims territorial rights to this part of the continent.'

'Right,' Charly agreed. 'And when Gasiorowski pointed out that the caverns would make perfect year-round submarine pens and the geothermal area could be tapped for heat and power so that a complete supply and repair depot could be built, the "Top Secret" stamp really came down hard.'

'I understand maybe the caverns have no ice in winter,' Gus said, 'but there is still the pack ice?'

'Submarines go under the water, Gus.'

He nodded. 'But how do they expect to keep a thing like this secret?'

'They'll try to keep it secret for as long as they can,' Charly said, 'at least until it's fully operational. After that, it's a *fait accompli*. What is anyone going to do if they do find out about it then? Bomb it? You won't get much more than a lot of angry words and hot air at the United Nations, which the Soviets will just ignore.'

'And the submarine base is just a start as far as Gasiorowski is concerned,' Grampion puffed. 'The power from the geothermal area will allow them to explore extensively, set up economic mining operations . . .'

'Put in missile silos,' Charly interjected.

'. . . and do what I said in the first place – build a small city and virtually claim an entire continent.'

'But they're not operational yet?' I asked.

Charly slumped on to a bunk. 'Not quite. The power plant is at about a quarter of its designed output and the construction on the first pens is complete but for the frills, but the connecting tunnels need a lot of work before they can be relied on. The way they look at the moment, they could easily collapse and cut the main caverns off from the power plant.'

I felt frustrated. All this going on and I hadn't been able to see anything of it except a little of the inside of one very ordinary building. 'I wish I could get a closer look,' I grumbled.

Charly raised her head from the bunk. 'I'm afraid you might get more than your wish. They need hands as well as brains. I think you and Gus will end up working in the tunnels.'

Charly's prophecy came true quickly. Neither Gus nor I minded that we were taken in the morning to be put on a work gang. We knew that if we were to escape, fight back, to have any chance at all, we had to have room to move and we had to know more about the workings of this fantastic base. But when we realized that we would be separated from Grampion and Charly, it didn't seem such an advantage. From then on, we were told, we would live with the rest of the workers while our two companions, because of their higher standing as scientists, would remain in the administration building.

But we didn't have much time to dwell on that problem. We were taken from our dome housing the soldiers' barracks and administration through a short covered way to another large dome which turned out to be a regular stalag, with an electrified perimeter chain fence and a secondary rolled barbed-wire fence inside it.

'They must use prison labour,' Gus whispered to me as we were marched through a heavily guarded double gate.

'They've had plenty of practice in Siberia.'

One of our guards barked something that I imagined meant 'shut up'. We did.

We were issued with some cheap cold-weather gear and plastic slickers at a quartermaster's store, and then taken to join a group of hollow-faced, beaten-down men being formed up outside one of the long huts that almost filled the space inside the wire. One or two glanced at us surreptitiously, but the rest just looked blankly at the mucky ground at their feet. Other groups were being formed in front of the other huts, and they looked in just as sorry a state as ours.

The sergeant in charge of us, a skinny rake of a man, stood huddled in a heavy coat, watching morosely. He didn't look in much better health than his charges and I guessed that an Antarctic posting wasn't the best the Russian army offered.

He slouched over to us and said, 'I'm Sergeant Chubokov. I speak English very well, that is why you have been put in this company, so do not think that I do not know what you are saying. Work hard and you can die in this hole in peace. Cause trouble and I will see to it you die in pieces.' His pinched mouth creased into a snagged smile as he realized that he'd made a neat play on words. 'You see. I speak English very well.'

With that, he gave orders to his corporal, and we were moved off without any attempt to keep us in much more of a formation than a bunched herd while he slogged along behind.

We went through another short covered way and again into a new dome. The power dome. I could feel the ground vibrate with the pent-up pressure of the tapped geysers that drove the steam turbines. There were huge pipes and giant valves everywhere; vapour hissed and rumbled into the tall stacks that allowed the excess to escape so that the whole thing wouldn't blow its guts out. It made you uneasy, a feeling that, for all the advanced technology used to harness this power, these great blowholes from the world's bowels could wipe it all away in one titanic flatulent burst. I was even more uneasy when we climbed on to a line of narrow-gauge railway cars and a little electric engine hauled us into what appeared to be the main tunnel leading to the coast and the submarine pens.

It was a natural tunnel, although many parts had been widened to take the pipes and cables crowded into it alongside the rails. Other sections expanded dramatically so that even the lights strung by the line couldn't penetrate the blackness. In these roomier galleries they'd built sidings so trains going in the other direction could pull off and let us pass. We went by many of these, filled with workers or construction materials. Once we ourselves pulled off to let a small enclosed railcar shoot by. I wondered if Charly and Grampion were inside enjoying its comforts.

Just to be inside anything but that cave would have been a hundred per cent more comfortable. I understood now why we'd been issued with slickers. The tunnel ceiling incessantly dripped freezing cold water you couldn't get away from. I didn't know whether it was condensation or the ice above ground melting with the unaccustomed warmth and then seeping through, and I didn't care. After half an hour, I just wanted to get out of it. But we remained in it all day, pouring steel-reinforced concrete pillars to shore up what seemed to be a dangerously weak section of ceiling. Every time one of the small trains rumbled by, pieces would fall and need clearing away. Safety gear was non-existent; only the guards had hard hats, and they kept well back from the worst areas. It was a project that should have been approached slowly and carefully. To build it so quickly they needed a slave-labour force to which accident and death were of no consequence. I reflected on this as I shovelled cement and concluded that none of the labourers here were expected, or would be allowed, to survive. Not as long as the project was to be kept secret.

After the train ride back through the tunnel at the end of the day, we stumbled, bone-chilled and incredibly weary, into the long prisoners' hut with the rest of our group. Sergeant Chubokov, who had spent the day in a warm hut erected on a flat car and used by the guards to get themselves dry, but who still looked as tired as the rest of us, pointed out our bunks. There were a pair of rolled-up indoor coveralls and two grey blankets on each.

'Take these,' he said. 'You can use the coveralls, too, while your other clothing dries. The men who owned it won't be needing it any longer. They've gone to the warmest place of all – hell!' He coughed out a laugh.

'You certainly have a way with words, Sergeant,' I said.

He nodded agreement. 'I should have been a writer, eh?' Then he left with the other soldiers.

Another group of workers was entering the big hut, back from whatever they'd been doing, but I didn't take much notice until Gus tapped me on the shoulder. I looked up to see a gaunt man, as haggard and drawn as all the others, but with fierce grey eyes that gave his face life.

'My name's Bill Claydon,' he said, 'from New Zealand.'

Chapter 20

For the next three days Gus and I laboured in the tunnels. It was brutal work, cold and wet and dangerous, and in that short time two men just dropped where they stood and died face down on the rock. The guards methodically took their particulars, stripped them, then hauled them into one of the many side tunnels and dropped the bodies into an old fumarole. The ground was too rocky or too frozen for burial.

But the majority of the work force wasn't as badly off as we were. Our group consisted of any poor bastard who had opened his mouth too much, started a fight, tried to escape, stepped out of line in any way. It was a punishment company, Claydon had said, but that was a bit of information Gus and I soon worked out for ourselves.

Claydon worked in the power plant where they made better use of his technical talents. Rourk, he told us bitterly, had been put there also, but he wouldn't stop fighting back, even if it was just to castigate the guards. They'd beaten him up several times, and when that didn't work, they'd put him into the punishment company, where he'd died. Life expectancy there was about three months. Rourk, he said proudly, lasted nearly six. He was a bloody tough Kiwi.

When I told him that Howard had seen the domes and stacks and how he had survived the trip back, he was amazed; and when I outlined how he had fought to organize a new expedition and led us back here, he nearly cried.

'When I first saw him,' Claydon said, 'I thought a good sneeze would knock him over, but Rourk said to give him a chance, he was tougher than he looked. I wish the old bastard was here to see how right he was.'

Gus and I told him the situation with Grampion and Charly and how again we were relying on Howard. 'But that's a pretty skinny hope,' I pointed out. 'If we're going to do anything, I think we'd better try to do it ourselves.'

That was easier said than done. Claydon filled us in on the layout of the operation and the security was well thought out and complete. Karakan knew his stuff. There were several domes: the smaller ones were used for supplies, vehicle storage and maintenance, and one as a hangar for the helicopters and a light plane; the larger ones were for troop barracks and administration, a prison compound, and the main power plant. The power plant dome abutted on the cliff and led directly into the tunnel, the major part of the geothermal area being in a maze of passages and tunnels inside the cliff. The domes were interconnected and the passages well guarded. Certainly no prisoners could go from one to another without an escort and our own compound was the only dome in which we were allowed any unsupervised movement at all.

Claydon knew the power generating area like his own reflection and we considered how we might utilize that knowledge. The possibility of getting in there by ourselves appeared to be about nil and the most we could accomplish if we did, Claydon thought, was to put the place out of action for a few months. I filed the information away, nevertheless. It would be better than ending up in a fumarole in a cave under the earth.

My most immediate interest, however, was why I hadn't yet

been questioned. I had expected them to start putting the screws on from the first day. They thought I was CIA and they would want to know just how much that organization knew about their little home from home. Why the delay? When I stumbled into our hut that night, shivering and wet, there were two guards waiting to take me to find out why.

'How do you like your work, Logan?'

'We could use a better union,' I said.

We were in the administration building not far from the room we had first been taken to. Dawson's lip had healed and the old smirk was back in place. He watched as the two guards shackled my wrists to two wide-spaced ring bolts in a beam slung above my head and my feet to two more in the floor.

It wasn't a big room, big enough to hold a metal bed with no mattress, a dirty wash-basin, a small desk and me, naked and spread-eagled vertically from the roof like a cheer leader in mid-jump. The shackles didn't lock but there was no way to release them without using two hands. When the soldiers had adjusted them to Dawson's satisfaction, he had them pull the beam up by means of a pulley arrangement so that most of my weight was supported by my arms and only my toes touched the floor. Having me stripped was a professional touch. Psychologically I felt much more vulnerable. Dawson was no amateur. It was too bad I didn't know anything worth while.

The soldiers tied the halliard to a cleat in the wall and went out. I was sweating. Fear sweat. Dawson came over to me.

'We're not going to kill you,' he said, and then added more as an afterthought, 'at least, we're not going to try to.'

'That's nice.'

'We're going to hurt you. And when we're not hurting you, we'll put you back down the mine. You enjoy it down in the drips, buddy?'

I said nothing.

He laughed. 'I guess you figure you're tough enough to take it. I doubt it. Not for as long as we'll keep you there. And what about Grampion? Not as young as he used to be. Or Charly? She likes being with the men, doesn't she? If the workers were too tired to appreciate her, I'm sure the guards wouldn't be.'

'Gasiorowski would have something to say about that.'

The laugh got harsher. 'Gasiorowski is just a tool; Colonel Karakan is in charge. And if I suggest that you, Gus, Grampion and Charly spend the rest of your lives in the punishment company, you can bet your ass that's where you'll rot. If, on the other hand, you co-operate, I'll see to it that everyone is treated well, and you personally – ' he gestured to the rack I was slung in – 'won't have to put up with a lot of unnecessary pain.'

It was an attractive offer. I think, if I'd known anything about anything, I would have been tempted.

'You haven't mentioned Howard,' I said. 'I take it he hasn't been as easy to pick up as you thought.'

That probed a nerve.

'That big-mouthed bastard, Pitt, tried to put the blame on Kokko and me for letting him get away,' Dawson complained, 'but Colonel Karakan is a career officer and I am a career officer. We see a little more eye to eye.'

'And isn't Pitt a career officer?'

Dawson spat contemptuously. 'He's a turncoat. Bought for money. He doesn't even speak Russian.' Nobody likes a traitor, it seems, not even the people he sells out to.

'I guess that dosen't make you much,' I said, trying to stir it up as much as possible to see what would happen. 'He was your boss.'

'We were working independently. Trying to set up two opportunities to get on the expedition. He worked through his contracts in mountaineering and film-making and I set up Bannister.'

It was ludicrous. I was hanging like something left over from the inquisition and he was doing all the talking. I could see now that it had really rankled that Pitt had taken command,

and he wanted to complain to someone who knew the background. I urged him on. It was better than being beaten up.

'How did you manage to get Bannister under your thumb?'

I thought he was going to go cold, but he really wanted to tell me how good he was. 'Bannister was easy,' he went on. 'He'd been trying to live the high life on a worker's wage and had got in over his ears in gambling debts. Since he handled all Grampion's business affairs, it was easy for him to dip into the till to pay off.'

'And you found out and told him "either or else".'

'Yeah.' He chuckled. 'I don't know whether he was more worried about Grampion putting him in jail or losing his upper-crust friends. Whatever, he was glad to get me on the expedition to keep my mouth shut, and then I hired Kokko.'

'Didn't he want to know what it was all about?'

'Not much. He was only interested in looking after number one.'

'Not quite. When you tried to eliminate me, he went sour on you and I think he would have poured it all out if he hadn't fallen over that cliff.' I'd liked Bannister, for all his weaknesses. But I wasn't expecting what Dawson said next.

'He didn't fall,' he said coolly, 'Pitt pushed him. When he shot out of the dining-room, I knew we'd have to do something about him, but the bastard got out of the house before Kokko and I could get to him for a bit of reasoning. I called Pitt and told him the situation and where Bannister had headed. He got over there pretty damn quick, I'll say that for him.' Dawson seemed pleased. 'I was giving the orders and for once everything went one, two, three.'

So the man I had seen in the trees hadn't been Bannister after all, it had been Pitt! Bannister was already lying in the surge at the bottom of the cliff.

Dawson looked at his watch and then at me. 'Well, what's it to be, Logan, the easy way or the hard way?'

The time for idle chat was over.

'The funny part of it is that I really am in this for purely personal reasons,' I said, not thinking it at all funny.

'It's like that, is it?' He didn't seem unduly unhappy. A little torture kept him from being bored.

I tried to shift my shoulders to relieve the strain, and automatically braced myself for the first blow. He noticed and smiled.

'Oh, I'm not going to work you over. Not my line.' He looked at his watch again. 'I'm just waiting for a friend of ours who's much better at it than I am. He's been looking for Howard and at the moment he's being bawled out for not catching him. He should appreciate someone to take his frustrations out on.'

On cue the door opened and Kokko lumbered in, his face red and his ears burning. He saw me hanging there and his straggly moustache twitched around his tight mouth. I wasn't Howard, but I was going to be the next best thing. Dawson spoke to him in Russian, presumably telling him that I hadn't agreed to their proposal, and something vaguely related to a smile twisted his mouth. Dawson sat down behind the desk and lit a cigarette while Kokko came up to me. He looked me up and down, savouring the vulnerable body he was going to pound into raw steak. Slowly, he reached between my legs, wrapped his big hand around my testicles, and squeezed.

I gasped as sick pain convulsed my abdomen. He squeezed some more and it flowed up into my head and tried to blow itself out through my eyes. He stepped back for a moment to let me recover a little, then that gorilla hand came back and engulfed a section of my quivering stomach and began to twist. Agony flowed into agony and I was almost glad when he smashed his fist into the side of my head and dulled my overburdened perceptions.

'No tricks to do with the thumb this time, eh?' he said.

'We can stop any time you decide to come clean,' Dawson said, calmly smoking.

There was nothing I could say that they would believe, so Kokko started to drive his fists into my stomach, ribs and kidneys, methodically working his way around me. The little food I had in my belly heaved up into my mouth and trickled down my chin. Somewhere in the back of my brain I wondered if he'd ruptured a kidney. It seemed ages before he let up, but he wasn't even breathing hard yet.

'Well?' from Dawson.

I spat a bit of vomit into Kokko's face for an answer. I wanted him to hit me in the head so that I would lose consciousness, and he wouldn't do that unless he lost his temper. It was the only way I could think to stop the beating and escape the pain.

I got what I asked for. The last thing I remember was his wild, blood-red eyes, and then my thoughts shattered as my brain crashed back and forth in my skull from his first smashing blow.

Pain. Throbbing, sharp, dull. So much pain that its very excess limited it. My mind was apart from it; knowing it, but aware of it second-hand as if it belonged to someone else. I was still hanging from the shackles, but as I came around I realized more people were present now than just Dawson and Kokko. I hung there and listened, not particularly caring.

'I'm afraid Kokko got carried away.' It was Dawson's voice.

'Goddamn it, Dyrsin, can't you do anything right?' I recognized Pitt. 'I've got to leave soon. The weather's right for the plane and we can't take a chance on leaving it any longer. But I need to know if the CIA knows anything about us.'

'You know it's not that critical,' Dawson said. 'They only had a whiff, nothing definite. I'm sure you'll be able to do your job adequately. Anyway, we should all be ready to make sacrifices and take chances for our country.' He sounded sarcastic.

The door slammed and Dawson laughed and said something in Russian. Probably to Kokko, I thought, but it all started to fall apart again and I drifted into blankness.

The next time I came round, the room was empty and my shoulder sockets were screaming. I took my weight as well as

I could on my toes to try to relieve them and felt the squelch of my own urine under my feet. Kokko had literally knocked the piss out of me. I couldn't sort out the overlapping pains very well, but as far as I could tell I wasn't permanently damaged. Kokko knew how to inflict the maximum amount of agony without killing the victim. I'd made him lose his cool when I spat in his face and he'd beaten me senseless. A Pyrrhic victory.

The raging thirst I felt made the time drag. I couldn't wrench my eyes away from the basin with its tap slowly dripping because of a worn-out washer. Then Dawson returned.

'Back with us, eh?' he said amiably, coming over for a closer look. 'Want to tell me your story?'

I didn't move.

'Didn't think you would. I never really thought a straightforward beating would make you talk, but Kokko has to get his jollies too. Now we're going to do it my way, but the big Finn should get some kicks out of this as well.'

I didn't know what the hell he was talking about, but then my mind wasn't exactly crystal clear. I started to get the picture when Kokko pushed Charly into the room.

'Logan!' Charly gasped when she saw me, my arms stretched like the central figure in a passion play.

'Shut your mouth!' Kokko snarled and pushed her across the room.

'You see how it's going to be, Logan,' Dawson said. 'Kokko's wanted to have your girl-friend's pants off for a long while, to say nothing of dreaming about giving her a good slapping around for putting him down in front of everyone. Now all his Christmases have come at once.'

I didn't know what to do.

'You might as well give us the story now, old buddy. You will eventually.'

'I don't know anything more. I was working on it as a freelance,' I lied desperately, trying to think of something I could tell them they would believe.

Charly was backed to the wall, nostrils flaring like any cornered animal. Kokko advanced on her while she crazily fumbled at the buttons on her shirt. What was she trying to do – make it easy for him? As he reached forward, spun her round and then wrapped his huge arm under her chin to immobilize her, it penetrated. She still had the gun in the binder round her breasts. But Kokko had her pinned from behind now with his forearm across her chest in such a way that it was impossible for her to reach that gun. Even if she did get it, Kokko would have it away from her in a second. She kicked at his shins, tried to scratch his face, but he laughed, enjoying himself, and calmly reached around, snapped open her belt buckle and pulled her heavy trousers down to her knees. Her underpants went with a rip, and then he plunged his hand up between her legs, his thumb going deep inside her, his fingers curled into her pubic hair. He lifted her completely off the floor, one hand clamped on the scruff of her neck to balance her, the other, between her legs, impaling her weight on his thumb. He shook her like a frail doll and held her out towards me.

'She pretty good screw, Adams?' he gargled in his broken accent. 'She feel pretty good.' He squeezed his thumb and fingers together so that Charly gasped and cursed him in her pain.

Her shirt was undone and I could see the binder underneath; and, quite plainly, the Beretta outlined between her breasts as she strained against her tormentor. To give her any chance to get it into action I had to get Dawson and Kokko's attention away from her for a second or two, particularly Kokko's. And it had to be now! Kokko would tear all her clothes from her in a moment and discover the gun.

'Charly was right, Kokko!' I yelled at him. 'Your thumb's the only thing you can keep up long enough for that kind of a job.' He was thick and it took some time to get through to him. 'No balls either, eh, stupid? Is that why you were so interested in mine?'

Kokko's eyes swivelled round to me and I could see Dawson in the background, laughing. He knew I was trying to provoke Kokko to get him away from Charly and he was amused at the futility of it. Kokko would just stop my mouth and go right back to what he was doing.

'They say a man's nose is like his penis.' I tried to goad him into attacking me. 'Looking at your little squashed mushroom, I'll bet it's hard for you to find enough to hold when you pi – '

He tossed Charly into the corner and came at me, a maddened gorilla, spittle squeezing from his cracked, cursing mouth. I hoped Charly was quick; Kokko wasn't going to pull his punches this time. Luckily, he was so enraged that his first blow missed my head entirely, and I managed to jerk away from most of the force of his second.

'Get away from him or I'll kill you!' Charly screamed. Kokko stopped in mid-swing.

'Kokko!' Dawson hissed, trying to back out of the way. 'Get that gun away from her.'

Kokko took a step towards Charly. She didn't look very dangerous with her pants around her ankles and a gun not much bigger than a toy in her hand, but when that gun came up rock steady and pointed through his left eye, he thought better of it.

'You, Dawson,' she ordered crisply, 'get Logan down, and don't be stupid. I can shoot both you and Casanova in whichever eye I choose in the time it takes you to do one stupid thing.'

The way Dawson moved, I knew he wasn't going to try anything, stupid or smart, and for the moment Kokko was unprogrammed. Dawson undid the rope holding the bar above my head and the shock as my arms came down was almost worse than the original torture. My vision trembled and shifted from red to black to normal as I fought to retain consciousness. If I passed out, it would be very hard for Charly to keep Dawson and Kokko in check. Slowly, the wobbling room steadied down and I called to Dawson to unshackle me

As soon as he freed me, he moved as far away as he could.

'Are you all right, Logan?' Charly said.

I wasn't sure. I felt like a hospital case. But everything seemed to move all right.

'I'm mobile. How about you?'

'I've had worse done to me in fun. Take the gun while I pull my pants up.'

Whatever mistakes the CIA had made in its operations, picking this woman wasn't one of them. I took the gun and turned to Dawson and Kokko.

'The soldiers will hear if you shoot us,' Dawson almost whimpered.

'I don't think anything that happens in this room would draw the slightest attention; shots least of all. Now lean against the wall.'

They quickly did as they were told; hands splayed out, bodies leaning in. Charly was decent again. I gave her the gun and picked up my clothes from where they'd been tossed into a corner. It was murder getting my arms into the shirt and pullover, but I moved them as much as possible to try to get them to work freely again.

I took the Beretta and frisked Dawson and then Kokko. Dawson was unarmed, but Kokko had a narrow-bladed, razor-sharp knife in a boot-sheath. I guessed he'd brought it along to use on Charly and me. I put it in my own boot and told Kokko to move over to the shackles I'd been strung in. There was a glint of fear now in those small, red eyes and he looked to Dawson for instructions.

'Do as he says,' Dawson ordered. As far as Dawson was concerned, better Kokko than him.

I shackled him in and had Dawson pull him off his feet. When he was up, Charly went over and drove her boot up into his groin. If his gasping, whitened face was any indication, it hurt him as much as it had me. I handed Charly the gun, picked up a chair, walked around behind him and smashed it as hard as I could across the back of his skull. He slumped in the shackles like a pole-axed bull.

Charly pointed the pistol at Dawson, who waved his hands futilely in front of his face as if they could stop even so tiny a bullet, but I said: 'We'll need him.'

'I wasn't going to shoot him. I just wanted him to keep the possibility in mind,' she said.

I went over to the heavy door, opened it a crack and peered out into the hall. I could vaguely hear voices from the guard-room at the end. Fortunately, our old room was the other way.

'Okay, Dawson, we're going down to get Grampion. I'll go first, then you, then Charly with the gun. If we're stopped, you're taking us back to the room down the hall. It's thin, but God help you if you don't make it stick.' He nodded vigorously. I knew he was scared enough to do what I told him, but I wasn't fool enough to hope that it would work if we were stopped. However, there was little else I could do.

Before we left, I rinsed my face off and sucked up as much water as my aching stomach would accept, then, after one last check, we stepped boldly out and marched down the corridor. It was only a few yards but I was sweating by the time we got there. I unbolted the door and we stepped into the relative safety of the room.

'Charly! Logan!' Grampion was fully dressed and looking worried. 'Are you all right, Charly? I tried to stop that cretin, Kokko.'

I noticed then that the side of his face still retained a blue-red mark where Kokko must have smacked him. Quickly I filled him in on what had happened.

'You can't get away, you know that,' Dawson said. 'But if you give yourselves up, I'll make sure you're treated well.'

I laughed. 'Whatever we do, Dawson, your only hope of living is to help us, because I'll make sure you die if you don't.'

By the look on his face, he took my point, and, I was reasonably sure that as long as his life was in danger he would do as he was told. I turned to the others. 'One of the domes is used for a hangar. They've got a light plane.'

I didn't mention that it had been nearly ten years since I'd been up or that I had only a dozen or so hours solo, and that in perfect conditions. However, if you considered the chances of being able to escape with a Sno-cat at six miles an hour, leaving a track you could see for miles, a plane, even in my hands, was a better bet.

'We can't leave Gus!' Charly said.

'I don't intend to, and Claydon is in the prison compound, too.'

'Claydon!'

'Yes, Howard's buddy. He's the one who told me about the plane.'

Grampion looked doubtful. 'How the devil can we get two men out of the prison compound and steal a plane? We'll have to have outdoor winter clothes, too. It'll be bad enough on the plateau, but the higher we go in a plane, the colder it will get.'

I'd been thinking about that. Claydon and Gus and I had talked about the possibility of damaging the power station; which Claydon knew exactly how to do if only he could get in on his own. A plan was beginning to form how that might be accomplished. I told Charly and Grampion about Claydon's idea.

'If we could get the steam running wild, it might cause a big enough diversion for us to get to the plane,' I finished.

'It would do more than that,' Charly said. 'That's why Gasiorowski was so happy to have a top geologist look over his operation. The entire cliff overhanging these domes is incredibly unstable; the whole system is, for that matter. All geothermal areas are shaky to begin with and having a continental-sized glacier grinding away on top doesn't improve it. I think that if the steam pressure was bottled up so that it finally exploded with enough of a bang, the whole thing would go, the tunnels cave in and the cliff face come down on to these domes.'

Could it be done? There was really nothing to lose. If we didn't escape we were certainly going to die, whatever happened. 'What do you think about the possibilities, Warden?' I asked.

'I'm no geologist, but from what I've seen of the cave system and that cliff hanging over us, I'd say the whole thing might collapse if you sneezed. Practically all their manpower is being used to strengthen the main tunnel and the caves where the steam geysers are.'

'I know,' I said. 'Gus and I have been helping.'

'Knowing it might work is one thing,' he went on, 'making it happen is another. How do we get in there?'

'We'll have to get someone to take us who won't be stopped.' I turned to Dawson. 'Where is Colonel Karakan at this time in the evening?'

His face was white. 'I don't know, he could be anywhere,' he said.

I took Kokko's knife from my boot, walked behind him, yanked his head back so that his carotid artery showed clearly in his neck, pulsing rapidly because of his thundering heart, and laid the keen edge across it. 'You know where he is, Dawson,' I said quietly, 'because I think he would have wanted an immediate report from you the moment I told you anything.'

He almost choked on the words but he got them out. 'In his office.'

'Get your coveralls on,' I told the others, 'so that you look as if you're going somewhere to work. We'll have to go up to Karakan's office the same way we came here.'

They slipped them on quickly over their other clothes and then Charly said to Dawson, 'Give me your jacket.' When he'd shrugged out of it and handed it to her, she draped it over her arm to hide the gun. 'Let's go,' she said.

I checked the passage again and we boldly stepped out, with Grampion and me in the lead and then Dawson, with Charly just behind, the hidden Beretta aimed at his left kidney. We met no one in the hallway on the lower floor, but just as we started to ascend the stairs to the upper storey, a soldier, unarmed and carrying a sheaf of papers, started down. I put my hand on the hilt of my knife, now in my sleeve where I'd slipped it to make it handier, and glanced at Dawson. He looked positively sick, and I realized that he was as worried about meeting anybody as we were; he knew that he'd be the first to go if there was an alarm. The soldier paid us little attention; Charly and Grampion were becoming familiar figures around the camp, and I guessed that prisoners like me with their faces puffed and broken weren't that uncommon. He bustled past saying something friendly to Dawson in Russian. Charly pressed the Beretta into Dawson's side, and he just grunted unintelligibly as we continued on up the stairs.

It was going to be difficult not being able to speak Russian, I realized. Fear for his life might keep Dawson from trying to cry for help to someone who didn't understand, but I doubted whether Karakan would be so easily intimidated.

We were at the door to Karakan's outer office. I adjusted the knife so that I could get it into action instantaneously and hissed to Dawson, 'Tell whoever is in there that you were ordered to bring us to see the colonel. And no shooting unless you have to,' I told Charly. 'If there's too much noise, we'll blow it before we've started. But if you have to – ' I nodded towards Dawson – 'him first.'

Her face was taut, but she said steadily, 'My pleasure.'

I opened the door and we walked in.

The fat corporal was there behind his desk, shirt adrift and busily writing on some papers. At first I congratulated myself that he was alone and then I saw the big trooper sitting in a chair in the corner of the small anteroom, his AK-47 assault rifle beside his chair. They looked up as we entered, the trooper without interest, the corporal with annoyance. I kept walking towards the trooper as the corporal said something questioning in Russian to Dawson.

'You take the fat one,' I said as conversationally as possible to Grampion.

The unsoldierly-looking corporal was no idiot. One look at Dawson's terrified face and he made a dive for his desk drawer and snapped a command to the trooper. But the trooper wasn't as quick on the uptake as the corporal, and as I slammed the knife up under his chin, he still had a look of incomprehension in his eyes. The blade scraped up his vertebrae into his skull and even that expression glazed over as he died.

The corporal had grabbed a Makarov 9mm pistol from his desk and was trying to pull the slide back to cock it when Grampion's meaty fist smashed into the side of his head. I didn't wait to see him fall all the way to the floor. I left the knife protruding downward from the trooper's throat and scooped up his rifle. Automatically, I slipped off the safety-catch and cocked the weapon as I stepped quickly to Karakan's door and threw it open.

There hadn't been much noise and he was looking only mildly irritated when I burst in. He was caught completely off guard, and when I bobbed the rifle in that gesture that every soldier knows, he put his hands slowly on to the top of his head. I glanced behind me into the anteroom; Grampion had the Makarov, one soldier was dead, the other slumped behind his desk, and Charly, still holding Dawson at gunpoint, had closed the door. The whole thing hadn't taken fifteen seconds; we were operating like greased cogs.

But the easy part was over; now we had to get Gus and Claydon free and all of us into the power plant – just for starters.

'Drag that trooper in here,' I ordered Dawson. 'Can you manage the other one, Warden?'

'Of course,' he said, and grabbed the fallen corporal by the collar. He was looking mightily pleased with himself.

While they hauled the two soldiers into the inner office, I moved Karakan out from behind his desk and relieved him of his service pistol. I handed it to Charly, who was glancing greenly at the haft of the knife in the dead soldier's throat.

'Can you use this?' I snapped.

She nodded, getting a grip of herself. 'Put that peashooter in your pocket then; this will be more effective.' She took the heavier automatic, checked the magazine and cocked it expertly. I was satisfied.

I caught Karakan eyeing the knife too, but not because it shocked him. 'I'll just put this out of temptation's way.' I pulled the blade free.

I was about to wipe it on the soldier's uniform before replacing it in my boot, when that uniform gave me an idea, and instead I wiped the blood on to my own pants leg. By the time I stood up, I had a fullblown plan.

Chapter 21

When we'd first headed for Karakan's office, I had intended to try to force him to have Gus and Claydon brought over, then to use him as a hostage to get to the power plant. Of course that would have alerted the whole garrison and therefore its chances of success were slim. It would be much better if we could get to our objective without raising any alarms and the soldier's uniform gave me an idea how it might be done.

I explained briefly, and then, taking Dawson back into the outer office, I left Grampion stripping the two fallen soldiers and Charly watching the colonel. When we'd first broken into his office, he'd fired a short burst of questions at Dawson which I told him not to answer. Since then, he had sat calmly and unafraid. No man to underestimate, I realized; fear for his life would not be enough to force him to help us if he thought we could really get away or in any way damage the base. However, the colonel's willingness to die to preserve the base or its secrecy might work in our favour if I could put it into the right perspective for Dawson.

In the outer office, I closed the door so that Dawson and I

were alone. There was no sneer on his face now.

'You've got an idea what we plan to do, haven't you, Dawson?'

'Blow up the power plant –' his voice weakened – 'which will smash the base – and escape in the plane.' He shook his head. 'Why don't you just try to escape in the plane?'

I'd certainly thought of it. It would have been much easier if we could have just marched out to the hangar with Karakan as a hostage and forced them to let us go. One look at Karakan showed how far we'd get with that.

'If the colonel thought we might escape, that knowledge of this base would get to the outside world, would he give his life to stop us?'

'Of course,' Dawson said immediately, and then realized the full implication of what that meant.

'Exactly,' I said. 'If Karakan thinks we have a chance of escaping, he won't hesitate to call fire down on to all of us, you and him included.'

There was fear in Dawson's face. 'He would too!'

'And if he thinks we are going to try to wreck the base . . . ?'

'The same thing!'

I poked the muzzle of the AK-47 into his stomach. 'Then we won't tell him, will we?'

'But he knows you're trying to escape,' he whined. He didn't like the idea of being caught in the middle.

'But he doesn't know how. What I want you to tell him is that we are going to try to escape through the tunnel to the sea.'

'There's nothing there but water and ice. You could never get away from there.'

'Right. If he thinks we're running into a cul-de-sac, that we are inevitably going to be caught, he won't be so quick with the grand gesture and get you and him and the rest of us shot.'

Dawson understood. This concerned his life. 'I'll tell him what you want,' he said.

I went over to the corporal's desk and rummaged around

until I found where he kept his telephone index. I deciphered Chubokov's name in Russian writing and pointed it out to Dawson.

'I want you to call him, tell him who you are, that you are acting for Colonel Karakan, and that he wants the prisoners Claydon and LaFlette taken to the beginning of the railway, where he will meet them with his own guard. And he wants them there in twenty minutes,' I added.

A slight gleam came into Dawson's eyes, so I said, 'And talk to him in English. He likes to practise. Tell him you'd heard he was very good and that you like to keep in practice yourself.' I took out the knife. 'And if you say so much as one word I think is out of line, I'll kill you where you sit.' The gleam went out, but I would have to watch his every step.

I stood behind him as he dialled the number with the point of my knife pricking him just under the ear. There's no bone there and he knew that the blade could slide into his brain as if it were soft butter. He called the operator and said Chubokov's number carefully in Russian so that even I could tell it was the right one. I took the phone from him as it rang until I heard the sergeant's familiar voice on the other end.

'No tricks,' I mouthed as I handed the receiver back to him, and there were none. He told Chubokov just what I wanted and did it in such a way that no one would ever think a quick turn of his head would kill him.

In Karakan's office, Grampion had stripped both soldiers and tied up the fat corporal, efficiently stoppering his mouth with a gag. I told them what I had done and what we were going to do now.

'What about him?' Charly gestured towards Karakan with his own gun. He watched her coolly from under his heavy lids.

'He's going to help us.' I turned to Dawson. 'All right, tell him that we are all going out of here in five minutes – Grampion and I will be dressed as soldiers – and we are going to the tunnel and through it to the coast. If he does what he is told, he'll live, if not, he won't. Now tell him that and nothing else!'

Dawson jabbered away in Russian and I watched Karakan's face intently. I didn't have the slightest idea what Dawson was saying and, for all his apparent fear, he might still choose the death-and-glory road. I watched Karakan's long face for a hint of that bleak resignation that would come if he was told what we were really going to do and he realized that to stop us he might have to forfeit his own life.

But his only expression was a ghost of a smile as he replied to Dawson.

'What did he say?' I asked.

'That he doesn't have much choice at the moment.'

I had to be satisfied. I didn't have much choice at the moment, either.

Grampion was already adjusting the corporal's uniform, and I hurried to get into the other while Charly kept her eye on Dawson and the colonel. In a couple of minutes we were dressed. Mine wasn't a bad fit, but Grampion, solid as he was, wasn't in the corporal's class.

'Just make sure your pants don't fall down,' I said. 'The greatcoat should hide the rest.'

I adjusted my helmet and carefully buttoned the greatcoat. This was no time to look unmilitary. Grampion did the same and he didn't look too bad even with the excess looseness. I ordered Karakan to put on his coat and cap and we were ready.

'You'll have to go first, Warden, and I'm afraid you'll have to keep your pistol in its holster, but leave the flap undone. Charly and Dawson next with that coat over Charly's gun, then the colonel, and then me in the rear. Dawson, tell the colonel that you will do the talking if any needs to be done and that he is to keep his mouth closed. If anything looks even slightly wrong, I'll blow a hole in his spine with my rifle.'

Dawson did as he was told and the colonel nodded.

Luckily, the door out of the front of the building by the main guardroom wasn't the only exit. I had been brought in earlier by a side entrance and that's the one we headed for.

Grampion in uniform, with the collar of his greatcoat turned up and his cap as low as possible, looked like a different man, and I hoped, with my helmet tipped forward and the rearranging that Kokko had given my face, I wouldn't be recognizable, either. Nevertheless, when we met two soldiers coming into the building just as we were leaving, my heart picked up its beat, and it wasn't until they'd stepped aside, smartly saluting, as we swept by, that I realized that I'd been holding my breath.

There were two ways to get to the power dome: one by way of the prisoner dome and one through a direct passage. Grampion led the way past the barrack buildings towards the direct passage. Soldiers saluted as we passed, but none took any particular notice. There was nothing odd about seeing their commanding officer touring the camp with just such a retinue.

As we approached the passage, the two guards there, seeing who was coming, threw open the wire gate and presented arms, their eyes straight ahead in accepted military fashion. Protocol before proficiency, I thought. It was no way for a guard to have to stand if he wanted to see anything.

I closed up on the colonel and whispered, 'Salute' – a word that an officer, whatever the army, would know. Karakan obligingly snapped his hand up to his brow as we passed through the gate. My hands were sweating, and as we marched through the relative privacy of the connecting covered way, I quickly wiped them on my coat. Karakan, seeing, smiled sardonically. He didn't think we had a chance.

We went past the guards at the other end of the passage. I expected things would get more difficult from here on.

The power dome was actually attached to the cliff face and it was almost filled with one, big, solid concrete building that housed the generators. Only one of these was working until the submarine pens became operational, but I could still feel the steady thrum in the ground beneath my boots. The geothermal workings were inside the cliff in the caverns. All the blowholes had been tapped, but until their vast steam power could be fully utilized, the excess was led to the stacks to prevent build-up. What Claydon wanted to do was close the huge valves at the geyser heads so that the pressure would rise and finally blow the machinery to pieces. But now we knew, according to Charly, that the resultant explosion would probably bring down the cliff above and bury the entire base. The initial idea had been to sow confusion to cover our escape; now, if we didn't get out of the way fast enough, we might kill ourselves as well.

We needed Claydon first. He was the only one who had any idea how to get to the valves and close them. The dome was only dimly lit, but I could see that the railhead leading into the main tunnel beside the generator building was empty save for a small engine and some wagons on a siding. I looked across the dome towards the entrance to the prison compound just as a party passed through. I recognized Gus's bulky figure and Claydon beside him. Then I recognized their escort, too.

How stupid I'd been! Of course Chubokov would bring the prisoners himself when it was a command from his own colonel. He would know me in an instant, and the chances were that he'd raise a commotion before he realized we had Karakan as a hostage. We were right in the open where the guards on the gates could see us, and there wouldn't be a hope in hell of getting to the power station once the alarm went up; Karakan himself would order them to shoot once he realized what we were trying to do.

'Quickly, head over behind that train,' I ordered Grampion.

He too saw Chubokov and the one other guard accompanying Gus and Claydon quartering towards us, but he didn't panic, just stepped out rapidly around the corner of the generator building, briskly military.

Chubokov saw us, of course, but since we said we'd meet him at the railhead, I guess he didn't see anything too unusual in our party ignoring him for the moment. By the time we got up to the train he was only twenty paces behind us, but now we had the building blocking the view from the guards at one passage and the bulk of the wagons hiding us from the other.

'Don't shoot unless you have to,' I called as softly as possible. 'You watch our friends, Charly, whatever happens.'

She eased away from Dawson so that she could turn easily and cover both men. Grampion stopped us where the shadows were deepest and we waited for Chubokov to catch up. I kept in the shadow as much as possible, with my head tilted down, lifted my foot and surreptitiously took Kokko's knife from my boot.

Chubokov had eyes only for Karakan. He marched past me and pounded to a halt in front of the colonel. Gus and Claydon were behind him and the other guard stopped almost next to me. I could see Gus look questioningly at Charly and then his eyes widened as he recognized Grampion in the corporal's uniform.

I didn't wait. Chubokov had barely opened his mouth to announce his arrival with the prisoners when I let my rifle topple, threw my arm around the guard's neck, and when his arms automatically came up to try to break the hold, reached around and plunged the knife up under his ribs into his heart. He was dead before the rifle hit the ground.

Chubokov's mouth was still open, but he was trying to unlimber his pistol.

'The sergeant, Gus!' I snapped, still holding the body of the guard.

Gus's great hands shot out, one pinning Chubokov's hand to his holster, the other almost encompassing the man's scrawny throat. He lifted him off his feet, squeezing and shaking him like a disjointed puppet at the same time. Chubokov's eyes bulged whitely and his whole body twitched spasmodically as Gus crushed windpipe, flesh, veins and arteries in one titanic grip. When he was dead, Gus dropped him in a crumpled pile, mouth still open, at Karakan's feet.

For the first time, Karakan's poise was shaken. His hand shook slightly as he nervously wiped the sweaty sheen from his forehead. He'd seen many men die, but he'd never seen one killed casually with one hand.

Gus's big grin flashed as he took Chubokov's pistol from its holster and stuffed it in his belt.

'Hey, Logan, we are making the escape, eh?'

I told Claydon to take the guard's rifle and all his spare clips too, and then looked around the end of the train to see if the soldiers at the gate had noticed anything. They were chatting quietly 150 yards away and seemed unconcerned. Gus saw my battered face as I did so.

He put a finger on my swollen cheek. 'You not going to be so good-looking if you keep putting your head in the way.'

'Kokko had a go at Charly and me.'

He turned quickly to Charly. 'Kokko hurt you?'

'Not so you'd notice.' She never took her eyes off Dawson and Karakan.

Gus's face darkened. 'I'll kill him,' he said quietly.

'Don't worry about it, Gus,' I said. 'He won't be bothering anybody for a long while.' And I quickly told Gus and Claydon what we were trying to do.

'You mean the whole cliff will come down?' Claydon asked.

'Most likely.'

His eyes gleamed. 'Bloody marvellous!'

'But you're the only one who knows the layout in the geothermal area and what to do when we get there.' I drew Claydon and Gus slightly aside and said quietly, 'And at the moment the colonel thinks we are trying to escape through the tunnel to the coast. That's fine with him; he knows we haven't got a hope that way; but he's going to get harder to handle once he sees where we're actually headed.'

Claydon nodded. 'You can get into the geyser area through the main generator building,' he explained, 'but the best way for us is to approach it more or less from the rear by taking a side passage from the main tunnel. Not many people outside the engineers know about it, but I had to work for a month in there and made a point of memorizing the layout. That way Karakan will think we're trying for the coast until we make our turn-off.'

'How far along the tunnel is the turn-off?'

'About three miles.'

I looked at the gaping tunnel mouth with rails, wires, pipes and ducts disappearing into its throat like spaghetti. It would seem odd to the gate guards if the colonel's party just walked in; and we also stood a good chance of meeting a trainload of workers coming the other way if we took the time to go on foot – and frankly my body was protesting at the thrashing it had taken and I didn't feel like walking three miles.

'We'll take the train,' I said.

I told Charly and Grampion what we were going to do, and she, Gus and Warden got the hostages and the soldiers' bodies loaded into the guard's van behind the engine while Claydon and I worked out the controls. It was completely electric in operation, running on an overhead cable and large storage batteries, and looked simplicity itself to drive. The motor started up with a quiet whine and Claydon went down the track to throw the switch on to the main line while I released the brakes and cautiously edged her forward. Claydon swung up into the cab with me and I opened the throttle and felt the little Toonerville Trolley surge forward. In a moment we were in the tunnel, its dripping walls flashing past us and the rattle of the bogies echoing hollowly in the confined space.

'It's not too far,' Claydon called, gazing into the dimly lit tunnel stretching ahead.

I throttled back but not much. I didn't want to meet another train before we got to our destination. In a few moments the tunnel began to widen and Claydon called to me to hold it down.

Suddenly we were in a large cavern that shaded off into blackness in its farther reaches.

'This is it. Stop here.'

I brought the engine to an unexpert jolting halt. 'Go and tell the others that this is the station,' I said, 'and get any flashlights that may be in the van. It looks dark out there.'

'What are you going to do?'

'I think it's time we started making a little commotion. Get everybody off.'

I watched from the cab until they'd all climbed down. Karakan was darting his eyes back and forth trying to orientate himself. I could see he thought something was wrong, but it hadn't dawned yet what it was. Once the others were clear, I took a big heavy-duty flashlight from its bracket, turned the engine-throttle up to full and hastily jumped clear as the train gathered speed and clattered off into the tunnel.

When I came up to the group, Karakan's face was white with rage and he was saying something vehemently in Russian. For a moment I thought he would try to attack me, guns or no. I unslung my rifle, snapped off the safety-catch and took aim at the bridge of his beautifully aquiline nose from a range of four feet. He closed his mouth with a grunt because I meant it and he knew it.

'Tell him,' I said to Dawson, 'that from here on he means less and less to us alive.'

Dawson translated what I'd said, but Karakan's attention was on the dwindling rattle of our train as it sped farther and farther along the track to the coast. It would never get there, I knew.

'Lead the way, Claydon,' I said, and prodded Dawson and the colonel into line as the gaunt explorer led us into a labyrinthine series of caves spreading from the far edge of the larger gallery we'd stopped in. As we were probing our way into the wet darkness, a long-drawn-out rumble echoed, seemingly interminably, from the rock walls behind us.

'God,' Grampion whispered, 'they won't be using trains in that tunnel for a while.'

'If the tunnel, she is there at all.' Gus had worked in the tunnels and knew how easily portions of them could come down.

'It should keep everybody busy for a while,' I said. 'They might even think the good colonel is in the wreck.'

Claydon led us unerringly from passage to passage, some so

low we had to stoop through them. As we moved on, the air got perceptibly warmer. We were approaching the geothermal area; a place where great gouts of steam and boiling water surge to the surface from the volcanic kettle below. To tap them for power and heat, to harness these titanic inner earth forces in the bitter bleakness of Antarctica, was a major engineering accomplishment. And now, I hoped, we were going to destroy it.

Claydon held up his hand. A faint light showed at the end of the tunel we'd just turned into. 'The geothermal area proper begins just ahead,' he cautioned. 'There'll be engineers about most likely as well as guards if there are any prisoner working parties on this shift. Watch out for some of the pools in the larger caverns, too. They're not just hot, they're boiling!'

When we got to where our small passage debouched, I eased ahead and had a cautious look into the fluorescent brightness of the larger cavern. It was a maze of concrete and huge trestled pipes that hissed and seethed with the pressure they were containing. The only geothermal installation I'd ever seen was in New Zealand, but it had been above ground, and although it was an awesome spectacle it did have regularity in layout. Here, because the different pressure outlets were located in a number of inter-connected caverns, the giant man-high pipes with their myriad streamers of smaller associated pipes seemed to twist and turn like writhing squids guarding the many entrances to hell.

I beckoned Claydon up. 'You know how to turn this off?' It had seemed so easy when we'd discussed it in the hut, but seeing that massive installation close up made me wonder at such an assumption.

'With a bit of help and no interruptions for about half an hour. All the wells are led into this main cavern,' he explained. 'You can't see them from here, but there are five big valves on the other side of the cavern that regulate flow, either directing it to the generators or bypassing it to the stacks to get rid of it and keep the pressure down. They shouldn't have been designed that way, but it's possible to close them all down and bottle the steam up completely.'

I looked out from our little crack in the rock at that weirdly lit hissing maelstrom of contained energy, a puny mortal gazing into Thor's workshop, and couldn't quite work up Claydon's confidence. But we had to try.

'Let's go, then.'

Claydon put a hand on my arm, still looking out. 'Watch for engineers or guards. We'll have to be careful.'

'Okay.'

I went back to the others. 'We'll walk out there as if we owned the place,' I instructed, 'but if the balloon goes up, shoot fast and don't miss.'

Karakan was very agitated; it was getting through to him what we were actually planning. He spoke rapidly to Dawson, who turned to me. 'The colonel thinks you are going to try to damage the plant. He warns that you'll never succeed.'

'Tell him we're just trying to draw off anybody chasing us by doubling back through the power dome.' He might believe it and I wanted to keep him from doing anything rash at least until we got to the valves. Dawson spoke to him and Karakan clamped his mouth shut, but his eyes were wild.

'Shoot him if he tries anything,' I told Charly.

We gathered ourselves together and stepped out into the main cavern. We didn't see anyone at first as we threaded our way among the pipes and catwalks, but on turning into one long open section, a man in a white coat holding a clipboard came towards us from the far end.

'Engineer,' whispered Claydon.

The man looked up, saw us marching towards him with Karakan in our midst, and slipped off along a catwalk. Keeping out of the colonel's way came second nature to the base people.

A moment later, Claydon turned off to the right, and suddenly we were face to face with the biggest valves I'd ever seen in my life. From them huge feeder pipes disappeared into a tunnel.

Grampion looked into its maw. 'Where does this go?'

'To the power dome and the stacks,' Claydon said.

'How the hell do you operate those?' I said, gawping at the gigantic valves. 'You can't just turn them off like a bathroom tap.'

'Hydraulics. It's not easy.'

We were so busy looking at the valves that we didn't see the working party of three prisoners and a guard until they were almost up to us. At first the guard didn't think anything was amiss – nothing odd about seeing his commanding officer and two other soldiers with a working party – but by this time Karakan had no doubts about what we were trying to do. He screamed in Russian, and after the briefest hesitation the guard snapped his rifle up to shoot.

Charly fired first and missed, but the bullet, spanging off a pipe near the guard's head, put his aim off and his shot missed Claydon. Gus killed him with two shots through the chest. He sprawled back into the pipes, his rifle flying from his hands.

'Karakan!' yelled Claydon, snapping a round at the colonel, who had taken advantage of Charly's shooting at the guard to dodge away at full speed. Dawson, as a reflex, took off after the colonel, but went down in our first fusillade, somersaulting as the 7·62 and 9-millimetre bullets smashed into his body. The three prisoners who'd been under the jurisdiction of the dead guard also took off, running as hard as they could in different directions. But Karakan, with his slight head start, disappeared into the maze behind us.

'I'll catch the bastard,' Gus said.

'No!' I stopped him. 'You could play hide and seek in here for ever. Even if he finds his way back through those tunnels to the rail line without any mistakes, it'll take him fifteen minutes or so; then he's got to get a group together and get back here. We'll fix the valves and try to get out through the tunnel to the power dome.'

I posted Grampion and Charly as lookouts while Gus and Claydon and I attacked the valves. They were absolutely massive; solid steel set in thick reinforced concrete. By a combination of hydraulic leverage and complicated gear trains, they could be slowly opened or shut – but oh, so slowly!

Initially Gus knocked the safety locks off with a huge wrench used to free reluctant valve wheels and then we began to wind and wind on the first three. It seemed to take for ever, but gradually the gauges showed the valve dropping towards the fully closed mark. Gus, spinning the heavy wheel, had his closed first and moved over to the next.

'That one last,' cautioned Claydon. 'These four are just draining off the excess steam, that one feeds the generator. When we shut it down the power goes off.'

'Are there emergency lights?' I asked.

'Some, but it's still going to be plenty dark.'

'To our advantage, I hope,' I wheezed as I heaved the last few turns to close my valve.

Gus had the fourth valve wheel turning when a burst of fire echoed over the hissing of the pipes from where Grampion was stationed. I heard the sharp clatter of the Kalashnikov Grampion had taken from the guard Gus had shot.

'Christ, it's only been about ten minutes,' Claydon said. 'Karakan couldn't have got back with reinforcements so soon!'

I grabbed my rifle. 'Gus, when you've closed that valve, start smashing the hydraulic cylinders and the gear trains while Claydon closes that last valve. When he's finished, smash that one too. Nobody will be able to budge those valves with the leverage system gone.'

Sweat was running down Gus's brown, block-like face from the strain and the heat in the cavern from the steam pipes. 'See what the trouble is, *mon ami*,' he grunted, 'we'll finish these off.'

I dodged off to where Grampion was hunkered down behind a plethora of pipes and steel. As I threw myself beside him, he got off a short burst.

'Who is it?' I asked.

'Karakan, I think,' he said, without looking up.

I took a quick look out. Several men in prisoner's garb were crouched or lying as far out of the line of fire as they could crawl.

'Another working party?'

'It would appear so,' Grampion said calmly. 'Two guards – just behind that big pipe.' He fired again.

'Blast! I thought Karakan would have to hot-foot it back to the tunnel to get help.'

'Probably sent that engineer we saw.'

Of course. Too easy. We'd have to get out to the power dome pretty soon or we'd be trapped between the two. If I was any judge of the man, Karakan would have sent orders to seal us off.

The sound of Gus's wrench smashing the gear trains clanged through the air and almost immediately I heard Karakan yelling something in Russian. He knew what that sound meant and he would do anything to try to stop it.

'Watch out! They'll try to attack.'

I left Grampion and scuttled over to where Charly lay grasping her pistol in both hands and peering out between two pipes.

'Looks like Karakan picked up some help without having to go all the way back to the railway tunnel,' I said.

'How many?'

'Grampion thinks two.'

'Karakan hasn't got a gun himself. They won't try anything but sniping until they get some reinforcements.'

The crunching of Gus's wrench was still ringing through the air when a sustained barrage of fire clanged and ricocheted from the metal around us, keeping us both completely pinned down. One of Karakan's men was giving covering fire so that the other could get to us from the side while we were forced to keep our heads down.

I twisted around just in time to see a soldier leap to a catwalk above us. I tried to bring my rifle up but the awkward position slowed me. He wasn't ten feet away and I could practically see up the barrel as he swung on me. A rifle cracked and it took a moment to realize that the searing smash of the bullet I'd braced for wasn't coming, that it was the soldier who was toppling off the catwalk on to the pipes below.

Claydon poked his head out from around a concrete support, his assault rifle still held to his shoulder. 'Come on!' he yelled. 'Let's get out of here. The valves are closed and God knows how long it will be before they blow!'

'Grampion, Charly, back!' I ordered, and sent a burst towards the spot that the other guard had been firing from – to keep his head down this time. We scurried back behind the relative safety of the valve block as Gus joined us.

'Only one way those valves going to open now,' he said, smiling, and jabbed his thumb ceilingward. 'Straight up!'

Grampion looked apprehensively at the broken machinery on the valves, behind which gargantuan pressures were quickly building. 'How long?'

'How do I know?' Claydon snapped. 'I just don't want to be here when they go.'

I looked into the tunnel that led eventually to the power dome. The first hundred yards was dead straight and then it gradually began to curve. The lights were already starting to flicker as the generators ran out of steam.

'How far to the dome?' I asked.

'About a mile and a half,' Claydon said quickly. 'They tried to keep it as straight as possible but they had to follow natural caverns in many places. We'll have to watch out for hot pools nearer the other end.'

'Right, you four get going and I'll bring up the rear.'

'But Karakan will probably catch you in the tunnel,' Charly protested. 'They could hardly miss!'

'Easier to miss one than five. Now get going!'

It was no time to be arguing over who was going to be a hero, and Charly knew it as well as anyone. She kissed me quickly on the cheek and the four of them pounded down the tunnel as fast as they could run.

The lights were flickering badly now. It wouldn't be long till they went out completely. I checked that the long flashlight I'd taken from the engine was still in my greatcoat pocket and took the moment's respite to change magazines on the AK-47. Karakan and the other guard wouldn't be sitting on their hands; the colonel knew he had to get to the valves if he was to assess and repair the damage. I looked at Gus's handiwork with the wrench and thought Karakan was going to be bloody mad when he saw it: nothing was going to put that mess back together outside of a full engineering team.

I edged around the concrete base of the valves and caught a flicker of movement through the pipes about thirty feet away. I let go a shot, more to keep them wary than with any idea of hitting anything. A shot from my left took a gouge out of the concrete and I ducked back, firing in that direction.

At that moment the lights failed completely, but I had a bearing on the tunnel mouth and began to sprint for my life down its pitch-black length, keeping one hand on the wall to guide me. It was a big tunnel but almost completely filled with the huge feeder pipes, and I knew that unless I reached the curve before Karakan and the guard got to the mouth, they could cut me down in its narrow confines even in the dark.

When I say sprinted, it's hardly true. The sharp, racking pains shooting through my chest and abdomen – a legacy from Kokko's enthusiastic beating – kept me to a jogging stumble. My breath came in more ragged gasps with every step.

I estimated that I had about twenty or so yards to go to the curve when the first shot filled the tunnel with its noise and the bullet flicked past me and clanged into something up ahead. I dropped flat, almost glad for the excuse to stop, and swivelled around, prepared to fire back if I had to, and hoping I wouldn't need to. Firing in that dark tunnel would reveal my location.

Just then the emergency lighting came on. It was nothing like the bright fluorescents that had filled the tunnel before with hard, garish light. These were low-wattage bulbs spaced thirty yards apart, just enough to stop you from falling over your own feet. I was lying in a pool of shadow and I guess it was that that made the guard hesitate; he must have thought for an instant that he'd hit me. He and Karakan were standing at the tunnel mouth directly under one of the emergency lights, and normally at that range and from a prone position I could have shot them both easily. As it was, with each breath I took burning its way in and out, I was lucky to hit the guard in the leg.

He went down with a cry and Karakan ducked out of the tunnel mouth, but not before he grabbed the fallen guard's rifle. I didn't want to duel it out with him, but scrambled to my feet and forced myself to run the last few yards around the curve. The others were there waiting, and as soon as I was out of the line of fire, Claydon spewed a burst towards the tunnel mouth.

'Logan!' Charly looked worriedly at my white face.

'I'm okay,' I wheezed. 'It's just that Kokko made it a little hard for me to do the hundred in under ten. I'm getting my second wind now.'

'The tunnel curves like this for about half a mile,' Claydon said. 'If we keep moving, I don't think they can get a clear shot.'

'Just Karakan now, but he's enough,' I said.

Gus let go another couple of rounds to keep the colonel on his toes and we hurried on into the dim tunnel. I *was* getting my second wind now, and my chest had settled into a dull pain that, considering our other troubles, I had no difficulty in ignoring.

When he'd seen the uselessness of trying to reopen the valves, Karakan came hotfooting after us. I didn't know at the time whether he just wanted to get revenge for what we'd done to his base or was trying to reach the power dome to get help to open the huge steam cocks, but whatever it was, he stayed close behind, firing occasionally, trying to ricochet his bullets around the curve.

Suddenly we debouched into a large cavern and in the feeble light of the two small bulbs that tried to illuminate it, I could see that its entire floor was a sulphuric, heaving mass of boiling water. The big steam pipes spanned it, anchored to the roof of the cave, and a narrow catwalk attached to their sides was the only means of crossing. The side of the catwalk was plated in steel to keep the boiling water from splashing on to anyone on it and it ended on a ledge that jutted out from the main tunnel that continued on the other side. From what I could see across the hundred-foot span in the weak light, the ledge was heaped with bags of cement, tools and a concrete mixer. Evidently, a work party had been making some repairs.

'It looks like the catwalk she has worked loose,' Gus said, testing it with his bulk. 'That ledge on the other side is breaking away too and the straps holding it are rotten from the acid in the water.'

'If we could knock it down, it would get Karakan off our backs,' Claydon said, breaking away one of the straps by levering his rifle under it.

We'd never get a better chance, I thought. 'Give it a try while I keep the colonel occupied.'

I squeezed myself into some broken rocks at the tunnel's mouth, looking back towards the spot where Karakan would have to show himself, while the others raced across the narrow bridge to get tools. In a moment they were hacking and prying at the catwalk's restraining straps, and it was beginning to sag in the middle.

I caught a glimpse of Karakan in the murk of the tunnel and fired a round at him. He dodged back round the curve so I couldn't see him.

Charly, Claydon and Grampion were working their way along the bridge towards me, breaking the straps, and Gus was on the other side on the ledge prying the footings loose with a big crowbar, when suddenly a burst of fire came from the tunnel on the other side and caught Gus in the back. He jerked upright, almost falling into the boiling water only inches below the ledge, then toppled backward over a pile of cement sacks.

'Gus!' Charly cried.

'Get down!' I screamed as she started back along the catwalk towards Gus on the other side.

Grampion pulled her flat on to the sagging catwalk with him and Claydon, and for the moment they were safe behind its metal sides. As I twisted around in my cramped position among the rocks, a figure darted out of the tunnel and threw itself behind the concrete mixer. He could have taken all the time in the world; I could only see the upper part of the tunnel entrance anyway, another stack of cement bags blocked the rest. To get a clear view you had to be on the catwalk, but the man behind the mixer had Claydon, Charly and Grampion effectively pinned down.

I saw a shadow of movement in what I could see of the far tunnel mouth and fired at the upper edge to try to keep back however many others were there. The man behind the mixer just about took my ear off with a return blast, and Karakan, behind me in the other tunnel, obviously realizing by the incredible rolling, re-echoing din of weaponry that he had reinforcements blocking our way, added his bit, blasting fragments of rock from my tiny sanctuary.

For the moment it was a stand-off. They couldn't get me, But I couldn't move, and the man behind the mixer couldn't get into line with the catwalk to shoot at Charly and the rest because I was covering the open ground he would have to cross. But that was little consolation when I thought about the closed valves and what was going to happen at any time: a searing blast of super-heated steam exploding first through the tunnels and caverns and then the cliff above us collapsing.

'Why don't you give up, Logan?' the call came across the boiling, dirty water.

You couldn't mistake that garbled accent anywhere. It was Kokko behind the mixer! I ground my teeth in frustration that I hadn't killed him. Now he'd killed Gus and, one way or another, would kill the rest of us.

'Give up and we go back to what we were doing,' he laughed. 'I have some more fun with Charly.'

'This whole place is going to blow up in a few minutes, Kokko,' I yelled. 'You'll go with us, too, you bastard.'

I heard him laugh again, and he chipped out a piece of rock above my head with a bullet. Probably Kokko only had a hazy idea of how the base ran anyway, I thought. He wasn't going to believe any stories of it blowing up.

I glanced out. My guts twisted when I saw the heavy concrete mixer moving! It must have weighed hundreds of pounds, but the big Finn was edging it along towards the catwalk, using it for cover. I fired at it but he didn't even pause. The bullets spanged uselessly from the thick metal as he closed the gap. Once there, he could pick the others off with one burst.

But Ari Kokko wasn't a man who wanted to kill quickly if there was a slower way. Gus had just about freed the end of the catwalk from the ledge before he was shot and that's what Kokko was interested in. Using the mixer as a shield, he took a crowbar and began loosening the remaining fixings. I could see the catwalk sag further until the boiling water lapped its underside. He was going to cook Claydon, Grampion and Charly alive!

'Okay, Kokko!' I yelled at him. 'We give up!' There was nothing else I could do.

But Kokko wasn't interested in surrender now. He continued to lever the supports free.

Grampion stood up on the catwalk to try to shoot, but shots from the far tunnel made him drop again. I fired, trying to drive back whoever was in the tunnel.

Then, like an apparition rising from the murk of hell, Gus heaved himself erect from behind the cement sacks where he'd fallen. I could see he was badly hurt, but his face in that misty half-light was demonic, his lips pulled back over teeth bared in pain and hate, his eyes glaring. Slowly he climbed over the sacks, his stare fixed upon Kokko lying unaware behind the mixer, breaking away the last bits of rock that held the catwalk.

One of the soldiers in the tunnel, seeing Gus rise up, dodged out, his rifle belching. In his hurry, he didn't take enough advantage of his cover and I shot him through the neck. Too slow. At least one of his bullets ripped into Gus's back, but Gus didn't even flinch so intent was he on Kokko.

The shots warned Kokko and he twisted into a crouch just as Gus got to him. He was in the open for just an instant, but the two closed so quickly that I couldn't get a clear shot. It was unreal. Two monstrous Titans straining in a flickering netherworld. Kokko was on his feet now, his huge arms locked around Gus's bullet-riddled chest. Even at that distance I could see the blood well into Gus's mouth. He coughed it into Kokko's face and wrapped his great hands around the Finn's throat.

Kokko reached up and with all his power, the muscles in his thick arms swelling his coat to bursting, tried to tear away those clenching fingers, those thumbs crushing into his windpipe; but Gus was a mountain, immovable, sucking the last of his strength up from his soul into his tightening hands. Kokko staggered and fell to his knees, eyes bulging. Gus, his whole being concentrated on the round, blood-spattered face in front of him, pushed Kokko back until he toppled on to the rock ledge, his head hanging over the edge inches above the cauldron. Then, gradually, he pushed that battered baseball head back and down. The Finn felt the searing heat behind his neck, and in a last maddened frenzy tried to heave himself free. His frantic writhing and clutching had no effect, and Gus, ignoring the scalding water rising over his hands, pressed Kokko's head slowly into the thickly bubbling pool. Even with his throat squeezed shut, Kokko gave a last whistling scream before he went under, his eyeballs popping with the heat.

It had been a spectacle out of myth and legend, and while it was unfolding, I felt curiously apart, caught up like a spectator in a dream of horror; there, but uninvolved. Reality shattered back with another whining shot from Karakan.

'Claydon! Grampion!' I shouted. 'Cross quickly. Soldiers in the tunnel!'

The catwalk swishing in the water must have been red hot by now. They were up, dancing across the swaying bridge, in an instant. Gus was still holding Kokko's head under the water and I fired over him to dissuade any soldiers in the tunnel from putting their heads up until Claydon, first across, was in position. He leaped to the ledge, stuck his rifle around the mouth of the tunnel and let the rest of his magazine go on full automatic. There was nowhere to run or hide in those narrow confines, and when the echoes had died, there was no return fire.

I put a shot down my tunnel to let Karakan know I was still operating. Charly and Grampion were dragging Gus away from Kokko and I shouted for them to get him behind the sacks and cover me when I made my crossing. I knew, as soon as Karakan saw me leave cover, he would come up quickly and try to pick us off across the pool.

With Claydon's help they got Gus behind the cement bags and yelled for me to come. 'But watch the catwalk,' Grampion yelled. 'It's just about to go.'

I got my legs under me, put a shot down the tunnel, and jumped across the tunnel opening and on to the catwalk. It was awash with boiling water now, and as I ran over it I could feel it give way beneath me. Grampion and Claydon poured fire into the spot I'd just left to try to keep the colonel at bay as I stumbled over the sinking bridge. Six feet from the end, I saw the last rock anchor go and, horrified, watched the catwalk begin to slither into the steaming, turbid water.

I jumped.

My whole being went into that jump. I dropped my rifle and threw myself up and forward. Had it been required, I might have flown; I think I could have; at that moment I could have done anything that would have stopped me from falling into that devil's pit.

I sprawled on the rock ledge, rolled, and dived behind the cement sacks with the others. Grampion was scrounging a spare magazine from the soldier I'd shot while Claydon watched for Karakan. Charly sat, holding Gus's head in her lap and quietly stroking his unruly mop of brown hair.

He looked bad. His hands and forearms were boiled flesh cooked to the bone; his chest was a sodden mass of blood, and since he'd been shot in the back, I knew that the bullets must have punched their way right through. Blood bubbled round his lips with each jerking breath through punctured lungs.

'Karakan!' Claydon said, quickly firing a shot and then cursing his miss.

I risked a glance over our barricade and saw Karakan wedging himself into the rocks where I'd been. The catwalk was down, only the far end still visible, the rest under the boiling pool. Karakan saw it too and a stream of Russian invective sizzled across the cavern. He couldn't follow so he blazed away his last rounds, threw his rifle in the pool, and ran back up the tunnel the way he'd come. He wasn't giving up, I was sure, but he had a long way round to get to us again, and I didn't envy him having to pass those valves.

I turned back to Gus. His eyes were open and he was looking up at Charly.

'It's going to be all right, Gus,' she soothed. 'We'll get you out.'

His voice was just a whisper. '*Ma petite Charlotte*, I think not.' His eyes turned to me. 'Logan, my friend, you make sure you look after her, eh?'

'Gus . . . !'

He turned his head slightly towards Grampion, his eyes crinkled up with a shadow of his old laughter. 'No lost city, but not dull either,' he said, and then the laughter was replaced with pain. '*Mes amis!*' he called to us, and the pain glazed away and he was dead.

Charly was sobbing. I pulled her to her feet and laid Gus LaFlette out flat on his back with his hand crossed over his chest while Grampion brought some empty cement sacks to cover him. We had nothing else to leave him but our love.

'Come,' I said, picking up the fallen soldier's rifle and turning into the tunnel. Gus had given us another chance, and I meant to take it. We left him lying in the eerie light of the cavern, a cavern soon to be his tomb. I hurried along at a jog; I didn't want it to be ours too.

We passed the three soldiers Claydon had shot. In the narrow, straight tunnel, they had no place to go but down, nothing they could do but die. I ran on, stolidly pacing myself, trying to husband my waning reserves of strength, the others close behind. We crossed more hot pools, twisted through what seemed this never-ending tunnel, but at least we met no more opposition.

'Hold up,' Claydon called. 'We're almost out.'

We stopped, breathing hard.

'There's bound to be all sorts of guards and technical people crawling over the generator building and the power dome,' Grampion puffed. 'How do we get past them?'

'There won't be much light,' I said. 'We'll have to try to bluff our way. Grampion and I as guards with two prisoners.' I pointed at the rifle Claydon cradled in his arms. 'You'll have to get rid of that. A prisoner with an AK-47 won't bluff many people.'

Reluctantly he laid the weapon to one side.

Just then we heard a distant rumble behind us. The tunnel floor jiggled severely and chunks of rock clattered to the ground from the walls and ceiling. The emergency lights flickered out.

'It's blowing up!' Charly cried.

The rumble growled away and the tunnel settled down.

'Just a starter, I hope,' Claydon said in an awed voice, while I hauled my flashlight from my greatcoat pocket. Its beam reflected from thick dust still swirling from the shaking, then, as we watched, it was swept away by a fetid blast of hot, steamy air; just a belch this time, but we knew that much worse was soon to come.

In one way, the preliminary shake-up helped us considerably. It threw the base into complete darkness for the short time it took us to reach the tunnel's end and enter the generator building. By the time the dim emergency bulbs came to murky life again, we were well away from the tunnel and making for the entrance. There were guards and engineering people everywhere. Even parties of prisoners milled about more or less unattended, waiting for someone to tell them what to do. But no one knew what to do except follow the feeder tunnel a mile and a half into the earth to see what was stopping the steam. After the last rumbling quake, no one was a volunteer for that. Our plan had been to cause a diversion to cover our escape and we'd certainly succeeded. No one was in the least interested in us as we hurried along in the semi-dark.

We got past the giant dynamos and into the lobby of the building. People were darting in and out and we fitted ourselves into the stream; but just as we emerged into the power dome, we came face to face with Gasiorowski and a train of technicians. His face was white and harassed and it took him a moment to recognize Charly, who was forced by the crowd to stop right in front of him. There was practically no light at all outside the building and I pulled Grampion back with me into the shadows, hoping not to be recognized but keeping our rifles ready.

He spoke to her quickly in French and didn't seem to be surprised to see her. She was escorted, after all, and he gave us the briefest of glances. In fact, he appeared quite glad to find someone who, if she didn't know what was going on, was at least scientist enough to be of some help.

Charly also replied in very expressive French. She waved back the way we'd come, turned valves with her hands, splayed her fingers up in the form of an explosion, and pointed up towards the top of the dome where outside and directly above poised the massive overhanging cliff. Gasiorowski's face began to twitch, and some of the men with him who either also spoke French or got the drift of Charly's sign language began to talk excitedly to the others in tones of fear and panic. While they were caught up with that, I took Charly's arm and officiously dragged her off, and the four of us marched into the darkness, leaving Gasiorowski behind, visibly nervous.

'What did you tell him?' I whispered to Charly.

'The truth. Except that I said that it was one of the working parties that sabotaged the steam valves. I told him it was due to blow any second, and when it did, the whole cliff over us would come down.'

'He looked like he believed it.'

There was another deep rumble that made the ground quiver beneath our feet as we reached the passage to the administrative dome, now unguarded.

'Not difficult to do with this going on. I also told him he'd better order the evacuation of the people here, at least get them out of the domes and into the valley.'

I nodded. I hoped we would manage to be among them. As we hurried into the passage, I looked back at what a short while ago had been a quiet, almost deserted dome. Now men were scurrying in and out of the generator building, setting up hand trucks to go into the rail tunnel, talking and moving apprehensively from one to another like ants whose nest has been disturbed.

We went through the busy administrative dome unremarked and along another short passage to the dome hangar where the aircraft were housed. There was usually a fair number of people working there, Claydon said, not prisoners but regular technicians and mechanics. Now it was all but completely dark and empty. Only two very worried-looking guards barred the entrance; everyone else seemed to have gone to see what had caused the blackout. Even the guards were more interested in learning what was happening than in stopping us, and as we neared them they began to fire questions at us in Russian.

'Take them quietly,' I whispered.

I rammed the barrel of my rifle into the stomach of the guard nearest me, and when he folded up, smashed the butt into the back of his head. Claydon and Grampion working together got the same results with the other man.

I stepped over the bodies and flashed my light around the dome. It was much smaller than the others, just a hangar, and it took only a moment to locate the plane. There were a number of helicopters in the dome and barrels of aviation fuel stacked towards the rear. Even so, there was plenty of room to move the plane out of the hangar once the main doors were open. When I'd ascertained that, I walked over to the craft and shone my light over it. I wondered if I would be able to fly it.

'Get those doors open,' I told Claydon and Grampion. 'I'll check out the plane. Charly, you find us something to bundle in, blankets, clothing, tarpaulins, anything that might keep us warm once we're out of here. It's going to be damn cold flying over the plateau.'

They went off and I circled the small aircraft once and then hoisted myself up inside through its three-foot by three-foot door. She had an air-cooled, nine-cylinder radial engine, a wing span of about fifty feet, combination wheel and ski undercarriage and, inside, pilot and co-pilot seats with another seat behind and more than enough extra room for cargo or other passengers. I slid into the pilot's seat and looked over the instrumentation. Everything was in Russian, of course, but that was the least of my worries; either you know what the instrument does or you don't, whatever the language.

I flipped on the switches and began to feel better. She was modelled very closely on the de Havilland Beaver aircraft both in size and cockpit layout, and I had done about ten hours in just such a plane. Ten hours over ten years ago wouldn't normally have overwhelmed me with confidence, but with the world about to fall in on us literally, any advantage was appreciated. I went over everything carefully. It was ready for flight except for one item. She was out of gas! The needles on both the main and auxiliary tanks read almost zero. God, I felt tired. Through the windshield I watched Grampion and Claydon hauling on the continuous chain that was slowly sliding the hangar doors open. Charly was piling gear under the wing ready to be loaded for our escape. We were all ready, freedom only the length of the runway away, and we couldn't move.

I felt the ground shake again and wished that the bloody thing would blow up and get it over with.

Charly poked her head in the door, throwing some bundles into the rear. 'Any problems?'

My voice almost broke. 'No gas.'

She didn't even pause from her loading. 'Plenty piled in drums at the back of the hangar. I think I even saw a small gas trailer with a pump.' She was gone again on her scavenging.

I must be tired, I thought. Of course there'd be plenty of gas about – it was one of the first things I noticed – and the equipment to handle it. I jumped out of the plane as Claydon and Grampion came back from the doors and felt the frigid air of the Antarctic swirl through the wide opening. I'd almost forgotten what it was like outside the domes, and after the heat of the tunnels the cold clutched icily and started me shivering. None of us would last long out there without the protection of the plane.

'We've got to gas her up,' I called, and they hurried after me as I ran to the rear of the hangar to get the pump wagon. It was bulky, but it ran easily on its fat pneumatic tyres and we soon had it jockeyed into position and the hose into the gasoline inlet. The midnight sun shone weakly above the valley and some of its light now filtered through the hangar doors to make our work a little easier.

It seemed to take for ever. Charly had loaded all she could find that seemed useful in keeping us warm for the journey and still the pump gurgled on. The four of us watched closely, trying to hurry it with prayers. The ground shook again, this time accompanied by ominous cracking from the cliff above.

'Surely that'll do!' Claydon urged, glancing up.

'We'll need every drop to have a chance of making it to McMurdo,' I said. 'Even full, I'm not sure whether it's got the range.'

Finally, the gas came up the inlet pipe and the automatic nozzle kicked off.

'Okay! Push that trailer clear while I cap it, and then everybody aboard.'

Charly helping, they pushed the trailer to the rear of the aircraft, but before we could board a familiar voice echoed in the dome.

'Stop! Dead! Don't take another step!'

Pitt, dressed in the same heavy clothing he wore on the ice with us, stepped from behind a nearby helicopter, a Degtyarev sub-machine-gun in his hands. Our rifles were propped against the undercarriage out of reach and Charly's pistol was in her belt, Grampion's in its holster.

'Throw those pistols down,' he ordered, and in a moment we were unarmed completely but for the knife in my boot. He came forward, face drawn, holding the Degtyarev steadily. 'I've been waiting for someone to fly me out in that plane and it's kind of you to fuel it up.' A low rumbling quivered the ground again and he glanced around worriedly. 'What the hell is going on, anyway?'

'We blocked the geothermal steam,' Grampion said. 'Any moment the entire cliff will blow out and bury this whole base.'

Pitt's face, already white with strain, went ashen, but he didn't lose control. 'Then I must hurry,' he said. 'You'll have to be my pilot, Logan. The rest can wait.'

'I won't leave them!'

'Either that or I'll shoot them down now where they stand!' he barked. 'Take me in the plane and they'll at least have a chance to run for it!'

He meant it. He wouldn't hesitate to kill.

'All right,' I agreed. There was always a chance if they were alive; dead there was nothing. And I still had the knife. Once I had him in the cockpit, I would try for him.

'More company,' Claydon said, looking towards the entrance-way.

Karakan, Gasiorowski and one soldier hurried towards us. Karakan and the soldier had rifles and all of them looked dirty and dishevelled; the colonel in particular was covered in dirt and mud, and a deep gash in his forehead was streaking blood down his cheek. He'd had a bad journey back through the tunnels. Chances had run out. I couldn't use a knife against four men.

When Karakan saw us, his lips drew back in a snarl and he raised his rifle; we were the people responsible for destroying his base and there was no cool control left in the man, only hatred. Even Gasiorowski, who'd now obviously been told that it had been us who'd jammed the valves shut, was screaming with rage. Once again I braced for the impact of bullets ripping into me, but before he could fire, Pitt knocked the rifle up and shouted that I was the only one who could pilot the plane.

Karakan didn't understand the English, but Pitt's intensity was plain. He paused. And then an incredible conversation took place with Charly translating what Pitt said to Gasiorowski in French, who then translated it into Russian for Karakan.

In the pause, with three languages being jabbered away, I noticed liquid swilling across the floor and under the three newcomers' boots. At first I didn't understand what it was because there was already a strong smell of gasoline in the air from filling the plane's tanks. Then I glanced towards the trailer tank. The light was dim, but from where I was standing it was plain enough. Someone was crouched behind the trailer hosing gasoline on to the floor.

Everything happened in a rush. Karakan gave a harsh laugh and said something in Russian, pointing to himself. Gasiorowski translated and Charly cried: 'He's a pilot himself, Logan!'

'I guess you're no longer needed, old buddy,' Pitt sneered, and both he and Karakan raised their weapons.

There was a flash of a match from near the gas trailer, and the next instant Karakan, Gasiorowski and the soldier were screaming in a roar of flames. Pitt stared wide-eyed for an instant, then like a crazy man swung his machine-gun back towards us.

I hardly heard the small crack over the flames as Charly

staggered him with a shot. I had completely forgotten the Beretta she had in her pocket! Pitt's heavy clothes took some of the impact out of the small-calibre bullet and he was able to recover himself and bring the Degtyarev back to bear on us, but Charly just kept firing, jarring him backwards until he fell sprawling into the inferno raging over the floor.

For a second or two we stared at the still, dark shadow that had once been 'Plum' Pitt shrinking in the leaping blaze.

'Oh God,' Charly moaned, and dropped the empty gun from her limp fingers. Despite all the killing, Pitt was the first whom she herself had actually gunned down.

Our brief tableau was interrupted by a figure stumbling around the tail of the plane slapping out small burn patches on his heavy parka and windpants. None of us recognized him at first until he yelled at us, standing like idiots watching the world come to an end, 'Let's get out of here, for Christ's sake!'

Howard!

We didn't have time for whys and wherefores then. If the cliff didn't fall on us first, the raging gasoline would soon blow us on our way. The wind slicing in through the hangar doors was keeping the flames away from the plane, but it wouldn't be long before the dome material and the rest of the gas caught and that would be that. Charly, Claydon and Grampion scrambled into the plane, but Howard paused.

'What about Gus?'

'Dead.'

He nodded once and climbed aboard. I was quick behind him. I strapped myself in and Charly clambered into the seat beside me and gave me a small grin.

'If you crash this darn thing,' she said, 'I at least want to be able to hold your hand on the way down.'

'I've got to get it up first,' I warned her.

I pressed the starter button and watched the two-bladed prop turn slowly against the compression, the motor whining to get started. The ground shook under us and I could see the wings vibrate with the shock. Stacked barrels of aviation gas toppled behind the plane and a large rent appeared in the roof of the dome. Finally the engine fired and the prop began to spin raggedly on its own. I adjusted throttle and choke and it smoothed out into a gratifying roar. The backwash blew the flames away from us towards the pump trailer, and as I released the brakes and the plane trundled out through the hangar doors, it went up with a whump and threw the fire in every direction. In an instant the entire interior was an inchoate mass of flame and black smoke fed increasingly by exploding drums of fuel.

As we rounded the curved side of the administration dome, I saw that either Charly's warning to Gasiorowski and his technicians had been heeded and they had ordered evacuation of the base, or its imminent destruction had become self-evident: men were streaming from the domes into the valley; soldiers, prisoners, technicians were running for their lives, all equal in the face of disaster.

'Where's the runway?' Charly gazed ahead worriedly.

I couldn't see it. The valley floor looked equally rocky and broken everywhere. 'Christ, there's got to be a runway!' I swore.

Howard leaned forward between us and pointed. 'That's it straight ahead. The broken look is just painted on so that it can't be seen from the air.'

And so it was. When you knew where to look, it was easily picked out. What had made it more difficult to spot initially was the fact that so many people were running along it.

'How can you take off with those men on it?' Charly cried.

I lined the aircraft up, set the brakes while I revved up the engine, checked the flaps and rudder, and when the plane was shuddering with restrained power, let her go. 'They'll just have to get out of the way,' I yelled over the engine noise as we picked up speed.

They did, scattering to the sides like refugees in a strafing attack. I paid them no attention. My whole focus was on the speed indicator and the memory of my instructor saying not to hurry the take-off. Nice and smooth is the way. But it wasn't the way I did it. We rose and bounced twice before I got her into the air and started climbing towards the upright tooth of the pyramid nunatak. Its jagged tip seemed to pass between our undercarriage, it was so close, but we missed – we were airborne!

I took in a great gasp of air and a ragged cheer went up in the plane.

I circled up, getting the feel of the aircraft, winding the trim to balance her and then, for the first time, looked down into the valley. Two of the domes were blazing now and all but one of the stacks had toppled, one crushing the prisoner dome. I doubted whether anyone was left inside, judging by the number of small figures streaming away up the narrow valley. As we watched, a crack appeared in the ice on the huge cliff overhanging the base; steam billowed up through the fissure and then, almost casually, a gigantic section slid down and the base was gone, the fire snuffed out beneath millions of tons of rock and ice. A huge wave of debris rolled up the valley but lost its momentum and settled before it could reach the survivors running for their lives. The lost city was gone, nothing left but a heap of rubble and a few wisps of steam. Gus's tomb, I thought sadly.

I swung the plane towards McMurdo.

Chapter 22

It was a long flight. Claydon navigated and it was only the blankets and spare flying suits Charly had found that kept us from freezing to death in the bitter chill high above the polar plateau. I was shattered and cold, and without the emergency rations that we found in the plane, and Howard's story, I would have collapsed over the steering column. We fluttered our way over the immense wasteland below, made brilliantly white by clear conditions. If the weather had been even a little bad, I don't think we could have made it. I didn't feel lucky; it was about time for a bit of help from above.

Howard told us how, after he had escaped from our camp with the dogs and sledge, he'd planned to attempt to make it back to Scott, but soon had to give up that idea. He'd seen the search parties and realized he didn't have enough food for himself and the dogs to make the trek and out-manœuvre his trackers at the same time. Instead he had made a wide swing and come back to the valley.

'I wasn't sure what I could do. I thought maybe I could overpower one of the soldiers that I saw occasionally outside, get his gun and go in and help you.'

'You'd have met half the Russian army,' I said.

'I soon realized that, so I holed up on the cliff, and when no one was about, came down and prowled around the perimeter. But there was no way in that wasn't guarded. I didn't know what to do.'

'But you still stayed,' Grampion said. 'After a few days when the hunt died down, you might have had a better chance to make it back to Scott.'

'Maybe.' Howard had that faraway look to his eyes. 'I didn't think about it. I wasn't going back alone again.' He smiled shyly, back with us. 'Anyway, I didn't have the chance. The whole cliff started to shake and I knew it wouldn't take much of that before it fell on to the domes. I sneaked down and scouted around waiting for something to happen.'

I glanced at Howard. How wrong I'd been to think he could leave men to die to save himself. He had known an avalanche was on the cards and still had calmly gone beneath it to try to help us.

He went on. 'When I came on the open hangar, I crept up as closely as I could to see what was going on. I thought I might be able to slip in unnoticed. Then I saw you and was just about to go in when Pitt appeared.'

'A traitor!' Grampion put all the disgust he had into the word.

'And a killer.' I told them how Bannister died and why.

'Poor Silas,' Grampion sighed. 'You and Charly did us all a favour, Howard.'

'I tried to get close to him. I thought I might be able to knock him down. Then the others came in.' Howard's voice grated. 'The gasoline was the only thing I could think of.'

'You're a bloody beaut!' Claydon roared, slapping him on the back. 'I told Rourk you'd make it back, but they didn't give him a chance to wait.'

There was a pause while we thought of friends, Gus and Rourk, even Silas. I felt no qualms at all about the men we'd destroyed.

Grampion broke the silence. 'Well, I'm coming back to Antarctica. Seeing those caves has made me even more certain about my theories. And I'd be damned glad if you'd do the organizing for me, Howard – and lead the expedition.'

Howard gazed out of the cabin window for a moment at the bleak but amazingly beautiful landscape below. 'Maybe I will,' he said pensively, and then laughed and punched my shoulder. 'If my wife will let me.'

'I'll spank her if she doesn't, Howard,' I said.

I made a perfect three-point landing on the strip cleared on the ice at McMurdo – two skis and the nose. The propeller snapped away, the undercarriage collapsed, and we skidded and slewed two hundred yards through the snow. We climbed slowly out, dazed and shaken, but all of a piece. There was no need to worry about fire. The tanks were empty.

As we waited for the running men and churning sno-mobiles to reach us from the station, I put my arm around Charly's shoulders and looked at the haloed sun that had been shining on us all these weeks. In Antarctic terms I supposed it had been a single day and it was not yet over, but it was more than long enough for all that had happened in it.

Alistair MacLean

His first book, *HMS Ulysses*, published in 1955, was outstandingly successful. It led the way to a string of best-selling novels which have established Alistair MacLean as the most popular adventure writer of our time.

Geoffrey Jenkins

Geoffrey Jenkins writes of adventure on land and at sea in some of the most exciting thrillers ever written. 'Geoffrey Jenkins has the touch that creates villains and heroes—and even icy heroines—with a few vivid words.' *Liverpool Post* 'A style which combines the best of Nevil Shute and Ian Fleming.' *Books and Bookmen*